The Boardwalk

Rehoboth Beach Reads

Short Stories by Local Writers

Edited by Nancy Sakaduski

A Playful Publisher

Cat & Mouse Press
Lewes, DE 19958
www.catandmousepress.com

Printed in the United States of America
10 9 8 7 6 5 4 3 2 1
ISBN-13 978-0-9860597-2-8
ISBN-10 0-9860597-2-2

PERMISSIONS AND ACKNOWLEDGEMENTS

"A Very Old Woman with Enormous Fins," Robert Hambling Davis.
© 2014 Robert Hambling Davis. Reprinted with permission.

"Awash," Emily Littleton. © 2014 Emily Littleton. Reprinted with permission.

"Boardwalk Bound," Kimberly Gray, © 2014 Kimberly Gray. Reprinted with permission.

"Come Fly with Me," Russell Reece. © 2014 Russell Reece. Reprinted with permission.

"Daisy Parade," Elizabeth Harner. © 2014 Elizabeth Harner. Reprinted with permission.

"Debut," J.L. Epler. © 2014 Jennifer Epler. Reprinted with permission.

"Elaynea and the Walk of Boards," Robin Hill-Page Glanden.
© 2014 Robin Page Glanden. Reprinted with permission.

"Forever Fifteen," Sandy Donnelly. © 2014 Sandra M. Donnelly. Reprinted with permission.

"Granny in Funland," Renay Regardie. © 2014 Renay Regardie. Reprinted with permission.

"No Business at the Beach," Dennis Lawson. © 2014 Dennis Lawson.
Reprinted with permission.

"Purpose," Nancy Michelson. © 2014 Nancy L. Michelson. Reprinted with permission.

"Stolen Heart," Terri Clifton. © 2014 Terri Clifton. Reprinted with permission.

"The Boardwalk and Dave Grohl," David Strauss. © 2014 David Strauss. Reprinted
with permission.

"The Case of the Artist's Stain," Joseph Crossen. © 2014 Joseph L. Crossen. Reprinted
with permission.

"The Edge of the World," Bruce Krug. © 2014 Bruce Krug. Reprinted with permission.

"The Great Rehoboth Race," Chris Jacobsen. © 2014 Christiana D. Jacobsen. Reprinted
with permission.

"The Keepers," Tiffany A. Schultz. © 2014 Tiffany Werner-Schultz. Reprinted
with permission.

"The Key to Winning," Mary Ann Glaser. © 2014 Mary Ann J. Hillier. Reprinted
with permission.

"The Old Colored Man Breaks the Law (Again)," Matthew Hastings.
© 2014 Matthew T. Hastings. Reprinted with permission.

"The Watch," Keith Phillips. © 2014 Keith J. Phillips. Reprinted with permission.

"The Ocean at Night," Heather Lynne Davis. © 2014 Heather L. Davis. Reprinted
with permission.

"The Window," Trish Bensinger Kocher. © 2014 Patricia Bensinger Kocher. Reprinted
with permission.

"There but for Fortune," Judy Shandler. © 2014 Judy Shandler. Reprinted with permission.

"Thunderbolts," Cathy Heller. © 2014 Cathleen S. Heller. Reprinted with permission.

"Untethered," Margaret Farrell Kirby. © 2014 Margaret Farrell Kirby. Reprinted
with permission.

Table of Contents

Daisy Parade, *Elizabeth Harner*..*1*

A Very Old Woman with Enormous Fins, *Robert Hambling Davis*........*9*

The Keepers, *Tiffany A. Schultz*..*17*

Untethered, *Margaret Farrell Kirby*..*29*

There but for Fortune, *Judy Shandler*..*37*

Thunderbolts, *Cathy Heller*...*49*

No Business at the Beach, *Dennis Lawson*......................................*57*

Debut, *J.L. Epler*..*69*

The Boardwalk and Dave Grohl, *David Strauss*..............................*79*

The Ocean at Night, *Heather Lynne Davis*......................................*85*

Purpose, *Nancy Michelson*...*95*

The Great Rehoboth Race, *Chris Jacobsen*.....................................*107*

The Case of the Artist's Stain, *Joseph Crossen*................................*119*

Stolen Heart, *Terri Clifton*..*131*

The Old Colored Man Breaks the Law (Again), *Matthew Hastings*......*137*

Granny in Funland, *Renay Regardie*..*149*

Elaynea and the Walk of Boards, *Robin Hill-Page Glanden*...............*157*

The Edge of the World, *Bruce Krug*..*165*

Forever Fifteen, *Sandy Donnelly*..*169*

The Key to Winning, *Mary Ann Glaser*...*179*

The Window, *Trish Bensinger Kocher*..*191*

Awash, *Emily Littleton*..*195*

The Watch, *Keith Phillips*...*199*

Come Fly with Me, *Russell Reece*...*207*

Boardwalk Bound, *Kimberly Gray*...*213*

PREFACE

These are the winning stories from the 2014 Rehoboth Beach Reads Short Story Contest, sponsored by Browseabout Books. Writers were asked to create a story—fiction or nonfiction—that fit the theme "The Boardwalk" and had a connection to Rehoboth Beach. A panel of judges selected the best stories and those selections have been printed here for your enjoyment. Like *The Beach House* (the first book in this series), this book contains more than just "they went down to the beach and had a picnic" stories. The quality and diversity of the stories is simply amazing.

We hope you enjoy this second book in the Rehoboth Beach Reads series.

For information on the contest, go to: www.catandmousepress.com.

ACKNOWLEDGEMENTS

I thank Browseabout Books for their generous support. We are so lucky to have this great store in the heart of our community. They have supported the Rehoboth Beach Reads Short Story Contest from day one and continue to be the go-to place for books, gifts, and other fun stuff.

I thank both the Rehoboth Beach Writers' Guild and the Eastern Shore Writers Association for their support and service to the writing community. These two organizations provide an amazing array of educational programming, and many of the writers whose stories appear in this book benefitted from their classes, meetings, and events.

I thank our judges, Rich Barnett, Sarah Barnett, Alex Colevas, Lisa Graff, Kristen Gramer, and Ramona DeFelice Long, who gave generously of their time.

Special thanks to Emory Au, who so beautifully captured the iconic Rehoboth Beach boardwalk in the cover illustration and who designed this book cover to cover.

I also thank Cindy Myers, Susan Ives, and Carolyn Colwell for providing valuable production assistance.

An extra-special thank-you to my husband and supply chain manager, Joe, whose support and encouragement I can always count on.

I would also like to thank the writers—those whose work is in this book and those whose work was not chosen. Putting a piece of writing up for judging takes courage. Thank you for being brave. Keep writing and submitting your work!

—*Nancy Sakaduski*

Daisy Parade

by Elizabeth Harner

Maddie smiled as she closed the door, wishing a good evening to the man in the black polo shirt and khaki shorts who delivered a bouquet of two dozen soft white daisies with a complement of baby's breath. Before she opened the card she knew they were from Justin.

Justin was the twenty-five-year-old investment banker whom she'd loved since they met more than ten years earlier during her family's annual vacation in Rehoboth Beach. The summer cottage next door to her grandparents' had been for sale that entire winter. When her grandmother told them that the house had sold in April, Maddie, a typical inquisitive teenage girl, couldn't wait for her beach week to arrive so she could scope out the new neighbors.

A white minivan had been in the carport when Maddie's family drove by and pulled into their own stone driveway. From the secrecy of the shaded front porch, Maddie had spent the first two days of their weeklong vacation with her blue eyes trained on the neighbors' front door. Like the surfers she'd seen who waited for the perfect wave, Maddie had watched with patience until she finally saw a figure exiting the house. Justin had a slender build and his brown eyes were hidden by a tousled mess of dirty-blond hair. His tan arms and legs protruded beyond the confines of his navy-blue board shorts and white undershirt. As he walked to the mailbox across the street Maddie had grabbed her flip-flops and followed, planning out the perfect "casual meeting" as she let the screen door slam behind her.

Now, at her home in Fairfax, Maddie closed her eyes and inhaled deeply to take in the aroma of her favorite flower. She hadn't seen Justin for six months. His business trip to Germany was scheduled to last six weeks, but delays and problems had come up that required his attention. It was early July and Justin hadn't been able to say whether or not he'd make it home in time for their beach week. Moisture grew at the corner of Maddie's eyes as she was again confronted with the heartache of being in love with someone so far away. The thoughtfulness of sending her her favorite flower reminded Maddie that this guy was worth it; he was the one, if only he were on the same continent. With a long sigh, Maddie set down the flowers and reached for the card:

My Sweet Maddie,

I know flowers are a poor substitute for my arms, but I hope their beauty will bring some comfort as I deliver bad news, yet again. I won't be able to make it back home until September, at the earliest. It kills me to disappoint you again, but it can't be helped. Even though I can't be with you, please go to the beach like we'd planned. I know you're thinking right now that you aren't going to go alone, but I know you won't be able to hold back your own curiosity, so I've arranged for a small surprise for you. Be at your favorite spot in RB tomorrow at 5 p.m.

Love always,
Justin

Amidst her tears of frustration at the thought of waiting another two months to see Justin, Maddie couldn't help but release a small giggle as she realized just how well her boyfriend knew her. She hastily grabbed a vase for the flowers, and with a grin on her face and a twinkle in her eyes she ran upstairs to start packing.

* * * * * *

Driving south on Surf Avenue, Maddie could see the Henlopen Hotel coming into view. The year's first glimpse of the ocean was just visible over the eastern horizon. This was Maddie's favorite place in Rehoboth Beach. Keeping one eye on the sweeping right turn, she saw it to her left: the flat surface of blue water, disrupted by small ripples and waves, as sparkles of light danced in the evening sun. She couldn't keep a smile off her face as she made a quick left into the parking lot and reached for her bag of quarters.

Standing next to the white bench where Maddie and Justin usually sat was a man in a tuxedo holding a daisy. When she walked toward him, the man greeted her with a smile and presented the flower. "Good evening, ma'am. Please take this flower and continue to walk south along the boardwalk. On your way, you are to stop any time you see a daisy. Collect the flower, take a moment to notice its location, and continue on your way."

Maddie was struck by the matter-of-fact nature of his speech. She wasn't quite sure how to respond. She took the daisy with a puzzled look on her face and said, "Thank you, but how am I ... ?"

"That is all the instruction I am permitted to share. Enjoy your evening," replied the man as he turned and walked away.

What are you up to, Justin? Maddie thought as she shook her head and breathed in the fresh, salty air that she loved so much. She continued down the boardwalk. Just ahead, Maddie noticed a daisy wrapped with a red ribbon around the metal fence that led up a small storefront staircase. As she carefully untied the flower she realized that this now-empty building used to be Yesterday's, a quaint, throwback diner where she and Justin had their first date.

His dad had dropped them off at the north end of the boardwalk and told them he'd be back in two hours. Maddie was so nervous to be on her first real date with a boy, with no parents or other friends to hide behind; it was just the two of them. They'd enjoyed burgers, fries, and real fountain sodas as they remarked about what life must have been like when restaurants like this actually existed. After dinner they'd walked up and down the boardwalk, people-watching and trying desperately to make small talk. Just as they passed by the restaurant again at the end of their walk, with five minutes before their scheduled pickup time, Justin reached over and held her hand.

Maddie could almost feel his smooth fingers interlaced with her own as a pair of squawking seagulls fighting over a French fry pulled her back to the present. Rather than Justin's hand, Maddie now held two daisies. She turned and continued south along the boards, keeping her eyes sharp and focused in search of a third. Soft, soapy bubbles distracted Maddie from her mission, popping against her legs as she passed the kite shop. She looked in and smiled at the young children begging their mother to buy them the latest summer gadgets.

As she approached Rehoboth Avenue it became more and more difficult for Maddie to spot anything other than throngs of vacationers. She saw families of all different backgrounds: young children swinging toys and stuffed animal prizes, teenagers grabbing at a shared bucket of Thrasher's, and older couples in hats, white windbreakers, and sneakers, walking hand-in-hand, but no daisies. Maddie walked slowly through the crowds, inspecting each bench and storefront, hoping to spot another speck of yellow surrounded by brilliant white petals.

Just as she passed the Candy Kitchen with a soft frown forming on her face, there it was: a fresh, solitary daisy in a vase on the Grotto Pizza hostess stand. Maddie tentatively walked over to the teenage girl manning the stand. Not wanting to sound crazy she said, "Excuse me, miss, is this flower here for a specific reason tonight?"

The hostess smiled and said, "You must be Maddie. Please take the flower and a slice to go. Enjoy your evening." With three flowers in one hand and a piece of swirled cheesy pie in the other, Maddie turned and walked across the boardwalk to the nearest open bench.

She sat facing the open-air pizza restaurant where she'd dined with Justin on more summer evenings than she could count. Stopping for a slice of Grotto was always a must, no matter how short their visit to Rehoboth. And if they could eat it on the boardwalk, staring out over the ocean, it tasted even sweeter.

After inhaling the perfect slice Maddie continued into the crowd of people, watching as they popped in and out of the shops and food stands along the boardwalk. The sun was starting to set; beachgoers were washing their feet as they came off the sand and it seemed as if everyone was heading to Funland. As she came to the first sand-colored pillar, Maddie was struck by all the sounds flooding the area. Kids were screaming with joy as buzzers and bells filled the night.

Maddie looked up at the first game, her favorite, the horse race. As the plastic horses bobbed their heads and made their way across the field, she saw it. Pinned to the top of the prize wall was another daisy. Maddie patiently waited to make her way up to the front of the line. Hesitantly she asked the boy running the game, "I'm sorry to bother you. My name is Maddie. I was wondering if that daisy hanging on the wall is for me?"

He smiled a devilish grin and replied, "It is, but I can't give it to you. You have to win it!"

"No way, really?" Although it was Maddie's favorite game, she'd never once been able to contain her excitement long enough to get the rubber ball into the holes as many times as was necessary to actually get her horse to the finish line first. This was one of Justin's favorite moments each year, watching Maddie try to win the horse race. He loved seeing her joyful anticipation build and he tried so hard not to tease her about her losing record. Maddie would try a few times, unsuccessfully, and then tell Justin to just go ahead. He usually won, but didn't gloat.

"I can't just have it, or pay you for it?" Maddie asked again.

"Nope, strict instructions, you gotta *win* it," the young man said, obviously enjoying his role.

"Oh my gosh, all right, here you go," said Maddie as she handed over a dollar.

"Okay, folks, we're playing for a large prize. At the sound of the bell ..." yelled the game operator.

The bell sounded and the plastic horses lurched forward. Maddie jumped with childlike enthusiasm and almost forgot to roll her ball. She had to concentrate. For the rest of the race she didn't even look up. She just kept rolling her ball and waiting for the bell. She sighed, thinking she'd be here all night and probably go broke before she'd be able to win her flower.

The bell rang and Maddie's eyes darted toward the wall, searching to see which horse won. It was hers! She looked around wondering, *How did this happen? Everyone else's horses are still at the starting gate. This doesn't make any sense. Is the game broken?* The boy handed her the daisy and, suddenly, all of the other players stood up, turned to her, and started clapping. Maddie looked confused for a minute, and then turned around to see everyone on the boardwalk standing still and clapping as Justin walked toward her and knelt down, a daisy in one hand and a ring in the other.

Elizabeth Harner is a high school English teacher in Gettysburg, Pennsylvania. While attending Bucknell University she was a staff writer for the school newspaper and intern for the university magazine. Creative writing has always been a hobby, but *"Daisy Parade"* is her first published short story. Rehoboth Beach is Elizabeth's favorite vacation destination and she has spent time there every summer since birth (thirty-one years and counting!), vacationing with her family at her grandparents' house in North Shores.

A Very Old Woman with Enormous Fins

by Robert Hambling Davis

After the May hurricane that swept the East Coast, Abe Hicks and his sixteen-year-old son Tucker were the first people on the beach by the Rehoboth boardwalk. They'd eaten breakfast at Sammy's Kitchen, and they wore their waders and fishing vests, for they'd both caught flounder after the last big storm two years ago. They planned to drive to Cape Henlopen Point and try their luck, but first wanted to scour the beach for washed-up bait. Abe headed toward a seething mass of hermit crabs. Tucker spotted something in the other direction. As he walked closer, he saw a humanlike figure sprawled facedown on the drenched sand.

"Hey, Pop, come see this," Tucker hollered in the wind, which was still gusting.

Abe walked toward his son, who stood wide-eyed, open-mouthed, over the strange-looking body. "What is it?" Abe said.

Tucker gave his dad a look that made him flinch, and then reached down and turned over the body. For a long moment they stopped breathing as they stood side by side, staring at a very old woman with a fish's tail. Her fins were bigger than those of the marlin Abe had caught off Key West five years earlier. Barnacles spotted her bony arms and the backs of her hands, and covered her breasts as if finding the most nourishment there. Her eyes, gray as the surf, gaped vacantly at the sunless sky.

"It's a mermaid!" Tucker cried, finding his voice. "A really old one. What should we do with her, Pop?"

Abe had fished for forty years and seen all kinds of marine life, but never the likes of this creature. His impulse was to carry her back into the ocean and let her go before anyone else saw her, but she looked dead, her body motionless, her eyes unblinking.

"I don't know," he said, and knelt beside the mermaid.

Seaweed stuck to her long white hair and a sand crab crawled through its tangles. Abe felt for a pulse on her wrist, her skin cold as a fish. He frowned and shook his head at Tucker.

"Maybe she doesn't have a heart," Tucker said. He opened his Swiss army knife, held it by her nose, counted to ten, and showed Abe the condensation on the blade. "Look, Pop, she's still breathing. What should we do?"

Did the mermaid need CPR? Abe wondered. Should he call 911? After all, she was half human and barely alive. He took out his phone, started to dial, then stopped. He didn't know what to do. The inland wind blew sand from her scales. Hungry gulls screeched overhead. No, she's not one of us, he told himself, and put his phone away. She came from the sea and should go back to the sea.

"Take her arms and I'll …" he said, then broke off as three boys and a girl with a black Lab bounded up, screaming and barking.

"What is it?" said one of the boys.

"A mermaid," said another. "Look at her tail and fins, dummy."

"Wow! A mermaid, a mermaid!" cried the third, clapping his hands.

"A senior citizen mermaid," said the girl.

They wore windbreakers that hissed as they crouched about the mermaid, ignoring Abe and Tucker. The dog sniffed at her fins and growled. Now more kids came running from the boardwalk. They shrieked and gawked and babbled. They took pictures with their phones, and texted and called their friends and parents, who by the time they arrived didn't see the mermaid for the crowd.

As things turned out, once the mermaid was resuscitated in a saline tank, the City of Rehoboth Beach claimed her as its own found subject. The city built a steel pier and a fenced-in Olympic pool by the boardwalk at Rehoboth Avenue and charged a five-dollar admission to see "The Marine Wonder of the World and Pride of Rehoboth Beach—Marian the Mermaid!" The mayor had named her after Maid Marian, Robin Hood's love interest, who was associated with May Day in English folklore. A dermatologist removed the barnacles from her arms and hands. A beautician untangled her hair.

When Tucker Hicks told his dad he didn't want to be in the spotlight, Abe claimed he was the one who'd found Marian. He downplayed the discovery, saying that if he hadn't found her, someone else would have. The media publicized Abe's varied life as a charter boat captain, building inspector, carpenter, projectionist, short-order cook, and divorced father. Tucker admired and loved his dad all the more for taking the credit.

Marian spent no time trying to adjust to the pool, looking first bewildered and then distraught by its confines. She swam ceaseless laps, her arms by her sides, and cut through the water with her tail fins like a dolphin, her white hair streaming down her back. She could swim a half hour underwater before coming up for air. Most people thought she was a mammal and were surprised that her kind hadn't been sighted surfacing offshore. Others speculated that she was the only mermaid on Earth, the freak offspring of an orca and her SeaWorld trainer, who'd then managed to return the fish to the sea where she birthed Marian. Marine biologists, linguists, interpreters, and speech therapists failed to communicate with her, and she didn't respond to the whale music her managers played by her pool.

"Whales have been hunted to near extinction," the mayor said. "Their music is too sad. Try some happy music. How about a polka?" he suggested, reminding people that he was the second generation of a family from Warsaw.

Marian's managers hired a polka band and dancers, but she kept swimming her laps, seeming oblivious to everything else. The managers tried other types of music, from fifties folk to eighties punk, doo-wop, heavy metal, grunge, pop, and rap, to no avail. Many people said she was deaf and that her human ears were remnants of sense organs she'd dispensed with long ago. Others claimed she had too much water in her ears to hear anything. There were even those who said she was an autistic mermaid, given her aloofness and compulsive swimming.

People from around the world came to see Marian, the one and only mermaid in captivity, this ancient sea goddess washed ashore in a hurricane. Boardwalk businesses set unprecedented sales, and hotels were booked a year in advance. When she refused her managers' attempts to feed her, tourists brought all sorts of food, including sardines, granola bars, lychees, cheese balls, and sushi, but she ignored these offerings and kept swimming her laps, as if the sheer energy she put into this pursuit would deliver her to the sea a hundred yards away. She swam in a fever that raised the water temperature twenty degrees and produced a steamy mist on cold nights.

Marian had been in captivity exactly a year when she finally communicated, revealing her true nature. On that sunny May afternoon, a record crowd gathered on the pier. A huge banner— HAPPY ANNIVERSARY, MARIAN!—draped the entrance, and bright clusters of balloons with her picture drifted in the breeze. A noted mythologist spoke about the origin of mermaids, citing Babylonian, Greek, and Roman legends. Abe and Tucker Hicks were there, dressed in their waders and fishing vests. At the mayor's request

Abe gave a short speech, saying how he'd thought Marian was dead when he found her, until he held his knife under her nose and saw the mist her faint breath had left on the blade. The crowd applauded him, and the mayor shook his hand on the stage overlooking the pool where Marian had surfaced for air. As she floated on her back, taking deep breaths, Abe sat down and stared regretfully at her desperate eyes and wilted lips. He recalled when Tucker had found her by the boardwalk after the storm and asked Abe what they should do, and how he hesitated as he watched the movie playing in his mind, the movie he'd watched countless times since then, while working or fishing or eating, or tossing in bed, trying to sleep. In his mind movie he told Tucker, "Take her arms and I'll take her fins and we'll take her back where she came from." Then they carried her into the surf and she leaped over the breakers like a sailfish.

"Mermaid Marian, this living gift from the sea, has turned Rehoboth Beach into an international resort," the mayor said. "Our boardwalk now attracts more people than the one in Atlantic City."

Abe half-listened, then tuned out the mayor completely as Marian, still floating on her back, took a long breath and held it, but didn't resume her laps, the manic pacing of her chlorinated cage. Instead, she turned vertical in the middle of the pool, flapping her fins with such force that her human half was above water. She opened her mouth and burst into song in a language no one understood. She was doubtlessly singing, though, as she raised her melodic voice and held her notes with the skill of a world-class contralto.

The mayor stopped speaking and the crowd stood transfixed by the song of this mermaid, who'd been mute for a year. Then the mythologist lurched back up to the microphone, shouldering the mayor aside, and exclaimed, "She's not a mermaid. She's a siren!"

Once he'd made this announcement, he jumped off the stage and hurried toward the pool with an urgent look on his face, the mayor following with the same look. Many of the men as well as the women crowded the edge of the pool, drawn irresistibly by Marian as she spun about in the water, singing in all four directions. Others palmed their ears, recalling Homer's *Odyssey* and the sirens who lured sailors off course to smash their ships on the rocks and drown. Yet the faces of the men Marian lured weren't those of lovesick victims seduced by a water nymph, but of gallant heroes rushing to a damsel in distress.

Why did she wait till now to break her silence? Many later speculated that she knew she'd have a greater chance of escaping her prison if she drew the biggest crowd before singing her plea for freedom.

Although the mayor and the mythologist and dozens of other men dashed to her rescue, it was Abe Hicks who led them all, opening the fence gate and diving into the pool in his fishing vest and waders. He was the first to reach Marian, take her by the hand, and swim to the side of the pool. The whole time she kept singing her song, whose lyrics, though incomprehensible to her human audience, were of a universal language that spurred men to her aid. The mayor, who'd championed Marian as the greatest Rehoboth Beach boardwalk attraction, knelt in his new suit beside Tucker, and the two of them pulled her from the pool, with an in-water assist from Abe.

The crowd cheered as Abe and Tucker carried Marian from the pier, across the beach, into the high tide. Many of those present would later swear she'd shed years on that walk, reversing her age so that by the time the father and son let her go, her top half was that of a beautiful young woman with ruby lips and raven hair. Like a fish caught and released, she didn't look back, but dove into the waves and was gone, returning to her home.

ROBERT HAMBLING DAVIS HAS BEEN PUBLISHED IN *THE SUN, ANTIETAM REVIEW, MEMOIR (AND) (NOW MEMOIR JOURNAL), PHILADELPHIA STORIES, SANTA MONICA REVIEW,* AND ELSEWHERE. HE'S BEEN NOMINATED FOR TWO PUSHCART PRIZES AND RECEIVED THREE DELAWARE DIVISION OF THE ARTS GRANTS, TWO FOR FICTION AND ONE FOR CREATIVE NONFICTION. HE WAS A FICTION SEMIFINALIST IN THE WILLIAM FAULKNER CREATIVE WRITING CONTEST IN 2002 AND 2012 AND A CREATIVE NONFICTION WINNER IN 2013. ROBERT HELPS DIRECT THE DELAWARE LITERARY CONNECTION, A NONPROFIT SERVING WRITERS IN DELAWARE AND SURROUNDING AREAS, AND HE CO-HOSTS 2ND SATURDAY POETS, A THIRTY-ONE-YEAR TRADITION OF MONTHLY POETRY READINGS IN WILMINGTON, DELAWARE. HE IS ALSO A FICTION EDITOR FOR *THE FOX CHASE REVIEW.* ROBERT WAS INSPIRED TO WRITE "A VERY OLD WOMAN WITH ENORMOUS FINS" AFTER READING GABRIEL GARCÍA MÁRQUEZ'S STORY, "A VERY OLD MAN WITH ENORMOUS WINGS," ABOUT AN ANGEL WHO FALLS TO EARTH IN A RAINSTORM.

The Keepers

by Tiffany A. Schultz

I've been on this boardwalk for hours. My summer-tattered sandals lie askew a few feet away, and tendrils of wind-loosened hair that managed to free themselves from the thick braid that rests heavily between my shoulder blades are now batting wildly at my cheeks and forehead. My stomach is growling like a rabid dog and I probably should have applied more sunscreen. What I wouldn't give for a peanut butter and jelly sandwich and a fresh coat of deodorant.

I'm from Wisconsin. My mother, Bobbie, was also born and raised there and in her forty-nine or so years on this planet, she has rarely, if ever, escaped the flat and smelly farmlands that dot the Dairy State's countryside. Sometimes, she and I get to Door County, which is still well within state lines, but it is about as close to not being in Wisconsin as Wisconsin is ever going to get. I think that's why she likes it so much.

"See, it is *just like* being out east," Mom said, trying to hide her surprise the first time we meandered our way up the Door County peninsula. She had found a small black-and-white magazine in a rusty wire bin next to the gumball machines while waiting to get an oil change one day, the glossy's headline declaring "Door County— Cape Cod of the Midwest!" After reading that, she could barely think of much else.

A couple of weekends later, we packed up the good old Chrysler Town and Country and hit the ground running, making a beeline toward the "thumb" of the state, which is where Door County resides. I remember that as we parked the car at the little drive-up motel in Bailey's Harbor, right off Old Cherry Road, my mom practically squealed in delight at its gingerbread and gumdrop charm.

"Room 15, if it's available, please," she requested of the desk clerk, trying to sound like anything but a first-time visitor. Reviewers on TripAdvisor had promised that the odd-numbered rooms had the best views, after all.

We made that trip a handful of times over the years, but now those trips are few and far between. Not enough time, not enough money, and sometimes, according to Mom, "not enough hens in the hen house," whatever that means.

But there is a part of me that wonders if it's all of that, or simply that she is too wrapped up in her love affair ... with Whitley Odette, her favorite talk-show host, to even think about leaving town. If she misses one batting of Whitley's daddy-long-leg lashes or the heaving chest of one emotional guest, there is no telling what might happen. Oh, I know there are DVRs, and there are most certainly TVs in almost every motel room in America, but she is obsessed and doesn't really spend a whole lot of time wading in the pond of reality, much less the pool of rational thought. The mere thought of *possibly* missing an episode sends her into a tailspin.

Every day at 3:10 p.m. I return from school, "Ma, I'm home" being my customary announcement. With the laundry long having been folded and her daily pilgrimage to the local produce market under her belt, she usually gives me a small squeak of acknowledgment from the living room, where she is perched atop our Dutch-blue Thomasville sofa, her hands folded neatly in her lap and a balled-up Kleenex tucked into the crook of her palm. Without fail, Whitley will make Mom cry for one reason or another.

One particular day, I rounded the corner and noticed she was unusually enthralled. Not in the typical "You get a flat-screen TV! And you get a TV! And YOU get a TV!" manic-Whitley Odette sort of way, but something that registered more as contentedness; the pencil-thin lines that naturally formed around her mouth and nose this day were uncharacteristically smooth and relaxed.

That day's show was "Whittling down with Whitley." It featured home makeovers and focused on ordinary people who were instructed to survey their possessions and divide them up into three distinct piles: the throwaways, the giveaways, and the keepers. I couldn't help but think that those three piles were a lot like the relationships and experiences we collect in our lives: the throwaways, the giveaways, and—if we're lucky—the keepers.

In any case, it caught my attention, so I plopped down next to her and dropped my backpack at my feet. The alternative was to get intimate with quadratic equations or clean my bedroom, both being the stuff nightmares are made of. And, I figured, maybe I could even learn something from this motley group of mad stashers.

Turns out, I tuned in right on time to see the first whittled-down family take a tour of their new and improved, crap-free home. The producers had carefully crafted the scene by piping in the song, "I'm Walking on Sunshine" as the stunned family completed their first loop of the upstairs. Right on cue, my mother started bawling like a baby.

"Is this the first time since you moved in that you've seen your … well, I guess it could be described most accurately as …" Whitley chuckled as her voice reached that baritone of excitement she was so famous for, "GREEN. SHAG. CARPETINNNNNNNNNNNG!!!!"

The camera left Whitley's giddy face and sloped downward to show her perfectly manicured toes, tucked into a perfect pair of Manolo's, standing on the family's perfect '70s-vintage shag carpeting. The camera operator panned back to the family, who were nodding in unison, in what could only be described as delirious bewilderment.

In the next segment, a woman from Oregon led Whitley by the hand to the guest bedroom, where her most prized possession, an at-home tanning bed, sat like an island amongst a sea of paper. "I just can't bring myself to throw it all away," she sighed, as she leafed through an old JC Penney flier. All the while, Whitley stood next to her, straddling a mound of "You may already have won!" sweepstakes mailers, while silently surveying what looked to be the aftermath of an F-5 tornado.

The JC Penney flier lady then led Whitley down her basement stairs, once again by the hand, through a maze of piled-up boxes of coffee filters, cereal, and tampons. The rows were stacked so high the camera operator had trouble keeping Whitley in frame as she tried to navigate the tight cardboard corners.

"But didn't you just tell me upstairs that you don't drink coffee or eat cereal?" Whitley asked with wide-eyed astonishment.

"Yeah, and I'm menopausal too, but I had coupons!" the woman exclaimed so loudly I thought her leathery face might crack. My mother could do nothing more than shake her head from side to side and dab at the corners of her dewy eyes.

Mom and I ended up spending the next thirty minutes transfixed, shoveling fistfuls of Crackerjack into our mouths without concern for calories, carbs, or sugar intake. I was a goner—completely sucked in by a bunch of hoarders getting saved by the big W. The before-and-after pictures of the reformed junk junkies, parading across the screen like beauty queens on a runway, were positively inspiring! Like one minute these collectors on crack were drowning in debris and the next they were being thrown a W-shaped life preserver. All that was missing was the Whitley roar of, "You've been saved! And you've been saved! And YOU have been saved!"

With ten minutes remaining, the last family, the McCormacks, made their packrat debut. Feeling a bit seasick by the oceanic proportions of people's junk, along with thoughts of my impending algebra homework, I reached down into my backpack; I knew I had an unopened can of Coca-Cola in the side pocket and felt like I needed an energy boost. I bent over to unzip my pack and felt my mother's hot meaty hand land on my shoulder. I looked up. Leading into commercial break, they were teasing viewers by showing an empty Dumpster in the McCormacks' driveway that, thanks to time-lapse technology, went from empty to overflowing in a matter of seconds.

While the commercial blared in the background, I was finally able to pop the top of my soda without being given away. I took a swig and the lukewarm mouthful went down like a big airy lump. Needless to say, belching ensued.

"Shhhhh," Mom put her index finger to her lips, "it's back on."

A wide-angle shot of the McCormacks' cluttered basement appeared, along with what appeared to be numerous sets of glowing eyes and tips of tails bobbing up and down. "That's seven, oh wait, eight," I snickered as I squinted to find the next one. "It's like playing *Where's Waldo,* the feline version." As if being a regular everyday hoarder wasn't enough, the McCormacks, it seemed, were cat hoarders as well.

My mother didn't so much as squeak, chuckle, or even shake her head in acknowledgment. Instead, we watched in silent agony as the entire McCormack clan, who could have easily been long-lost members of the Kennedy family, showed Whitley their "humble abode," as the sweet-as-pie Mrs. McCormack put it.

"Doesn't she look just like Laura Petrie?" Mom mumbled, forgetting I was not one of her girlfriends, who might have known that little nugget of '60s pop culture trivia. Mrs. McCormack had a petite figure, which was made even more darling by a pair of navy cigarette pants, along with a choker of creamy white pearls, a lacy pink tank, and a pair of blush-colored ballet flats that could only be described as "just so." Her perfectly coifed hair, worn in a shoulder-length bob, was also classically understated; all of which made it impossible to imagine her as anything but domestic. Mrs. McCormack quite obviously spent a lot of time tidying herself, but no time at all tidying her home.

"Re-ho-both Beea-ch," Mom said moments later, as if she were learning a foreign language.

I looked back at the TV and saw the words "Rehoboth Beach, Delaware" scrawled in a happy font underneath the faces of an equally happy McCormack family, which included Mr. McCormack and three boys, who were spitting images of one another, with broad but crooked smiles and thick mops of sun-kissed hair, which they kept side swept across their ample foreheads.

"Re-ho-both Beach," she repeated over and over.

"Yes, Mom … Rehoboth Beach. It's in Delaware, apparently, and the McCormacks live there," I said, my patience wearing thin.

The screen was now aglow with exterior shots of the McCormacks' cute-as-a-button Cape Cod, complete with a cookie-cutter corner lot and white picket fencing. Eventually, the shot widened to show an entire Mayberry-like street, all the homes with the exact same quaint beachiness about them. The camera then crisscrossed the two blocks it took to reach its final destination—a long, unevenly planked and sun-weathered boardwalk spanning the length of the shoreline, where Whitley just happened to be standing in a wide-brimmed hat, oversized sunglasses, and perfectly creased linen pants. She was greeting fellow boardwalkers with her telltale high-glossed lips and toothy grin, all while doling out muffins and pastries that had been purchased from the town's bakery.

"Well now, isn't that just the cat's ass," Mom hissed, her excitement tainted with just the slightest bit of jealousy.

The camera then cut to one of Rehoboth's many boardwalk joggers, who was holding a gigantic bran muffin with both hands like it was a bar of solid gold. "This is the biggest thing to hit Rehoboth Beach since … well, since ever," the woman exclaimed. "And I'm not talking about the muffin!" She snorted and turned away from the camera, pointing a frenzied finger at the talk-show maven, who stood not twenty feet away, shaking hands with and hugging passersby.

If it's possible to hear someone's heart flutter in excitement and break simultaneously, that's exactly what I heard Mom's do.

* * * * * *

It was, by every indication, an ordinary summer afternoon. Mom was in the living room, tickled pink to be watching Whitley interview Brad Pitt. While Mom was cooing like a mourning dove in heat over Brad's dreaminess, I was sitting at the kitchen table painting my toenails the most delicious shade of hydrangea blue. Moments later, I heard an unintelligible scream, almost like the moo of a sick cow, followed by a thud like a clap of thunder that brought me to my feet.

"Ma … what's wrong?" I said, bursting into the living room. There I found Mom, sitting in a heap on the floor with the remote control clutched in her right hand, stabbing fiercely at the air in the direction of the TV screen.

I turned around and saw Whitley's pleasantly plump face staring back at me. She was distorted in a blurry mess that was the result of the DVR pause button, but still completely recognizable. I grabbed the remote from my mom's hand and pushed the rewind button in quick, rapid pulses. After a few seconds, Mom came out of her zombie-like state and told me I had gone back far enough. I hit play and heard the telltale boom of Whitley's voice.

"It's my twentieth season, peopllllllllllllllle," the queen of talk teased from within the confines of our fifty-inch flat-screen. (The new season was set to begin in two short weeks—I knew because Mom had placed a big red smiley face on that date on the calendar that she kept on the front of the fridge.) "And you won't believe what I'm up tooooooooooooooooo ... and where I may show up," she concluded with a wink.

For the next sixty seconds, a montage, comprised solely of images from seasons past, flashed across the screen in rapid succession. Clambakes and hoedowns, Faith Hill concerts, camping in Yellowstone. Icy shots of Patrón lined up on a polished silver platter and hiking the Grand Canyon in her army-green Bermuda shorts, her knobby knees appearing to buckle with each wobbly step.

And there it was, right after a photo of Whitley blowing out candles atop a three-tier birthday cake: an image of a white bench in front of gently swaying beach grass on sandy dunes. At the bottom corner of the frame sat the empty basket that once held all those precious-as-gold breakfast pastries. It was a scene that only someone like my mother, who had an unhealthy obsession, would have recognized.

* * * * * *

"Whitley would never lie or deceive or anything of the sort," the breathy words tumbled out of Mom's mouth as we furiously packed our suitcases the following morning. Thanks to a small fund she kept squirreled away for "emergencies," we filled up the gas tank, indulged in a box of mini powdered-sugar donuts and still had enough for a "thrifty" (Mom hated the word "cheap") seven-day quest.

"But Ma, we don't even know for sure if or when she is going to be back in Rehoboth," I said within the first five miles, already flipping through the pages of an old *People* magazine. "Remember," I said, clearing my throat in order to call up the right Whitley intonation, "where I mayyyyyyyyy show up." I slapped the magazine shut and rolled my eyes. "The key word being 'may,' Ma." Mom's only response was to roll her eyes right back at me and then we exchanged a series of exhales.

The 1,127-mile journey started by cutting diagonally across the "palm" of Wisconsin and then dipping into the northern-most tip of Illinois, where we rounded the southern-most tip of Lake Michigan. I thought getting into Indiana would be a relief, but it turned out the flat and gray landscape of the nowhere-nothing state made me sort of sleepy and homesick. So the decision was made that just after crossing into Ohio we would stop and get a $59 room for the night. *Thrifty.* Of course Mom was grateful for the little things, like the fact that it included a hot shower and free breakfast. I, on the other hand, was a little less enthusiastic. "Seriously?" I groaned as we opened the door to a room that reeked of cigarette smoke and wet dog.

"WWWD," Mom proclaimed as she pushed passed me, her head bopping from side to side, I'm sure keeping beat with some happy tune playing on endless repeat in her head. When I didn't respond, she began "What would …" I got it and joined in, "Whitley do?" Mom gave me a hard, satisfied nod.

I chuckled. "Whitley wouldn't be caught dead in this place, much less *do* anything."

Mom placed her suitcase on the bed and began unzipping it. "Well, she certainly wouldn't be complaining about it," she said, as she retrieved her toothbrush and one of those little tubes of travel toothpaste. "She'd make the best of it; she always does."

* * * * * *

The following morning, I made the best of it by filling up on free Apple Jacks and cheese Danish before we hit the road. We again headed straight east, angling south just outside of Newton Falls and continuing on through Pennsylvania and Maryland. By late afternoon, we crossed the Bay Bridge, finally arriving in Rehoboth, just as the boardwalk was lighting up for the evening. Before refilling the car with gas, before checking into our *thrifty* Dewey Beach motel, before even taking a much-needed potty break, we parked the car and ran to the very spot on the boardwalk where Whitley took the picture … and snapped a selfie.

Then we took a potty break. But after that, we covered every inch of that boardwalk—a bucket of tangy vinegar fries, a pocketful of watermelon saltwater taffy, and giant cones of creamy custard serving as our trusty companions.

* * * * * *

Fast-forward two days and the giddiness of our arrival has faded into a distant memory, at least for me. My vision is blurry from lack of sleep and my growling stomach has now reached a fever pitch. As I sit here on the boardwalk, holding vigil of sorts—you guessed it, no sign of Whitley—I wonder out loud if the universe is mocking us.

"The universe gives birth to your wishes every moment of the day, if you let it," Mom says, staring out from underneath a sun visor she bought from one of the Penny Lane shops. I close my eyes and silently, but quite seriously, wish for Whitley to be spat out from the marshmallow-like clouds above, like a newborn baby, into my mother's awaiting arms. I quickly add that if she happens to be holding a slice of Grotto's pizza and a peanut butter–chocolate swirl cone, that would be great, too.

An hour later, Mom decides she's going to head to the local bakery, the one Whitley got the muffins from for the makeover show. She intends to stake it out in case any of Whitley's entourage should need a carb fix.

"Tell Trixie," I say, knowing from years of watching that she is Whitley's best friend, "I said hi." I stick my tongue out at her as she turns to head down the boardwalk. Mom turns to see my sour tongue pointed at her and her only response is to smile and raise her eyebrows in possibility.

* * * * * *

Of course we never did see Whitley, or Trixie, or any members of the Whitley Odette entourage while we were in Rehoboth, simply because they weren't there. My mother refuses to believe it. She just thinks they were very busy with their "shooting schedules" and other miscellaneous things.

"You know Whitley and her treadmill—it's practically a religious experience for her," my mother says on the ride home, somewhere between Pittsburgh and Akron. "I bet she had to work out like a fiend with all that pizza and custard everywhere."

"Uh-huh," I utter, gazing at the passing landscape out the car window.

"Amen," Mom says.

I look over at my mother, who is now motioning the sign of the cross and muttering something unintelligible, and can't help but notice how beautiful her naïve smile really is.

WWWD? She'd make the best of it ... she always does.

And with that, I decide that my only response is going to be to nod happily in agreement. Despite cheap *(thrifty)* motel rooms, blistered feet, and spotty meals; despite sunburn, too much taffy, and the complete absence of Lady W; I decide to make the best of it. I slide back in my seat, smile, and with a Whitley-like sense of purpose, move this adventure from the "throwaway" to the "keeper" pile.

Tiffany Schultz is a humor columnist, features writer, short story enthusiast, and aspiring novelist. She has work appearing on a monthly basis in a suburban-Chicago community living magazine, and her short story "Right Before His Eyes" was published in *The Beach House*. Tiffany, a born and bred Midwesterner, uses her fond memories of vacations spent out east as a kid as the inspiration for her beach and boardwalk writing adventures. Alongside her husband and two children, she visited Rehoboth Beach for the first time in 2014, but plans on making many return trips in the future.

Untethered

by Margaret Farrell Kirby

Throw your dreams into space like a kite, and you do not know what it will bring back, a new life, a new friend, a new love, a new country.
—ANAÏS NIN

Nora hadn't been back to the beach or the boardwalk since that day, but had so often relived every detail that it was as if it were permanently etched in her mind. She could still feel the texture of that morning: how happy she thought she was, how unaware of what was to come. It was a Saturday, the middle of July, the last day of their yearly beach vacation.

Brad, after his morning run, was reading the *Washington Post*, having his coffee; the children—six-year-old Clare and ten-year-old Paul—were eating bags of Cheerios in front of the TV. She blew kisses and went out to get her bike to ride to the boardwalk, her turn for some time alone.

Once on her bike, she looked back at the house they'd rented on Chesapeake Street for the past ten years: an aqua-blue clapboard house, white shutters, window boxes full of pink petunias beginning to get tall and leggy, sea grass, annuals and perennials of all colors in the front yard, so different from their house in Bethesda, a staid colonial with a manicured lawn and shrubs lined up perfectly on each side of the maroon front door. Just looking at this house, she experienced an inner expansion, a freedom; she felt untethered from her ordinary life.

She'd ridden her bike each morning of the vacation over the bridge across Silver Lake into Rehoboth, to the end of the boardwalk, and parked it in a bike rack on Prospect Street.

After walking to the Henlopen Hotel at the other end of the boardwalk, she wandered back toward the middle and picked a bench, that day in front of the Atlantic Sands hotel. It being Saturday, the boardwalk was especially busy.

Her routine was to alternate—face the ocean for a while, then flip the bench to watch the boardwalk. She loved the morning movement: storefronts being opened, walkers and joggers out for their morning exercise, strollers being pushed, dogs being walked, families riding bikes. She watched the parade of beachgoers emerging from the streets, laden with chairs, coolers, beach bags, and umbrellas as they headed to the beach.

She often felt like a voyeur, looking at faces, listening to conversations, trying to steal glimpses of the lives around her. That morning she listened to a couple on the next bench arguing, clearly in a bad mood and angry, a contrast to the prevailing atmosphere; aside from the occasional tired, cranky children or surly teenagers, the boardwalk radiated a contagious lightness of spirit.

That July day, she looked at the deep extravagant beach-blue sky dotted with colorful kites waving gently in the breeze, taut against their strings, amid white gauzy clouds, not a dark one in sight. Hearing the background noise of the waves breaking on the shore and the sound of seagulls, and feeling the gentle warmth of the sun, Nora was content, relaxed, lost in her reverie. She occasionally glanced at the angry couple sitting quietly on their bench.

"Hi, Nora."

She looked up, startled to see Brad standing there, in his shorts and T-shirt, holding two carryout cups of coffee. She looked at her watch. It was ten o'clock; she wasn't due back to the house until eleven.

"What are you doing here? Where are Clare and Paul?" she asked.

"They're starting to pack, I told them we'd be back soon and would go to the beach."

Nora was surprised; it was unusual for him to do something so spontaneous. "How did you know where I'd be?" she asked.

"You always end up on a bench somewhere on the boardwalk; I parked my bike on the end and walked until I found you."

After the initial surprise and a brief twinge of annoyance—this was *her* time—she smiled at him. "You must have missed me," she said, as he sat down and silently handed her a cup of coffee.

She looked at him. He was staring down at his hands, which were wrapped tightly around his cup, his face hidden from her view.

"What's wrong?" she asked.

As he began to recite a string of sentences, his voice was so low she had to move closer to hear him. He'd been unhappy, feeling boxed in; he needed some time alone to sort things out, wanted to move to an apartment for a while. He looked at her after he finished his litany, his eyes unreadable behind sunglasses.

Speechless, uncomprehending, she stared at him. It was as if something unforeseen was coming toward her at high speed.

She studied his face. Tanned from their vacation, he looked handsome. His hair was brown, curly, and beginning to turn gray. College sweethearts, they had dated since they were twenty; after graduation she'd gotten a job as a kindergarten teacher, Brad had gotten his MBA and then a job as an accountant. After getting married at twenty-five, they worked for five years, then started their family and had two children, spaced four years apart, just as they had planned. Everything seemed to fit perfectly.

She tried to get her mind to work. All she could think to say was, "You're kidding, right?" After there was no answer, she asked, "Is there someone else?"

"No, no," he answered. "Only a therapist who's been helping me sort things out."

"You've been seeing a therapist?" she asked, incredulous.

She began to feel hot. The sun was getting higher, no longer so gentle but now glaring and harsh. Her legs were sticking to the bottom of the boardwalk bench. The happy throngs of people now annoyed and taunted her with their smiles and laughter.

"I don't understand. I thought we were happy." She was nauseated, her head started to hurt. "The kids, what about the kids?" she asked as she began to grasp the implications of what he was saying.

"We'll figure it out, make it work. I've thought about it."

"You've thought about it? How long has this been going on in your head?" she asked, trying to keep from yelling.

She looked at him, the once familiar face she loved, suddenly foreign. She looked at the next bench, at the couple she'd been watching. They were smiling now, unaware of the seismic shock that had occurred on the bench next to them.

He looked away. "I really tried to make it work."

"You tried to make it work!" she yelled now. "How in the hell did you do that? You never said a word to me."

"Nora, please," he said, as he looked around, clearly embarrassed as people walking by turned to stare.

She jumped up, took the lid off her cup of coffee, poured it on the bench, watched as it ran and pooled on the glossy white paint, watched with satisfaction as it seeped toward his shorts, his tanned hairy thighs. The couple on the next bench openly stared.

She wouldn't let the tears start until she was away from him. She knew she had to get off the boardwalk, away from everyone. She passed Dolle's and looked down Rehoboth Avenue; too many people, with Saturday-morning shoppers and lines already at Thrasher's.

She walked to the next block and down Wilmington Avenue, past Penny Lane, unsteadily threading her way back to her bike. Past her favorite stores and restaurants—each beloved landmark tainted and ruined.

For a long time after that day, it was as if a protective layer of skin had been peeled off, leaving her raw and exposed. The pain she felt when she thought about the boardwalk was searing; she felt a double sense of betrayal—not only at what he had done, but the fact that he'd done it there. She equated it with the loss of her innocence in a way, her illusions about her happy life.

She couldn't imagine how she'd blindly lived in such a cocoon of self-delusion. How ironic it was that he felt boxed in, she thought. She was so used to accepting and living with her own sense of being boxed in. He, detail-oriented, logical, rational; she, scattered and disliking of order; she'd tried to meet his expectations. They had adjusted, or so she thought.

She pictured the dishwasher after he loaded it. Everything exactly in its place: the knives, spoons, and forks, handles down; the plates, dishes, and bowls facing the same direction. She pictured him frowning at her efforts—some handles up, some down, the plates and dishes here and there. She didn't have his spatial sense or need for order.

He complained about other things, like how she put the toilet paper on the roll. He showed her how to do it, but Nora couldn't remember—it never made sense. And it never seemed that important.

Maybe it was an accumulation of the things she did that annoyed him, or perhaps there was something glaringly wrong with her that she couldn't see. In the end, Nora never really knew the reason.

After the divorce was settled she began to refashion her life. She let him have the staid colonial, moved to a two-bedroom condo, found her life easier and freer. Brad had the children every other weekend; they alternated school breaks and summer vacation. With time for herself now, she took meditation classes, did yoga, and began painting again. She kept teaching kindergarten.

Eventually, she realized that she had changed, had made a fundamental shift, had formed a new foundation. She was no longer that naïve woman on the boardwalk.

She took pleasure in little things, like loading the dishwasher with no one correcting her. She made new friends, laughed more, was able to recapture her buried spontaneity. She became almost grateful to Brad for liberating her, unboxing her from his rigid expectations, for the unintended consequences of what he had done.

One day, she glanced at a picture she had on her dresser, one she had taken of Brad and the children sitting happily on a boardwalk bench with a bucket of Thrasher's fries. She felt a twinge of longing, a yearning to go back, a realization of how much she missed it.

As the two-year anniversary of that fateful day approached, Nora realized that Brad would have the children that week, on a Busch Gardens vacation. She called the Atlantic Sands and rented a room facing the ocean.

The first morning there, she ventured out of the hotel onto the boardwalk and found an empty bench. The sound of the waves breaking on the shore, the squawking of the seagulls, the feel of sea breeze, and the subtle smell of the ocean, brought her alive again to the texture of the boardwalk. There were sounds of laughter from a couple on the next bench. She inhaled deeply and smiled.

Her cell phone rang. She looked at the caller ID: Brad calling from Williamsburg.

"Hi, Brad," she answered. "How are you all doing?"

"Yesterday was nice, we spent the day at Busch Gardens, had fun. But it's raining today. How are you doing?"

"Good," she said. "Who wants to talk?" Usually Clare and Paul argued over who would be first.

"If you have a minute I'd like to talk to you."

Crap, she thought. She wasn't going to tell him she was sitting on the boardwalk. "About what?" she asked.

"I've been thinking. I was thinking before this trip." He was talking in halting, disjointed sentences, so unlike his usual crisp and efficient way of making his thoughts known. "Actually Clare and Jack and I would like to come to the beach, I could rent a couple more rooms at the Sands ..."

"Wait," she interrupted him. "What are you talking about?"

"Well, the kids are bored here. And we have four more days of vacation. They miss the beach. I do too. And I want to talk about us."

"What about us?"

"I think we should get back together. I decided I was just going through some kind of midlife crisis; I'm over it now. It would be better for the kids and better for us financially. We can talk when we get there."

He sounded so sure of himself, in charge, insistent, saying the words she had once so longed to hear. It was as if he were offering a dog a bone, certain the treat wouldn't be rejected.

She looked up at a kite bobbing in the sky, back and forth in the wind, straining at the end of the line, tethered to the one holding the string.

"Nora," he said. "Are you there?"

"I'm here," she said. "I'm here."

She took a deep breath, still looking at the kite. "No, Brad, you can't come. We're divorced, I'm happy with my life; this is my vacation. If Paul and Clare are bored, take them home. Tell them I love them and I'll call them later."

She pushed the "off" button on her phone, stood up, and looked out at the expanse of the glimmering ocean. Then she turned around and headed to Thrasher's to stand in line.

Margaret Farrell Kirby is a member of the Rehoboth Beach Writers' Guild and has taken several of their classes in different genres over the past two years. "Untethered" is her second published piece. She divides her time between Silver Spring, Maryland, and Rehoboth Beach, Delaware. She is appreciative of the talented and supportive teachers at the Writers' Guild, and also for the writing opportunities and encouragement from Cat & Mouse Press.

There but for Fortune

by Judy Shandler

There he is again, I note as I begin my morning run: a small frail man with scruffy beard and wild hair, always holding a Styrofoam cup. Presumably it's filled with coffee, or maybe something stronger, although I am pretty sure he would not refuse a misguided offer of cash for it. Each day he claims the same spot on the boardwalk, setting up his tattered campstool just outside the public restrooms one block north of Funland, container in hand. Maybe he's got a prostate problem. Out of the corner of my eye I see him grin maniacally and tip an imaginary hat as I approach, so I lock my eyes straight ahead and concentrate on my stride.

Rumors have him a homeless Vietnam vet, an eccentric millionaire, even an undercover cop; you name it. With his unfailing position as sentry by the bathroom entrance, some add "pervert" to the list. Plenty of benches line the boardwalk on the ocean side across from the restrooms, so why would anyone lug a grimy campstool to claim squatters' rights, right there? I say he's a harmless oddball providing a little bit of local color.

Whatever. I mentally plan for the end of the month when my three sisters will join Rob and me for a week, two trailing husbands, and all lugging countless duffel bags and vacation gear. They will turn our vintage two-bedroom cottage on Rodney Street into the real estate equivalent of a clown car, but more fun. We'll exchange glances and crack up each time my next-door neighbor Gladys looks over from her front porch to ask, "Where in the world do you *put* everybody?"

I am working on my mental to-do list when suddenly a bicycle cuts in front of me, and we collide, hard! The crash of metal is followed by a thud of flesh and bone on the boards. I am down in a flash of spectacular clumsiness, as is the teenaged rider. Passersby rush over, and one offers me a hand. "Thanks," I gasp.

Both my knees are bloodied and stinging. You forget how painful a skinned knee is, something "made all better" with kisses and Superman Band-Aids, but I can tell you, skinned flesh hurts like hell. My right palm, too, is scraped raw. A bead of blood makes its way down my leg.

The young girl lifts her head to onlookers, who ask if she is okay. She is lying awkwardly alongside her fallen bike, like a marionette cut loose from its strings. Wearing jeans, she is better protected than me. She appears dazed. "Is my fault," she apologizes to no one in particular, "My fault. *Izvinitye*. I em so sorry."

The girl rises and steadies herself. When she reaches to upright her mountain bike, we hear a quick metallic rattle and see the gear chain lying in a pool on the boardwalk. The derailleur, now dented, will no longer thread the chain.

She bursts into tears. "I heft to be at work," she says, sobbing. "What heppens now to me? I need job." She's a pretty, dark-eyed girl whom I assume to be an exchange student far from home, and my heart goes out to her. She looks lost, and confused, and scared. A woman in the small crowd reaches over to pat her shoulder. "Sorry, hon. Want to use my cell?" She shakes her head no, and cries harder.

"Let me take a look," says a voice from behind. It's the weird guy, the bathroom geezer! This marks the first time I have heard him speak, or seen him stand, or acknowledged him on any level, so I am as stunned by his sudden presence as I am appalled by it.

Folks give him a wide berth as he squats to examine the mangled bike. The wind lifts his wild tangled hair, making it wilder still, and surreptitiously, from behind, I scrutinize the details of his strange appearance. As does everyone else.

Surprisingly, his shirt and pants are well laundered, albeit bizarrely mismatched and woefully threadbare. His canvas shoes sport a many-layered rainbow of splattered paint. I note with irony that he would surely take first prize in a costume contest for "bum," right down to the stained bandana stuffed into his frayed back pocket.

"Yup, it's busted all right," he pronounces, and the young girl wails in despair.

"I need to be et work, need to vatch kids." She motions to her left. "The Heffles, I am babysitter." She collapses in misery. Embarrassed, a few folks inch away. I, too, feel helpless.

"Welllll," the old guy offers tentatively, "I may have a solution." He looks up and grins foolishly, and I consider that this guy may be certifiably nuts. How in the world can he, or any of us, possibly help her?

"*I* have a bicycle you can use," he announces, almost theatrically, with a sweep of his hand, "in my garage, just a couple blocks away. You could keep it until yours is repaired."

The girl's head jerks up. She stares at him, eyes wide.

Murmurs of assent ripple through the small audience while I am still processing "I have a bicycle, in my garage." Is that even possible? This guy has a house? Nearby?

Within minutes, a chorus of approval erupts among nodding heads. One man claps, and soon everyone applauds this strange man's extraordinary generosity, while suddenly I am watching a movie in my head featuring Norman Bates. Or maybe Freddy Krueger. Not to be an alarmist, but has no one considered he may be completely delusional? And where, exactly, is this old weirdo planning to take her?

"That's not a good idea," I blurt to the young girl.

Her eyes remain glued on the old guy.

I appeal to the crowd. "She doesn't even know …"

"I take *your* bike?" she asks her benefactor. "How? Vhere?"

Within minutes the bystanders depart, exchanging high-fives, and the curtain comes down on this brief unscripted drama. But I remain skeptical. Something is off. Like a Roman emperor, I rule thumbs-down on whatever he's up to. I try to catch the girl's eye but she gives me her back.

He leans closer, speaking softly; I catch a few fragments: "… south onto Winslow … garage unlocked … number 314 … sure, happy to help …"

I back away. Neither the old guy nor the girl acknowledges me. I am relieved that he will not go with her to his house; that is, if he actually has a house—which I doubt. She is probably going on a wild-goose chase, but she will be going alone.

"Thenk you, thenk you!" she calls after a few steps, waving. "You are good man! Thenk you so much!"

The old guy tips his invisible hat to her as he drags the crippled bicycle back to his bathroom sanctuary. He drops it unceremoniously and it clatters to the boards. Easing back into his campstool, he lifts his Styrofoam cup in a toast. "Happy to help."

With that I hobble home to Rodney Street for bacitracin, a few gauze packs, and maybe a couple Superman Band-Aids.

What's this lunatic up to? And what will happen to the pretty, dark-eyed girl?

＊＊＊＊＊＊

Rob insists I have misjudged the old coot. In fact, more than once over the last couple of days, he has accused me of being overly suspicious. And elitist. He is convinced everything I witnessed should be accepted unconditionally; the girl will keep her job thanks to the kindness of the strange old man on the boardwalk. "Sure, he's eccentric," he says. "So, what's the problem? When all is said and done, he still reached out to help the girl, right?"

My pal Marge and I are not so sure. Like me, Marge can easily conjure a few horrifying abduction scenarios from what I've told her, and she has been combing the papers for breaking news of a missing Russian au pair. How would we know what has happened over the past few days? I'm still badly bruised and haven't run on the boardwalk since the accident. Did the old guy lure the girl into some kind of trap? Who knows what has since transpired, good or bad?

The big questions are: Do we believe the old guy lives nearby and could he have actually helped the girl? Or was he conspiring to trick her for some devious purpose? Or is he simply crazy as a loon? Rob says yes to "A," Marge to "B," and I to "C."

Marge and I decide on a drive-by as soon as Rob leaves for work.

Both of us expect 314 Winslow to be a ruin of a house, judging from the old guy's appearance. Actually, Marge is envisioning the old house in *Psycho*, with dilapidated winding stairs leading to a house of horrors high on a hill. When I remind her there are no hills in Rehoboth Beach, she acquiesces with, "Point taken." Personally, I suspect "314 Winslow" was the random creation of an addled brain, with no connection to the guy on the campstool. Still, after three days on the sofa, I am up for an adventure. We go.

We turn onto Winslow and there it is, number 314, a modest bungalow in need of paint on a small and poorly tended lot amid several upsized and modernized beach homes. The name "Galek" is spelled out on the mailbox in faded stick-on letters that had once worn a reflective finish. At the end of a crushed-shell driveway reaching into the overgrown backyard, a detached garage materializes. We park.

Marge rings the doorbell while I slide low on the front seat. The boardwalk guy would have clocked in for his bathroom vigil by now, so if someone answers, it won't be him. The squawk of a raucous laughing gull shatters the morning silence as a Jolly Trolley glides by.

Marge waves me over. Coast clear.

Looking more like Ethel and Lucy than Rizzoli and Isles, we two sleuths scamper onto the front porch. We crouch in front of the windows, peering inside, eyes shaded, but see nothing that either announces or disclaims the old guy's habitation. Or the girl's, thankfully. The rooms are sparsely furnished but tidy, with yellowing shades pulled unevenly across the front windows. We see a pair of plaid loveseats facing each other, two ladder-back chairs, and a few unadorned tables. No television in this room, no books or magazines. Detective Marge adds, "No blood trails." Check.

Looking more like Ethel and Lucy than Rizzoli and Isles, we two sleuths scamper onto the front porch. We crouch in front of the windows, peering inside, eyes shaded, but see nothing that either announces or disclaims the old guy's habitation.

She elbows me to follow her to the garage, primed to find "hard evidence." Maybe she's expecting a frantic young girl, bound and gagged with wild terrified eyes? A torture chamber?

We are midway to lifting the unwieldy garage door when we hear, "Can I help you?"

I freeze.

It's the next-door neighbor, still in his bathrobe, poking his head out his back screen door.

"Uhhh … we wanted to leave something for … Mr. Galek," I stammer, releasing the heavy door with a thud. "Just wondered if we should leave it here, in the back." My face flames red.

"Something for *Mr.* Galek?" he frowns, scratching his head. "Shoot, the Galeks are long gone. Him maybe two, three years ago; her, this past fall." He eyes Marge. "You say you've got a package for …"

"Not a package, exactly," she corrects, brushing her hands together briskly. She strides to his back stoop and extends a manicured hand in introduction.

"Marge Williams," she offers, flashing a smile like a beacon.

He strokes his chin. "Um, Hank."

She launches into her pitch as I listen, transfixed: She's a real estate agent scouring the neighborhood for a client, and she adores this charming diamond in the rough. It's a Craftsman, yes? Just perfect. Exactly whom should she speak with about the property?

She glares at me to play along so I close my mouth and try to look officious.

"You ladies will probably want to talk with Miz Galek's pop. He moved in to help near the end."

Marge cocks her head in question.

"Cancer," Hank continues. "She was dying piece by piece, and with the husband moved out, Noah came down. He did everything for her. *Everything.* He's the one you'll need to talk to; but I can tell you, he'll not be interested in selling this place any time soon."

He steps backward into the house, pulling the screen door after him, but Marge reaches to catch it, all smiles. "No harm in trying," she coos, inviting herself in. And within minutes, she has the owner's name officially recorded in her Day-Timer: Noah Turchev.

Walking back to the car I tell Marge we are spinning our wheels here. The old guy at the boardwalk can hardly take care of himself, let alone someone else. Whoever lives at 314 Winslow, it's not him.

* * * * * *

We each get to work on our computers, and within a day we have compiled a few interesting factoids:

Noah Owen Turchev: Born in Slobozia, Rumania, 1941.

Arrived New York City, 1950, with parents and two older brothers, Leon and Gregor.

Earned BS from the University of Maryland, College Park, in 1964. Psychology.

Law degree, 1967, University of Baltimore. Passed the bar same year.

Title attorney, Columbia, MD, 1968–1977.

Married 1972, Howard County, MD, to Emilee Jordan.

Real estate attorney, Lewes, DE, 1978–2005.

Public records list six properties in Sussex County, one of which is on Winslow Avenue. Four lost to foreclosure.

Wife Emilee, deceased, 2000.

Only child Eleanor Galek nee Turchev, deceased, September 2014.

Turchev was an attorney?

Like I say, no way the old guy on the boardwalk is Noah Turchev.

* * * * * *

The doc removed my bandages first thing this morning, and I am good to go, literally; I've already laced up my Nikes. Rob has taken the day off and we are going for a late-morning walk. Before the bicycle incident I used to run three times a week. Now I'm afraid if I don't start to move this creaky body, my joints will set like cement. Worse, I have gained three pounds. And my sisters arrive this week. I need to get moving!

To satisfy my lingering questions about the old geezer and the young girl, Rob proposes the following itinerary: We'll walk through the neighborhood, get on the boardwalk at the Avenue, head south past the public bathrooms to scope it out, go a few more blocks, and then turn around. We'll see what there is to see and maybe connect a few dots for my report to Marge. As a bonus, I will burn some calories today. I am psyched.

I call Marge. She launches into her latest theory and says don't bother going to the boardwalk because the old guy will be gone, exposed as a pathetic houseless, bike-less fraud. We'll see no whacky bathroom monitor because he'll have crawled back into whatever filthy box he crawled out of.

I hold the phone away from my ear and wince. Her voice continues. I disconnect with a quick "Gotta go."

It feels great to be outdoors getting exercise. Even more fun because Rob is with me. The sky is painted brilliant cerulean with cotton-ball clouds tinged pink. We start strong, going east on Rodney and left onto Bayard, but I am winded by the time we turn onto the Avenue. We see families unloading their coolers and Wonder Wheelers as far as the eye can see, as they set out for their day in the sun. We pick up our tempo and head east.

You know you have reached the ocean block when the air fills with salty sea breezes redolent of caramel popcorn, funnel cakes, and pizza. I never tire of it. I watch small children skip with gleeful abandon into Candy Kitchen; I soak in the comical reactions of folks at The Ice Cream Store reading flavors like "booger," "bacon," and "I don't give a fork" with amusement. I spy slender teens feigning abject boredom as they scan the horizon in search of other slender bored teens. I love it all, and I stop for just a moment to take it in.

"You okay?" Rob asks.

"Better than okay," I say with a smile.

We resume our walk, recharged, taking long strides with elbows pointed. The beach is a mosaic of sound and color, with tourists and locals arriving and departing, grabbing a soda here, a burger there; lathering sunscreen, strolling the boards, tossing fries to the gulls, people-watching on benches. As we step onto the boardwalk, I slow again to inhale the magic of Rehoboth.

Again, Rob misinterprets: "Had enough?" I tell him no, I just need to soak in the scene. The ocean is calm today, a shimmering lake of emerald dotted with frothy pearl breakers. Kids carry plastic pails to and from the water's edge as sandpipers skitter past, and boisterous gulls strut the sand. I take one final look at the tapestry of blankets, umbrellas, and beach chairs, and at "ready, set, go," we jump-start for the third time our compromised attempt at a power walk.

I look straight ahead and almost immediately see the old guy. He is standing by his campstool chatting up the Russian girl. I elbow Rob. "That's him! And that's the girl! Hurry!" I take off, and Rob follows.

She is straddling a red ten-speed with drop handlebars and a black leather racing saddle. The two of them seem to be sharing a joke and the music of her laughter fills the air. As Rob and I approach, she leans in to hug the old guy before pushing off, and he tips that fantasy hat of his in farewell. "So long, Anya," he says as she pedals away.

I am beaming at seeing the girl. She looks so happy. And I will admit to being blown away by that bicycle.

"See you tomorrow!" she calls with a backward wave. "Good-bye, Noah, my friend!"

I stop dead in my tracks. *Noah?*

Rob backs up and slides his eyes to me. "Ahem," he says; meaning, of course, do I see how unkind I have been? He puts his arm around me. "Judge not, lest ye be judged," he whispers, grinning, "because, there but for fortune …" I flush with embarrassment. Rob holds me close.

With that, he turns toward the public bathrooms and tips his own imaginary hat back to Noah. Noah's face erupts in pleasure!

"C'mon," Rob nudges, "let's go talk to the old guy."

Yes, I say to myself, Rob is right. It's time to meet Mr. Noah Owen Turchev.

And that's exactly what we do.

JUDY SHANDLER WRITES A WEEKLY COLUMN FOR *DELAWARE COAST PRESS* AND TEACHES NONCREDIT CREATIVE WRITING CLASSES AT WILMINGTON UNIVERSITY'S REHOBOTH BEACH SITE. SHE HAS PUBLISHED ARTICLES IN *DELAWARE BEACH LIFE* MAGAZINE AND THE *CAPE GAZETTE*. HOLDING AN MA IN CREATIVE WRITING, JUDY IS CURRENTLY A MEMBER OF THE REHOBOTH BEACH WRITERS' GUILD. "THERE BUT FOR FORTUNE" IS HER FIRST PUBLISHED WORK OF FICTION. SHE AND HUSBAND DON ARE ENJOYING SEMIRETIREMENT IN HISTORIC MILTON, DELAWARE.

Thunderbolts

by Cathy Heller

Kate swears they knew we were following them that night. She claims that she and Lauren put some extra wiggle in their step and flipped those long waves of hair on their shoulders in an enticing way.

Ron and I know we were being discreet and that we fell in well behind them on the boardwalk at Wilmington Avenue where we smoked, loitered, and checked out the girls. We watched them turn onto Stockley Street and then rushed to make the turn so we didn't lose them. They entered a house halfway down the block.

Kate says they were looking for us the next evening. However it happened, we were stupidly fortunate.

When Ron called out, "Hey, will you answer a question for us?" Lauren took the lead and came our way. Now here is the stupid part. Ron's question was, "Kenny and I were just wondering. What color is the bow on your bra?" Lauren, who was used to dealing with brothers, lost no time in responding that she wouldn't be caught dead in any bra with a bow or lace. Ron then said, "I don't believe it. Prove it."

While Kate and I looked on skeptically, Ron and Lauren trotted down the steps and ducked under the boardwalk. We turned to face each other at the same time and I was instantly lost in her eyes and her smile, so I did the only logical thing. I wrapped her in my arms and planted a long, hard kiss on those smiling lips that responded softly as I felt her arms move in around me and her body seem to melt into mine. I felt such power, like I had been struck by a thunderbolt. So the first words I said to her when we pulled apart were, "Ah, I think I'm in love." She held out her right hand and said, "I'm Kate."

I took that hand in my own and we walked down the steps to the beach and later got comfortable under the boardwalk. Lauren snapped a Polaroid picture of us when we joined her and Ron on the boardwalk as our first evening together was ending. Kate wrote "June 1, 1969" in bold letters at the bottom of that picture. We would always remember that night.

The next night I was waiting on the boardwalk at Stockley Street holding a bunch of daisies that I had picked from the neighbor's garden. I had tied them with a thin blue bow that matched the small one that was on the front of Kate's bra. Kate hung the flowers on a nail to decorate our special spot under the boardwalk. Our spot was cool, soft, and welcoming. We fell in love as we listened to the ocean and the people enjoying a stroll above us.

We were there often over the next ten weeks that summer. Ron had his little niche carved out as well and it seemed he had a new girlfriend every week. Always the practical joker, he would hold on to one end of a dollar bill and push it between the boards. When an unsuspecting person above went to grab it, Ron would pull it back and say, "Oh, no, you can't catch me," in a high screeching voice that would usually result in a fit of laughter. Ron always wondered why his girlfriends didn't want to return. He had his space decorated nicely. So what if there were pictures from Playboy that would be taken down by younger boys as soon as he fastened them to the boards.

I used my Boy Scout pocket knife to carve "Kate and Kenny '69" into the soft pine board. The spot would offer us protection from the storms we both loved to watch. Once, we saw a water spout form and move along our beach. We would speculate on how often lightning struck the sand or the lights on the boardwalk.

One night, we were digging in the sand and I pulled up something that looked like a root. Kate said it was just petrified dog poop and told me to stop digging. I showed her that it was hollow and easily broken and kept digging to find another piece. When I showed it to Ron's uncle, who taught science, he explained that what I had found was called fulgurite. It's a kind of glass that is formed when lightning strikes the sand. In Latin, *fulgurite* means thunderbolt.

Kate thought that was pretty magical, like a sign from above. She said that we were destined to be together; our chance meeting was like a lightning strike. Ron and I had written a song about girls being sent to us from heaven, but he now changed the words and sang about digging for thunderbolts and finding love.

Ron, Chuck, David, and I were musicians who had a decent garage band. We always brought our guitars to the parties. It was all innocent fun. Yes, there were the pilfered bottles of wine or hard stuff that were passed around, and Ron was the first to bring grass, but we kept each other in line.

Ron's uncle submitted one of our band's tape recordings to a local radio competition. When we were interviewed at the studio, the host announced, "Today we have with us Kenny and Ron, who do lead guitars and vocals, with Chuck on bass and David on drums. They make up a band called … wait a minute, I didn't catch the band's name." We began to laugh because the truth was we could never agree and changed our name as often as Ron changed girlfriends. But we heard Ron blurt out, "The Thunderbolts" and it stuck. It wasn't long until we got a gig at the local hot spot. Then we began getting calls for gigs in Milford and even Dover.

Kate, Ron, and I became part of a group of friends that came together only that summer. Some were local, some were summer visitors, and some only joined us once or twice at our beach parties.

One night, a group of us was huddled around a bonfire on the beach. We felt the magic of the sand, the ocean, and the music that we created. Summer was coming to an end and we were talking about our plans for fall. It seemed we were living a magical dream.

Suddenly, we saw a flash of light and heard what sounded like an explosion. A thunderbolt had struck somewhere on the beach. How I wish that Kate and I had been able to escape to our spot under the boardwalk, but we were at Deauville, just north of the boardwalk's end. As we scrambled to the cars, it began to hail. Kate wrapped herself in a towel from the backseat and said, "Please take me home." I took off just a little too fast.

What happened next is a blur. It was a combination of the powerful rear-wheel drive and the dirt and hail on the lot that sent my car into a fishtail that spun out of control.

Our life as a couple ended that night. When I took flowers to the hospital the next morning, Kate's father met me at the ICU waiting area. He told me that Kate was sleeping and that visitors were limited to family. "It's over, Kenny. As soon as she is stable, we will move her to Philadelphia. We can only hope that she will heal enough to start college in September. She can have a new beginning."

I started to talk but her father cut me off. "Kenny, your irresponsible behavior led to this. I have already consulted my attorney and if you try to contact Kate you will hear from him, so let's just keep this simple. Understand?" As if I had a choice. I handed him the flowers and asked him to give them to Kate. He said that flowers were not allowed in ICU. I gave them to a nurse on my way out.

That day's paper ran a picture of my Camaro with the passenger side wrapped around a pole. I turned on the TV, lay on the sofa, and watched the blades of the ceiling fan spin around overhead. At least they were in a controlled spin, *unlike my life right now,* I thought. I wouldn't ever believe that this was what Kate wanted.

* * * * * *

All through college, we kept The Thunderbolts going strong. I always felt that part of me was missing but, nevertheless, I found success. Ron and I both got real jobs after graduation and we used some of our money to pay for recording sessions and sound editing. We were lucky enough to open for Eric Clapton's band as a last-minute replacement when he played in Philadelphia. We signed a record deal with a small record label as a result of that gig.

It was early summer in 1973 when we performed at the Bottle and Cork. At the end of the evening, I looked up and found myself gazing into the eyes that had captured me four years earlier. Kate stood there, extending her hand to shake mine. I heard her say that she enjoyed the show and I felt my lips brush her cheek. I think I said, "Good to see you." When she flashed her wide smile, my heart skipped a beat. I had to remind myself to breathe when I saw her parents standing beside her.

Her father had not changed a bit, still looking stuffy in his jacket and tie. He put his hand on my shoulder and called me "Kenny-boy." He led me off to the side while commending me on my success and post-college maturity.

I thought I was going to be sick. I was speechless and struggled to say, "I guess I'm doing all right, Mr. Sanders. How are things with you?" He said that after all these years he had come to terms with the accident. He had found peace as he watched Kate heal. He was proud of how well she had done in college and in finding a job, but something wasn't right. Her smile just didn't come as easily and her spark didn't glow like it had before that terrible night. And then he asked me to come to the house that night for a nightcap.

The band already had the night planned. We always went to a diner that served breakfast all night. Tonight we had to discuss contract renewals. David was being courted by another band,

Chuck had a baby on the way, Ron was happily rolling with life as it happened, and now I had something weighing on my mind. I ended up excusing myself and drove to the boardwalk to reflect on what I really wanted.

I sat in the spot where Kate and I had planned a future of loving each other. I took in the moon and the power of the ocean waves and breezes before I worked up the courage to walk to that clapboard house just down the block. I rang the bell with a trembling hand.

Kate's parents welcomed me in. Kate was sitting on a loveseat in the living room. She put her glass of white wine down on the table and covered her mouth with her hand. She clearly hadn't expected to see me. But I caught a flicker of a smile in her eyes as her parents tried hard to make me feel comfortable. There was polite conversation. They were trying to decide if they were going to sell the house or renovate it.

When I reached the point that I thought I was about to burst from tension, I asked if I could take Kate out for a walk. Her father said, "You'll have to ask her." She took my hand, jumped to her feet, and said, "I thought you'd never ask."

Hand in hand like the two teenagers who fell in love during our magical summer, we rushed as fast as we could to the beach. Kate hit those familiar weathered boards just a step ahead of me, so I caught her in a bear hug and spun her around for a kiss. A powerful, electric-like charge struck us again as it had in 1969. We were laughing, crying, and just giddy. We pulled apart and I looked into her eyes and said, "Ah, I'm still in love." She smiled, held out her hand, and giggled when she said, "And I'm still Kate."

We found our special spot under the boardwalk. With her finger, Kate traced over the letters that still spelled out "Kate and Kenny '69." I used my Swiss Army knife to carve "and '73" beside it. Then I added a lightning bolt.

CATHY HELLER WORKED AS A READING SPECIALIST FOR TWENTY-NINE YEARS IN PENNSYLVANIA. SHE CREATED MANY STORIES, POEMS, AND SILLY SONGS FOR HER STUDENTS AND COLLEAGUES. SHE HAS PUBLISHED TWO POEMS AND IS HONORED THAT "THUNDERBOLTS" IS HER SECOND PUBLISHED SHORT STORY. HER FIRST, "OLD TIMER," WAS PUBLISHED IN *THE BEACH HOUSE*. CATHY ENJOYS THE OCEAN AND THE INDIAN RIVER BAY. SHE AND HER HUSBAND MAKE THEIR HOME IN OAK ORCHARD. SHE ALSO ENJOYS THE SPLENDOR OF OUR NATIONAL PARKS. ALTHOUGH SHE SPENT MANY HOURS ON THE REHOBOTH BEACH BOARDWALK WHEN SHE WAS YOUNG, SHE NEVER VENTURED UNDER THE BOARDWALK LIKE HER CHARACTERS.

No Business at the Beach

by Dennis Lawson

There she was, sunning herself on a lounge chair by the beachfront pool at the Atlantic Sands Hotel. I stood on the Rehoboth Beach boardwalk, peering at her from thirty feet away through the metal fence that separates the public from the pool. The fence's metal slats were thin and widely spaced so that the hoi polloi like me could look in with envy. Beth was sitting upright and facing me, but she didn't react to me standing there and watching her. Her eyes were probably closed behind her giant sunglasses.

It was late afternoon. The summer sun remained strong and it beat down on my scalp. My hair is almost all gone on top. I should wear a hat, but none of them work for me. A ball cap is lame, a fishing cap embarrassing. The only hat I like is a fedora, but then people would think I'm a professional killer.

Which I am, but it's not something I exactly advertise.

I walked along the fence to the Sandcrab Bar, which is the Atlantic Sand's outdoor cocktail lounge. Around the side, a short flight of stairs leads up to the pool. But unlike the pool, the bar is open to the public. At night, the bar gets lit up by a bunch of tiki torches and there's always a crowd. Right then business was slow. I stepped under the canopy and greeted the bartender, a thin, tired-looking brunette, probably late thirties, who managed to give me half a smile.

"Jack and Coke," I said. The bartender went to work. That one was for Beth—I remembered that she liked them. I'm a fan of whiskey, but not so much Jack Daniels. I was hoping for Seagram's VO, but no dice. "And a Canadian Club on the rocks," I added.

The bartender laid the drinks on the counter and didn't bother to give me a price. I pulled a twenty out of my billfold and handed it to her. As I picked up the cups, she finally gave me a smile. I'm sure the drinks were more expensive than they should be, but that still had to be a decent tip.

I went straight for the stairs to the pool. The bartender had already moved on to a new customer. And I looked like I belonged there. Not only did I have two drinks, but I was dressed nicely—white polo shirt with thin multicolored stripes, khaki pants, boat shoes, aviator shades, and a gold-tone Casio wristwatch.

Even with decades of experience behind me, I had to gather my courage to keep a smile on my face as I approached Beth. She was in her twenties when we met. Now, she'd have to be almost fifty, but she was as gorgeous as ever. Her curves filled out a two-piece black bathing suit. A gold ring connected the cups on top, and another gold ring hitched the bottom across her soft thigh. She seemed to be dozing. A pair of high-heeled slippers waited beside her chair. A young man who looked to be fresh out of college occupied the next chair. He didn't look all that happy to see me approach with two drinks. His lily-white chest practically glowed.

"When did the stork drop you off?" I asked.

"What's that supposed to mean?" he replied.

Beth stiffened. Then she casually lifted her sunglasses up and perched them in her red-dyed hair. "Aloha, Frank. It's been too long. I wouldn't expect to see you here today."

"Oh? And why is that?"

"It's the Preakness, silly. Don't you always go to Baltimore to see the race?"

She had me there. "I'm impressed you still remember."

"I didn't know you'd end up looking so much like Hunter S. Thompson."

"Is that a compliment or an insult?"

"I've always found tall, intelligent madmen alluring."

I smiled at the kid, who looked annoyed. I had no doubt that he was already crushing on Beth, and crushing hard. It's the only way with her.

"Listen, kid, I'm sorry to interrupt your tête-à-tête. I have some business to discuss with our friend Beth here. Time to run along."

He looked at Beth to see what he should do.

"It's fine," she said to him. "I'll credit your account and we'll spend another day together. Don't worry, it's a long summer."

The kid wasn't happy but he pulled on his T-shirt. He gave me one more spiteful look before walking away and going down the stairs toward the bar. I kept watching until he moved a ways down the boardwalk.

"This Jack and Coke is for you," I said. I handed her the drink.

"My favorite. I guess you remember some things about me, too." She took a generous sip.

I put my drink down on a little table between Beth's chair and the one the kid was in. I raised the kid's seat to its upright position and made myself comfortable. I had a sip of my whiskey. It brought back some good memories. I pushed them aside.

"You told him that you have business to discuss," Beth said.

"I do."

"You know the rule. No business at the beach."

She wasn't kidding. That was one of our organization's policies. You could certainly do business in vice—that was Beth's trade—

because the fun stuff was okay. It mainly referred to the nastier stuff—no killing, no kidnapping. And no working out business with other families and organizations.

"Hopefully it's just a simple misunderstanding," I said.

Beth had a couple swallows of her Jack. Her cup was more than half empty.

"Thirsty?" I asked.

"Get on with it."

"Tell me your sins, Beth."

She was quiet. We watched the people go by on the boardwalk, the waves washing along the shore. Then she said: "You want to talk business? Go ahead. Do your talking. And make it quick, because you're already costing me money."

"It's my understanding that money isn't an issue for you. On account of holding out on the boss."

She turned on her side and watched me. Out of the corner of my eye I could see her twisting a strand of hair. She waited until I looked at her. "Just so I understand. I inherit something, left for me in a will by a man who wanted to see I at least got something while his frigid wife and worthless kids got the rest of his estate, and I'm supposed to cut a check to the boss? Is that really how things operate?"

"Yes, that's really how things operate."

"Give me a break." She lowered her voice to a harsh, angry whisper. "I'm one of the best earners he's got. How many honey-traps have I set over the years? How many of them are still paying, even after all this time?"

I hated to stop her while she was on a roll. Her angry words sent ripples along her soft flesh. I enjoyed more of my Canadian Club. Then I reached down to the little clutch she had stowed beneath her chair. I looked over the flower pattern and opened it. She watched me but didn't say anything or try to stop me. Hotel key-card, some cash, lipstick, mascara, a little mirror, and two airport-sized bottles of booze: Jack Daniels, of course, and Absolut vodka. Both had broken seals and were around three-quarters full. I closed the clutch and put it back down.

"We know you've been working with some of Chen's boys," I said. "You're going to have to tell me a better story."

She downed the rest of her Jack. "Fine. Buy me dinner. Let me just run up to my room and put something on over this."

"No dice. I like you without a gun. We can get you something at the five and dime on our way to Grotto's."

She glared at me as she put her sunglasses back on. Then she grabbed her clutch and slipped into her heels. Her balance wasn't good. I took her arm and led her down the stairs.

Evening was settling around us on the boardwalk. The waves brought a gentle breeze. At the five and dime, Beth bought a long dress to wear over her bathing suit.

"Why not get a pair of flip-flops?" I asked.

"I've got an image to maintain. How am I supposed to make money? Especially since apparently I'm not giving enough away."

"Cute," I said. And I meant it. We both knew her time on this earth was numbered in hours and minutes, not days and years. But she wanted to act like she was being wronged. I respected her for it.

We continued along the boardwalk, among the families, friends, and couples, like we were a couple ourselves. We had known each other for a long time; we came into the organization together. Back then, I was trying to make it as a private eye. I was digging up dirt on Judge Kowalski, a Wilmington judge who was popular with the community and especially beloved by the local police force. His wife had gotten sick of him stepping out on her and had employed me to dig up enough dirt to make divorcing him a breeze. When I realized that he had taken up with a dancer from a go-go club on Route 13, I offered the dancer a slice of the pie if she would double-cross him. Beth happened to be that dancer. The police and the DA's office hated us, but the organization sent us a lot of warm words. Turned out we had skill sets that were very profitable, if we were willing to swallow our conscience. And, in some ways, our pride.

We got pizza at Grotto's and fries at Thrasher's and then headed for an empty white bench. I slid the backrest so we would be facing away from the beach. I figured the only reason she wanted to go for a walk was so one of Chen's people could tail us. I had noticed three people—two men, plus a woman—who could be tails, but didn't have anyone locked in yet. Beth was eating like she was enjoying it, which was a good sign—it meant the tail was on to us. I was looking forward to meeting this person.

"This feels like old times," Beth said. "Out on the prowl together. I feel like such a big deal, considering you'd give up the Preakness for me. Are you still as obsessed as you were back then?"

"I've got a decent amount riding on it and I expect to come out pretty well. Now let me ask you a question. Why do you need Chen's gang to help you with your inheritance? Why isn't the boss good enough for you?"

She sighed and drank her soda. "Always business. You were like this back then, too."

"And you were too clever for your own good. I know. Move the story along."

"It's simple. Chen's an art collector. Especially older American stuff. Mr. LaRue's collection is right up his alley. Chen's paying me half the market value, but I'm still making a killing."

"So what are we talking about here? Give me a number so I understand."

"Fifty grand."

No way she'd toss the organization aside for that amount. She was barely trying. Now I was kind of insulted.

"Let's talk about how we can make things right. I want to walk off this pizza. Let's go down to Funland. It's been a long time for me."

"What is this, some kind of date?"

"Yeah, why not? We never really had a date. Might as well try now."

The sun was getting lower, and the beach was clearing out, but there were still plenty of people on the boardwalk. We passed the Greene Turtle and came to the Playland arcade, the one with the mechanical Zoltar fortune teller out front.

"Think if we'd asked him about us thirty years ago, Zoltar would've predicted where we'd end up?"

I didn't reply. She made a mistake in stopping us like that—it forced the dimwit tailing us to suddenly turn and look at a Whac-a-Mole game twenty feet away. The thing about a tail is, you don't want him to stand out. Not too tall, not too short. But in reality, that eliminates a lot of people. This guy was as average as they come, for a beachgoer: muscle shirt, baggy cargo shorts, flat boots. Okay, the boots were a little out of place. And the lack of style was just embarrassing.

"Are you happy with who we are, Frank? If you could change who we are, would you?"

She caught me off guard with that one. All of my doubt about taking her out came creeping back. I had to focus on the job at hand.

"We are who we are, Beth. You're the same person you always were. I'm the same person I always was, deep down."

"Really? You were always a killer deep down?"

Focus. "Only as necessary. I can be your friend tonight, if you want me to be. Now come on. We'll be lost in the crowd at Funland. We can talk there and work things out."

Funland hadn't changed, at least not that I could tell. Bumper cars. Kids in rocket ships. Horses spinning around on a carousel. Screams coming from the haunted mansion. The tail was getting close, so I had to make a move. I leaned over a metal fence in front of the helicopter ride. Beth did the same. I casually took a pair of handcuffs out of my pocket and cuffed her to the fence.

"I need to use the bathroom for a moment," I said. "I don't feel like having to search for you when I get out."

I walked into the bathroom and pocketed my sunglasses. A dad was shepherding his little boy out. That left me alone—luck was on my side for the moment. I pulled on a pair of leather gloves.

My pal in the muscle shirt walked in. His hand was in his pocket, presumably on a gun. He didn't have time to draw before I smashed his head against the wall. While he was still dazed, I got behind him and wrapped an arm around his neck. I forced him into the last stall. I only squeezed his neck until he passed out—remember, no business at the beach. I sat him on the toilet, flushed for good measure, and after exiting the stall, I used a quarter to jam the door closed. In the moment of calm that followed, I took off my gloves and caught my breath. The carousel's happy tune played in the background. I whistled along for a few bars as I went on my way.

Beth was where I left her. She looked surprised to see me. Again, I was insulted. "You underestimate me," I said. I stuck the key into the lock and released the cuffs. "Now something tells me that Chen doesn't send a goon to keep an eye on you unless we're talking serious business. Chances are that I'm going to kill you either way, but you might as well at least try to talk your way out of it."

We walked out of Funland. She didn't sob at all, but a few tears escaped from behind her sunglasses. The tears left multicolor streaks from all the eyeliner and eye shadow she was wearing. She was a little too conspicuous on the boardwalk, so I led her out onto the beach. The sky was gray and we had a stretch of sand all to ourselves. When we got close to the water, I pulled her down beside me. To anyone looking out there, we were just a romantic couple trying to get some privacy. I looked at my watch.

"Sorry I don't have a drink to offer you," I said. "Feel free to have one of yours. Start talking."

She slipped her shoes off and dug her toes into the sand. "You've heard about the art museum selling some of their paintings to get out of debt? Well, LaRue was on their board of trustees. Some of the other trustees were seriously considering selling LaRue's favorite painting in the whole collection. He was outraged. So I convinced him to steal it. The timing was perfect, because the painting wasn't on view. And LaRue thought he was just borrowing it. I told him that my people would slip it back into the collection, after the museum sold enough stuff. Then LaRue had an unfortunate accident. The whole plan worked. The painting he left me in his will was a nice gift, but it was nothing compared to the masterpiece we got out of there. Chen really is an art collector; I've been working with him because he's going to be my fence."

"Going to be? So you've still got it?"

"It's hanging above the bed in my hotel room. 'The Nymphs' by Alfred Burnside. It's a scene of five women in long white dresses dancing out in the woods. If you know anything about art, you know that it's an American reaction to the British pre-Raphaelites. I know I'm talking another language here, but it's pretty rare stuff. Here's a translation: millions of dollars."

Now I needed a drink. But I didn't really trust hers.

"And the unfortunate accident?"

"I'm not just a honey-trap, my dear. I've got other jobs as well."

I always considered Beth my equal, but I never knew she was a killer as well. My mind was reeling.

"Why make this move? What is it that you didn't have?"

"How about a life of my own? How about always having to work for someone, taking orders, having to report on every last thing I did? For a long time I enjoyed the life. But at some point, it became hollow. I want to be my own boss. I want to live for me. I still don't know how you guys got onto me."

"That was the easy part. We've got a guy inside Chen's organization."

"They're the ones who have it the worst. The two-faces."

Looking at Beth, I felt responsible. I helped bring her into this life. And for her, it wasn't worth living any more. "I think we can work out an angle," I said.

She smirked at me. "Oh, yeah? What's that? Turn everything over to the boss man?"

"Isn't it worth it for your life?"

She was quiet. The water rolled gently and the sky got darker. "I could use a drink," she said.

"You and me both."

She opened her clutch and took out the Absolut vodka. "The Jack is drugged," she said.

"At least you ruined some Jack and not something good like VO."

She gave me a small smile and tipped the Absolut against her mouth. I watched her throat pulse with a swallow. Relieved, I took the bottle from her and had a swallow myself.

I'm not a fan of vodka, but I could still tell there was something very wrong with it as it went down my throat. Beth spit out the vodka that she'd held in her mouth, and now she gave me a much bigger smile.

I could feel my central nervous system beginning to shut down. I automatically reached for the snub-nosed .38 holstered under my shirt, but Beth grabbed my wrist before I got close. With her other hand, she pulled a small knife out of one of her shoes. The blade pressed against my throat, and I fell backward. Beth lay down beside me. We looked like two lovers whispering sweet nothings to each other. The blade remained against my throat.

"You're not dying," she said. "If you fight the effects, you should be able to stumble out of here. You're going to feel like crap tomorrow, though." Her lips came up to my ear. The sound of her breathing was like a seashell pressed close. Or was that the ocean? I think I heard her say, "I decide what makes my life worth living, sweetheart."

Then she was gone. Some number of minutes later I managed to get to my feet. The effects of the laced vodka were easier to overcome when I was walking. I don't remember much about how I got to the boardwalk, except for some reason, the bright orange Dolle's sign was burned into my retinas. Every time I closed my eyes, I saw it. The less said about the rest of the night and the next day, the better.

Later that week, I got a bottle of Seagram's VO in the mail. That was the last I heard from Beth. I didn't catch much hell for failing to take her down, because she was well-liked. No one in the organization really wanted to think of her as a target.

Chen was another story altogether.

DENNIS LAWSON RECEIVED AN INDIVIDUAL ARTIST FELLOWSHIP FROM THE DELAWARE DIVISION OF THE ARTS AS THE 2014 EMERGING ARTIST IN FICTION. HE GOES BACK AND FORTH BETWEEN REALISTIC FICTION AND CRIME TALES. WHENEVER HE WRITES ABOUT THE BEACH, GANGSTERS SEEM TO GET INVOLVED. FOR "NO BUSINESS AT THE BEACH," HE INTENDED TO WRITE A STORY ABOUT A PRIVATE DETECTIVE IN THE MOLD OF PHILIP MARLOWE—BUT THEN THE NARRATOR ALMOST IMMEDIATELY DECLARED HIMSELF TO BE A KILLER INSTEAD. DENNIS'S STORY "FAIR WARNING" APPEARED IN THE PREVIOUS REHOBOTH BEACH READS ANTHOLOGY, THE BEACH HOUSE. HE ALSO HAS A CRIME STORY IN THE AUTUMN 2014 EDITION OF THE FOX CHASE REVIEW. HE AND HIS WIFE, BETH-ANN, LIVE IN NEWARK, DELAWARE, WITH THEIR DOG AND CAT.

Debut

by J. L. Epler

Less than a mile each way—that's all it was. From the Boardwalk Plaza Hotel on the north end, past the intersection at Rehoboth Avenue, down to the turnaround at Prospect Street, and back. Joanna knew it wasn't the distance that was the problem. It was the memories.

"Never mind that," she said to herself, checking her hair in the rearview mirror as her car idled at the red light on Route 1 in the early summer heat. "Today is different. And *I'm* different," she added assertively. She opened up the calendar on her phone, glancing back up quickly to see that the light hadn't changed yet, and clicked on today's date: June 6. She typed in "Debut," and then rested her phone back on the empty passenger's seat just as the light turned green.

As she drove slowly into town, she noticed the lack of chaos that usually accompanied summer weekends. *The locals haven't gone into hiding yet,* she thought. She saw a smattering of vacationers who were taking advantage of the empty parking spaces and open restaurant seats before the real crowds came into town.

Joanna knew all of this because she had grown up in Rehoboth—well, actually just outside of it, in Angola. When people asked, she just said "Rehoboth," partly to make them jealous and partly to avoid the quizzical looks when she started to explain where Angola really was. *After all, I did work here every summer,* she reminded herself. In the first few summers she was old enough to work, she became a game operator at Funland, wearing the signature red shirt and khaki shorts.

But in her senior year of high school, she blossomed into a skillful swimmer, tall yet agile, which prompted her to try out for a coveted lifeguard position in Rehoboth, which she easily won. She wore the bright red swimsuit with pride, and waited patiently—more patiently than she should have had to—for the automatic upgrade in social status that usually came with the position. She chuckled to herself as she pulled into the parking garage underneath the hotel. *I spent my entire adolescence in a color that was all wrong for me.*

But many things were wrong for her during that awkward and painful time in her life, when she would do anything to cancel out the pregnant pauses of others who observed her with a curious eye. She could sense their awkward confusion as they glanced at her as unobtrusively as possible, as if she were a mystery that they just couldn't figure out. Their puzzled expressions said it all: *something was off.*

Thankfully, twenty years had shifted the town's population, but there were some holdovers. A handful of Joanna's ex-coworkers hadn't left the resort town for bigger and better opportunities. Instead, they had moved up into management, or become part owners in the businesses they frequented as teens. It was those people Joanna secretly hoped to see tonight.

For her special night, she spared no expense. She reserved an oceanfront room at the Boardwalk Plaza so she would be able to hear the ocean. She also saw value in the hotel's proximity to the boardwalk, where she planned to debut her new look. Much was at stake tonight for Joanna, and she needed a room that would provide a quick entrance or exit, depending on how she viewed it.

Once she was settled in her room, it took her nearly two hours to get herself ready, but she had come to enjoy the process that once seemed so tedious. Over the past few months, she could eliminate several steps thanks to the work the doctors had done. She took her time, applying her makeup and doing her hair as the sound of crashing waves and crying seagulls came through the sliding door of her oceanfront room. But her stomach started to turn on her as the sun exited over the western side of the hotel. She paced nervously, trying to channel the person she was now before stepping out onto the catwalk, which tonight came in the form of the boardwalk.

Looking up and down the wooden strip, Joanna noticed that the boardwalk was fairly empty except for where it intersected with Rehoboth's main avenue.

"Well, that's disappointing," she said aloud, but moved forward anyway onto the center strip that was lighter and angled differently than its adjacent parts. "Almost looks like the yellow brick road," she smirked.

Joanna felt regal in her new outfit, especially the wedge sandals she had bought just for this occasion. Despite the unevenness of the planks on the boardwalk, she moved in them with ease, thanks to weeks of practice going up and down the sidewalk in front of her apartment, which was also uneven due to the old tree roots that had upended the blocks of cement into slanted sections. She paired the sandals with a cute summer skirt that was a creamy yellow, bright but not obnoxious. Still uncomfortable with the shape of her arms, she layered her print camisole top with a billowy gauze blouse that came to her elbows and tied shut in the front in two places. The blouse showed a faint outline of her figure without too much detail. "Slight reveals" of the human form were often more intriguing than the real thing. That little piece of advice came from *Glamour*—or was it *Elle*? She had spotted it in the stack of beauty magazines at the doctor's office and had quickly torn it out and shoved it in her purse before the receptionist at the front desk could notice.

With each step down the boardwalk, Joanna's shoulders started to rise from their earlier protective position, and her downward glance leveled off to where she was looking straight ahead. The smell of the sun-warmed wood of the boardwalk flooded her instantly with a sense of nostalgia.

She stopped in at Obie's, despite her lack of hunger and thirst, to have a drink at the bar. Adults were there, and she wanted to be among them. She ordered a glass of nondescript Chardonnay from the young bartender. Red wine would stain her teeth. The sound of sportscasters calling a baseball game on the TV screen competed with the chatter among the patrons. Joanna set her gaze on the ocean, which was visible only from the elevated bar inside. If she narrowed her gaze directly on the water, she almost felt transported to some warm Caribbean island bar. The view was that good. But the cacophony of sounds was too familiar to escape the fact she was not anywhere but Rehoboth Beach.

She turned her attention back to the atmosphere inside. The bartender was nice enough. He was a young man—attentive and polite—but Joanna could tell that she was the type of woman he wouldn't spend time getting to know, despite the good tip he might get for trying. She was aware that her dress and demeanor suggested a more maternal feel. Still, she wanted to engage someone here, so she sipped her wine slowly in hopes that an opportunity would occur. It did, but only as she was paying her bill. A middle-aged couple, dressed in matching Hawaiian shirts, sat in the two seats to her right, within her view of the ocean.

"I think we are in your way, aren't we?" the woman asked, as she noticed Joanna lean back on her bar stool to scan the ocean. She had just given the bartender her credit card.

"Oh no, I'm heading out anyway. It is some view, isn't it?" Joanna added in a lighthearted tone, wanting to assure them that they hadn't interrupted her.

"Yeah, it's great," the man said as he smiled and looked down at Joanna's shoes. She was now standing, and her natural height, in combination with the shoes, was an unusual sight.

Did he just give me the once-over? Joanna thought.

"Wow, did you play basketball?" the man asked reverently.

"George! God, what kind of question is that to ask?" the woman admonished. She then turned to Joanna. "Ignore him. He's a man. He has no filter."

Joanna thought this was funny, but she immediately turned her gaze to him and responded gently, with a warm smile, "Actually, I was a swimmer in high school and was quite good at it."

"I guess you were." He smiled back.

The woman added, "Are you from around here?"

Finally, Joanna thought.

"Yes! Why? Are you from around here?" She leaned forward, as if doing so would propel her into the intersection of the past and present she was hoping for.

"Nah. We're from Dover."

"Oh," Joanna said, deflated. She distracted herself from her disappointment by signing the bill the bartender had just brought back, ignoring his untimely friendliness now that he could sniff out a reason to be so. Instead, as she signed, she noticed how nice her nails looked this evening. The manicurist had done an exceptional job yesterday.

Joanna politely said her good-byes to the couple and very consciously shaped her exit, knowing their eyes were still on her as she descended the small set of stairs that led back to the boardwalk. She resisted turning back to check, and instead put a little extra flare in her stride to stoke her confidence.

When she passed the Rehoboth Beach lifeguard station, which had closed for the day, she paused for a few moments, paying homage to the work she had done there for three summers in her red suit. The windows of the small building reflected the dunes to her back, and the outline of her shadow within that reflection appeared authentic to her. She smiled, and imagined what that would look like on the darkened silhouette.

The clouds were burnt orange now, and Joanna no longer needed her sunglasses. Removing them was like removing an additional filter. As she passed the main intersection with Rehoboth Avenue, Joanna decided to sit on a white bench for a while to watch people. Her heart stopped momentarily when she saw a familiar face walk past and sit down on the next bench. The man was famous around here, in an oddly Delaware sort of way. Back when she was young, all of the kids knew him by sight too. Some mocked him privately; some felt sorry for him. Joanna had tried to help him after her shift on the beach one afternoon. He had stood there, she noticed, day after day in the same spot with binoculars, searching for something. When she approached him and asked, he said he was searching for his lost dog. What Joanna didn't know at the time was that his dog had been lost for years, but he still looked for him at sunset every day that he could. He was friendly enough, though, and his futile search resonated with her. By the end of the summer, she just waved to him guiltily, and he always waved back.

Joanna debated whether or not to approach him today. Would he recognize her as the lifeguard who tried to help him find his dog? Probably not. And she couldn't be sure of his state of mind, either. He was already pretty old twenty years ago. As she observed him now, he glanced toward her and nodded his head to acknowledge her. She nodded back and smiled at him weakly. She noticed he still wore the binoculars around his neck.

This encounter with a familiar face ushered forth a somber mood for Joanna, one she had not anticipated tonight. Rather than triumph, she felt inadequate again. She decided against talking with the old man and instead went into Funland. The staff still had on red shirts, and the rides, with the exception of a few, were still in their familiar places. On a whim, she bought three solo tickets to go on the teacups, a ride she had been on as a child and one she worked as a teen. She loved the signature daffodil lamps that loomed large over the periphery of the ride. The line was short, and she got in a cup by herself. It was an awkward fit with her size, and she wasn't sure how to navigate it gracefully in her skirt. She was uncomfortable when the ride started, but within minutes, the ride's magical effect allowed her to release her worries about sitting ladylike in her skirt. She succumbed to the blurred lines, colors, and sounds as they whirred by.

When the ride was over, she continued south on the boardwalk. This section was lined with residential homes, all lit up and lively with the sound of music and conversation that competed with the sound of the surf. Night was falling as Joanna reached the turnaround at Prospect Street. In an effort to prolong what was turning into a disappointing debut, she sat down on the very last white bench to sulk. It was quiet. Too quiet. She opened her purse and brought out her phone, which became the only illumination except for the flickering street lamp and the crescent moon. She scanned her recent posts to Facebook and her text messaging, trying to figure out whom to engage in conversation.

"Having a great time in RB!" she wrote on her page.

Several "likes" came in, along with comments from her friends.

"Jealous."

"What's the weather like?"

"Next time bring me along!"

"How do the new shoes feel?"

Joanna let the virtual conversation continue without posting a response. She pulled up her text messages again.

Charlee, Joanna's friend in Philadelphia, who knew how far she had come, saw her post on Facebook and at that moment, texted Joanna.

"You doing okay?"

Joanna let the ellipsis blink for a while as she pondered her response.

"Nothing happened. I didn't see anyone who recognized me." Joanna confided, not hiding her disappointment.

"Sorry, love. Send me a selfie. I want to gaze upon the gorgeous new you."

Joanna smiled, feeling validated for the first time this evening. It was dark, so she wasn't sure how the photo would turn out, but she sat up straight, reapplied her lipstick, and shot the picture. She looked washed out from the flash, but the beach grass behind her framed the image nicely. She clicked on the picture and sent it to Charlee.

The night air was cool, much cooler than she had anticipated. A stiff wind kicked up from the east as she got up to head back north, toward the hotel. She felt it sharply through her flimsy gauze blouse and at first crossed her arms in an effort to shield herself. The gusts continued and she felt her body instinctively tighten and curl in upon itself for protection. As she approached the commercial section of the boardwalk, gold letters against a deep blue backdrop caught her attention under the fluorescent lamppost and she glanced at it reflexively as she passed. The sign read "Star of the Sea."

Yes, she thought. She released her protective grip on her blouse and defiantly untied the two bows that kept it together, letting it billow and blow open against the wind, her arms and upper body now exposed for all to see, and judge. *This is who I am.* She raised her arms to the wind and the blouse caught it like a kite and slipped off of her arms, untethered. She watched as it danced and twirled, not caring where it would eventually land. Instead, Joanna walked proudly toward the lingering crowd at Rehoboth Avenue, absorbed in her thoughts. She noticed someone approach, but thought she would just walk past.

"Excuse me," the woman said.

As soon as the woman's voice registered, Joanna worked to shift her attention back to the scene around her. This person in front of her was no one she recognized.

"You look familiar. I saw you earlier at Obie's, but I just couldn't place you," the woman said.

Joanna's earlier desire to connect with the past had dissipated several streets back, so the question sparked no response from her.

"Do you have a brother or something? Maybe he was lifeguard in the late '80s?" the woman asked as a last resort.

Joanna's heart skipped a beat, and her original indifference immediately turned. She felt her face grow hot. She peered into the blue eyes of the woman, searching past the graying hair and the onset of small wrinkles around her mouth and eyes, surveying a body that had certainly been cared for but that had also felt the effects of time.

"He was tall, like you, and was a fantastic swimmer. I worked with him, and you resemble him so much. I just had to ask; I am so sorry to bother you," she added, and then began to walk away.

Joanna, still stunned, started to smile, and then laugh. *I have no idea who that was,* she thought, still laughing.

Jennifer Epler is a member of the Rehoboth Beach Writers' Guild and is active in other local writing groups. She has been selected to participate in several writers' conferences and retreats, including Stony Brook University's Southampton Writers Conference and the Delaware Division of the Arts' Writers Retreat in Cape Henlopen. Her story "The Replacement" was published in *The Beach House*. She resides in Wilmington and Rehoboth Beach.

Judge's Comment:

"Debut" deals with a serious topic that is deeply personal, without leaving the reader feeling heavy-hearted. Readers will identify with the narrator's feelings of insecurity, and feel as though they're right there with her as she makes her way down the boardwalk.

The Boardwalk and Dave Grohl

by David Strauss

It'd already been a long, hot day in Rehoboth. We'd actually gone to the boardwalk for the kiddy rides, a chance to get out of Ocean City for half a day—from the insanity of Coastal Highway and the 300,000 others crammed in high-rises and block after block of bright white concrete condominiums, all stacked here, there, and everywhere, to the beaches and those blue rental umbrellas like pushpins on a corkboard—to visit the relative quiet of small-town Rehoboth, with its actual beach houses and cute cottages, a real community. But, let's face it, I'd come along for the chance to sit in Dogfish Head to quaff a few pints, to get away from the kid and the wife and the oppressive heat for a bit while she window-shops, and to sit at a bar like I used to when I was young and spent my summers living and working in Ocean City, when life was unencumbered by such things as strollers and wipes, juice boxes and diaper changes.

It's barely noon and the kid is crying because of the heat. My dream of Dogfish Head is gone with the knowledge of a ninety-minute wait (and, sadly, no 90 Minute IPA) and so we soldier on down Delaware Avenue, passing the young people spilling out of shops, the kids hand-in-hand, barefoot teens on skateboards, and everyone seemingly moving against us—or more to the point, we're three small salmon swimming upstream and the current is swift and the kid can't get comfortable and whoever thought pushing a stroller in this August heat into these August crowds was even close to a good idea needs to have his head checked—and so we move on past Kohr Brothers *(later, later, after lunch)* to the boardwalk, fighting more crowds and then the mob of the carnival crazy kiddy rides, and of course all he wants is to spin in those mini PT Cruisers zipping round and round, and so being the good dad, I oblige, Mommy snapping pictures of a smiling child and his sweaty father. And it's all good, this whirlwind of colors, the sights and smells of summer at the beach, until the cars come to a slow stop and those little woodies begin moving backward, picking up momentum until we're flying at some unsafe speed in reverse and I'm being slammed against the side of the door, my son giggling with glee, until I feel as if I'm going to lose it, swirling tight circles, that sick feeling on an empty stomach, and we're sure getting our money's worth here, this ride without end, until, thank God, it comes to a slowly spinning halt. But then, there's that helicopter sky ride, more spinning, but thankfully slower, and a few games (like throwing money away), and *honey, we're only here once a year and it'll really make his day if you just ride it with him one more time,* and so more puke-inducing woody cyclones and then, unsteady on my feet, I learn that the family has decided on lunch.

We emerge into the bright white glare of sunshine and heat and begin picking our way along the boardwalk, sights set on Grotto's, but not even to the Candy Kitchen on the corner, we're mobbed by more people, more strollers, and those seagulls circling and dipping and I'm sure they've got their sights set on me, and so we turn around and go with the flow, not certain of our destination, but life seems much easier when you're just one of the lemmings. We veer off at Wilmington Avenue and begin strolling along, fewer people and less noise, but not much action, until I spy the Ram's Head and recognizing this from Annapolis, and still envisioning a cold draft on this summer's day, suggest this as our stop. We check to make sure they have cuckoos (chicken nuggets) and fries for Liam, and thankfully they do, and so in we go.

The place is relatively quiet and I'm eyeing the taps when the hostess sees us, that forever-cheerful "how many in your party" she's offered a million times over the course of this summer, and then she sees us, the child and that erector-set stroller, Dad in his stupid polo shirt, and Mom with her humid hair a hot mess, and, still smiling, directs us to a room in the back of the place with two television sets, no bars, and not one other single soul.

We pass by the bar and I'm rubbernecking at the tap handles—it's all Fordham, and I've settled in my mind on an oyster stout to kick it off, and then we're back in the back, settled at our four-top and the room is quiet, a baseball game on mute, the collection of necessities beside our son, his books and crayons and apple juice box, which I'm stabbing with that silly little straw until it punctures and squirts all over my hand and forearm, and my poor wife is pawing at her head trying to straighten those wild curls, to fix the unfixable; she just can't throw in the towel and give up and go native with a hat and a ponytail and so she insists on straightening those curly locks every morning until she is again disappointed by the defeat of humidity, and she's got that look and Liam can't find his Hot Wheels car and is getting upset and where is that waitress. Another dagger: Mirella, my lovely wife, can't find her license—which means I'll have to drive back to O.C., and the waitress approaches with a smile and a request for drinks and Liam is busy bothering Mommy for his car and Mommy is busy digging through her purse and Daddy just stares at the beer menu wondering what might have been, smiles sadly, and orders an iced tea. Mirella mumbles her water order and another for our son, who is ready for his cuckoos now and so we go ahead and order them for ASAP, and then as the waitress disappears Mom and Dad finally exhale, slumping in their respective chairs.

The back room is eerily quiet.

So I'm feeling sorry for myself with my unsweetened iced tea and my sticky forearm, that unsettled stomach and this day and how nothing has happened as planned, the way it had unfolded in my mind, and instead of exquisitely crafted microbrews and beach pizza, I'm sucking on unfresh iced tea and waiting for some chicken wrap or something—I can't recollect. I'm thinking of an exit strategy, a way out of this town without round two of the boardwalk mob and then another upstream stroll along the other side of Delaware Avenue, when I notice another family with another child being escorted to the exile of the back room—the kid room. They've got the same basic setup, though their child is younger, husband and wife, one set of grandparents, and they set up at a table across the floor from ours and now we're a group of two families in the forgotten back. But this guy, the child's father, is different, not the typical Rehoboth-mold dad like me (today); he's decked out in baggy surf trunks and a T-shirt, tattoos and long, straggled hair, and I'm watching him and a light is going on and then before he even takes his seat, I realize I'm sharing the room with Dave Grohl and his family. Dave Grohl. Nirvana, Foo Fighters, drummer, guitarist, all-around rock god.

Grohl takes his seat so that the two of us are facing each other from across this empty space, and I'm already thinking of what to say to him, how to approach and get an autograph, possibly a photo; planning how to turn this day around so that I've gotten something out of this trip, when he locks eyes with me for just a second and gives me that half-nod, that *I know you know* look, and smiles, and then he's chatting with his group and giving his child his attention and just like me, Dave Grohl is just being a dad and a husband on vacation with his family. And then I watch the waitress bring him an iced tea and I know that I've already gotten my something out of this trip—in fact, I've had it all along, and an autograph or a photo would only cheapen it. And so for a half hour or so, I share an experience with my family and his family, and I understand that this, the insanity of finding the parking space and the traveling caravan of strollers and supplies, the push and noise of the crowds, the swirling rides and overpriced everything, and yes, the unfresh iced tea and sticky apple juice forearms, Dogfish Head and Grotto's, Kohr Brothers and the Sea Shell Shop, Gidget's Gadgets and Browseabout Books—it's all part and parcel of this strange American pastime we call summer vacation, and I'm one of the lucky ones because I get to experience this wonderful mess every year, am blessed to share this with my son just as my father shared it with me, and so, on our way out from the back of Ram's Head I turn for just a half-second and watch one of the great rock 'n' roll heroes of our day as he passes his experiences on to his own child. Then we're out into the white light and August heat, heading toward Kohr Brothers, and I smile to myself and hoist my son onto my shoulders, holding tightly to his knees while he messes my hair, and my wife takes my hand as we happily join the crowd of tourists strolling the boardwalk on this summer day in Rehoboth Beach, and a soft ocean breeze washes over us, while unbeknownst to all (except me), Dave Grohl sits in a quiet room enjoying a simple lunch with his family.

David Strauss grew up visiting Ocean City and Clearwater Beach every summer. He spent his college summers living and working in Ocean City, Maryland, and has had poetry and/or short stories published in *The Scarab, The Damozel, Self X-Press,* and *Dirt Rag Magazine.* In 2013, his first novel, *Dangerous Shorebreak,* was published through CreateSpace. He lives in Bel Air, Maryland, with his wife, Mirella, and son, Liam, where he teaches US history.

The Ocean at Night

by Heather Lynne Davis

Before Mr. Zee can settle onto a wooden stool at Obie's, Bobby has already poured him a double vodka tonic on the rocks. He slides it past several other patrons to the man with the black moustache that curls up at the ends.

"Nice night," Bobby says to the middle-aged man.

Zee nods his bald head and raises his glass, his motions slow and formal. "To your health."

His accent is heavy, Eastern European or maybe Mediterranean, Bobby thinks. He's asked the guy a hundred times where he's from, but the answer is always the same: *everywhere.* Judging by how much the guy spends and how often he comes in—almost every night—Bobby figures he's got money. Could be a Russian businessman, involved in import/export. Or maybe he's mixed up in something sinister—hence the secrecy.

Whatever the explanation, he leaves great tips, so Bobby is happy to have him. On a lot of nights, the guy stays until closing, watching people on the boardwalk or talking with half-drunk customers. Some nights, he wanders off to visit the handful of other bars on the boardwalk. All the regulars know him, but no one seems to know much about him.

Zee sips his drink and follows the last few minutes of a beach volleyball game under the floodlights. Then he stares at the black ocean and the tattered clouds passing over the moon. The early June air hangs humid and dense.

"There will be storm tonight," he says to no one in particular as a younger man sits at the bar two stools down.

The young man with curly brown hair scowls, his shoulders hunched. Red rims his blue eyes.

Zee studies him.

"Bourbon, neat," the young man says.

"You desire to get drunk quickly," Zee says. It's not a question.

The young man glances at him. "I'm really not here to talk," he says.

Zee strokes his goatee. "Try rum in Diet Coca-Cola. Carbonated, no sugar. That will intoxicate the most fast. I read, study." He motions to Bobby. "A rum and Diet Coke for this man. It's on me. Your best."

Bobby smiles. "You got it, Zee."

"Thanks, but I don't need it," the young man says.

Zee moves closer. "Who is she? I can tell your bond with this woman is strong. Or you would not need to drown yourself."

The young man looks at the bartender for help. Bobby pretends to be busy washing a glass.

"Look, I don't want to talk about it right now."

"I was in love more than once," Zee says. "Two times."

The young man doesn't want to encourage the odd stranger, so he stays quiet, stares at his drink.

"I loved first one so much, I thought I could not live without her. When she left me, I almost did not go on. Do you know what kept me going?"

As the young man downs his bourbon, he realizes he's too tired to fight.

"No, what?"

"Curiosity."

"Curiosity?"

"I was not done with world and world was not done with me. As much as I wanted this woman, I knew world was bigger than anything I could imagine. End of one thing always beginning of another."

The young man shakes his head. "I think it would be easier if she left me. Maybe we should just stop trying."

Zee frowns. "What is your name?"

"Max."

"Max, do you love her?"

Max closes his eyes and squeezes his forehead. He sighs. "Yes, I love her so much it scares me. But we keep failing. She thinks I blame her."

"Why are you here, at beach?"

"We were going to celebrate."

"So you cannot celebrate anymore?"

Max grabs the rum and Coke Bobby hands him.

"No," he says quietly.

"Whatever you have lost, you must find way to persevere," Zee says. "You think this is end of your story together?"

Max looks more closely at the swarthy man with eyes that seem old and young at once. "It can't be the end. I just don't know where we go next."

"It is easy. I will tell you. Take her a red rose. Sit together in front of ocean at midnight. Speak your fears into the wind. Can you do that?"

Max is starting to feel drunk, his nose numb and the edges of his vision soft. He thinks Zee must be crazy, but he'll humor him. "I guess."

"Then you will move forward."

Before Max can say anything else, Zee stands and throws a hundred-dollar bill onto the bar.

"Change?" Bobby asks.

"No. Cover his tab." He gestures toward Max.

"Got it. Calling it a night?"

"Time to move on," Zee says.

Outside, in the misty darkness, Zee strolls the boardwalk until he finds Max's young woman at the south end, well beyond Funland.

There's almost no one else around this late at night. He feels her before he sees her. Her sorrow is so raw, it almost stops him in his tracks. Wide-open emptiness. Despair mindless as the sea. Aching without end. Emotions he has not felt for a very long time.

A woman of maybe thirty looks over at him hazily. If she were not lost in grief, she'd be more nervous about this stranger getting so close to her in the darkness.

She's sitting cross-legged on the white bench, facing the ocean, her cropped black hair blowing across her face. He clears his throat, careful not to startle her.

"Excuse me, miss. Would you happen to have a tissue or napkin?"

A woman of maybe thirty looks over at him hazily. If she were not lost in grief, she'd be more nervous about this stranger getting so close to her in the darkness.

"Uh, maybe. Let me look." She unzips a shapeless cotton bag and rummages around. "Here's one."

Zee takes it from her and blows his nose loudly. "Excuse me. I must be allergic to these salty breezes." He starts to sit. "Do you mind if I rest for a moment? I have a long walk back."

"Go ahead. I was just leaving."

"May I ask you something before you go?"

"Sure," she says in a tired voice.

"Do you think ocean at night is good or bad?"

She wonders why this weird old guy had to bother her tonight of all nights. Maybe she should just walk away. Instead, she gazes at the line where the water meets the sky. She can barely make it out. "It's not one or the other. It just is."

"Ah, yes. I agree. But this is my favorite time on boardwalk. Sun is gone. Moon plays on waves. Children are home, dreaming. So beautiful. So quiet."

A tear rolls down her left cheek.

"You cannot tell a lie when you are looking at the ocean at night," Zee says. "Did you know?"

She shakes her head.

"It seems like you have lost something."

"Yes. Two times now."

"You want a child."

She looks at him, stunned, her vision watery. "How did you know?"

"I too have lost things. Many things and people when I came to this country. I had to learn to persevere. Now I watch."

"What's your name?" she asks.

"They call me Mr. Zee. What is yours?"

"Olivia."

"That is lovely name."

She doesn't know why she's talking so openly to this stranger about their losses, the stupid attempts they keep hanging every hope on. His voice is rich and deep, soothing. "I waited too long. My eggs are old or bad or something. We don't care about money. We don't want fame or power or a big house. Just a baby. It should be easy."

"Where is husband?"

"We had a fight. I think I'm driving him away."

"Do you love him?"

She frowns. "Yes, but I don't know if it's enough. You know?"

"Say good-bye," Zee tells her.

"I don't want to let him go," she says.

"No, not to husband. Say good-bye to children who left. Did you say good-bye?"

She likes the man's face, the wrinkles at the corners of his eyes, the smile lines around his mouth, even the small gold hoops in his ears. Before she can protest, he takes her hand and pulls her up. They walk to the closest path down to the sand.

"Come," he says. "Let ocean take sadness away."

She doesn't believe it will, but goes anyway. She kicks off her flip-flops and lets her feet sink in the cool sand, thinks how Max will scold her when she tells him she went to the water with a strange man.

Then her feet are wet. She lets the waves crash around her ankles. Zee stands back while she talks to the night, to the starlight and the moon, to the constant motion. She thinks how nothing ever stays the same. How the tides wash everything away.

"I love you, my little ones," she says. That much she knows is forever.

* * * * * *

The next morning, Max and Olivia splurge on breakfast at the Boardwalk Plaza Hotel. Max eats ravenously, like he always does when he has a hangover. Even though his head is pounding, he feels cleansed. A family of four waves at them from a bicycle surrey as they roll by. Olivia sips her coffee and thinks about how ridiculous Max looked last night when he finally came crashing into their hotel room, plastered, with a plastic rose he had obviously stolen from a Grotto's table.

He had insisted they go back to the beach and sit near the water together. He said she needed to tell the wind her fears. She had blabbered something just to shut him up. On their walk back to the hotel on Wilmington Avenue, he had puked three times. After he brushed his teeth and swallowed some ibuprofen, they had crawled into bed together, exhausted.

It was the first time in three days they slept curled against each other, calm and quiet, not angry or in tears. As they drifted off, a wild storm let loose, leaving the sea air light and fresh in the morning.

Max hasn't mentioned the strange guy from the bar and Olivia hasn't mentioned the man who led her to the ocean. They both wonder if maybe they imagined him.

After they finish their eggs, bacon, and blueberry scones, Max and Olivia stroll along a boardwalk that looks so much different today than it did yesterday. All the same stores and benches and dunes are there, but the shadows are not quite so dark. The growing crowd seems less annoying.

She steps closer to the mannequin in its old-fashioned wooden case. He looks like a gypsy—black goatee, gold earrings, turban. He seems familiar, probably from all their visits to the shore.

They pass Dolle's and the gazebo, then the ice cream shop and displays of hermit crabs in cages. In their newfound closeness, Max and Olivia feel fragile as sea creatures without their shells. Olivia squints inside the arcade as they pass. A commanding voice makes her jump.

"Give Zoltar your treasure. I have much wisdom to share with you."

"Oh my god," she says. "It's the creepy fortune teller. He scared me."

Max laughs. "I remember this guy. Hey, Zoltar, what's up?"

Olivia raises her eyebrows. "Honey, I don't think he can hear you."

"Want to know your fortune?" Max asks, pulling out his wallet.

"They're always so lame," Olivia says.

Max notes the fear in his wife's voice. "Hey, you're gonna hurt Zoltar's feelings."

She steps closer to the mannequin in its old-fashioned wooden case. He looks like a gypsy—black goatee, gold earrings, turban. He seems familiar, probably from all their visits to the shore.

Max inserts the dollar bill and waits. Zoltar waves his hand over the crystal ball until a ticket pops out below.

"What does it say?" Olivia asks, wrapping her arms around her husband.

Max looks down at the ticket, and then back at the machine, his brow knit. "No way," he says, staring at the ticket, turning it over.

"What?" Olivia says, her heart hammering for no reason at all.

Max takes her face in his hands and kisses her lips, then hands her the ticket. He watches her eyes get big as she reads it.

Perseverance is the key. Your lucky number is three.

HEATHER LYNNE DAVIS RECEIVED AN MA IN CREATIVE WRITING FROM SYRACUSE UNIVERSITY. HER POEMS HAVE APPEARED IN JOURNALS SUCH AS THE *CREAM CITY REVIEW, GARGOYLE, POET LORE, PUERTO DEL SOL,* AND THE *SONORA REVIEW.* HER BOOK, THE LOST TRIBE OF US, WON THE 2007 MAIN STREET RAG POETRY BOOK AWARD. HER STORY "THE GHOST OF HENLOPEN AVENUE" WAS PUBLISHED IN *THE BEACH HOUSE.* SHE IS AT WORK ON A YOUNG ADULT NOVEL AND LIVES IN THE SHENANDOAH VALLEY WITH HER HUSBAND, THE POET JOSE PADUA, AND THEIR TWO CHILDREN.

Purpose

by Nancy Michelson

The hour hand on the antique brass clock tower was in shadow, as the sun had begun dipping a bit in the west, but the air was still warm on the August night. The hour hand pointed to seven as the white-haired woman entered the boardwalk from Baltimore Avenue. She made her way straight across the wooden planks to a bench positioned where she could observe the comings and goings of the families, lovers, friends, or occasionally, a solitary soul. Many of them were so familiar to her. Their movements were as varied as their characters and appearances. The bench offered the perfect place for people-watching, and the locals knew that the seven o'clock hour was the ritual time for the woman to come and do just that.

She was singularly interested in the actions of one couple—a man and a woman in their mid-forties, whom she knew intimately. The woman had nondescript brown hair and light blue eyes; the man had golden brown hair and startling blue eyes. Athletic, energetic, they sped by in a brisk walk, absorbed in their conversation. She knew that it would take them approximately a half hour until they came into sight again, upon their return from the other end of the boardwalk, the end closest to Silver Lake. Approximately, because they sometimes paused along their promenade to do some of their own people-watching, or to indulge in an ice-cream cone. One time, they had impulsively paid for tokens and pretended that the ride through the funhouse had not seemed much less scary to them as adults than it had in childhood. Their timing was also affected when they stopped to talk with someone they knew. That happened quite frequently, and it was clear that they enjoyed these interactions. There was always a lot of laughter. But then again, they usually seemed to find humor in most of what they encountered on a summer evening's walk on the boards. Rarely, their dialogue was much more serious; on those few occasions it could involve raised voices, and even tears, and those times tugged at the aging woman's heart.

On this particular evening, the elderly woman's attention was drawn to someone else: a girl at the Baltimore Avenue entrance. She appeared to be in her late teens. The girl had thick, long, lustrous chestnut-colored hair. The woman thought, *I once had thick, long hair, but it was more of a mousy brown.* The girl was slim but curvaceous. The woman supposed that the last time she had been that slim was before puberty, a good fifty—no, wait, sixty (?!)— years ago. Definitely no curves. She had been nothing like the girl. Her own eyes had been a faded blue. Not like the deep penetrating brown of this beauty.

The girl stood looking toward where the woman sat, and hesitated. Her entire demeanor was that of indecision. Or was it disappointment? She began to pace, and as she did, her irregular circles came nearer and nearer to the woman's bench. Finally, the girl stood next to the bench, shifting her weight, changing her pose. She looked intently out across the waves now, although the woman was aware of how the girl repeatedly glanced sideways at the bench next to hers.

"Would you care to sit?" the woman asked her. Her words surprised herself; she wanted immediately to take them back. Fortunately, she didn't have to.

"No, thanks." The girl took out her phone and began rapidly scrolling, still glancing at the adjacent bench. It was occupied by young parents overrun with tumbling children dripping chocolate and vanilla stickiness all over themselves, the parents, the bench, and the boardwalk. It would not be long before the family would be ready to move on, but the woman could not imagine the girl would risk the damage to her form-fitting white shorts *(way too tight; way too short)* from the ice cream souvenirs left on the bench.

As the woman had predicted, the young family soon scrambled noisily off to their next adventure and the girl lowered herself carefully onto a seemingly clean spot on the bench. She flipped the back so she could continue gazing out at the waves, then sat sideways, facing somewhat toward the woman, her arm draped over the bench back. The woman's eyes widened as she saw the girl's fingertips graze a brass plate in the center of the wood. It was unusual for the plate to be affixed to the ocean side of the bench back. The plate was shiny—new—and that's when the woman realized that she need not be offended by the girl's refusal of her offer to share *her* bench. The girl had deliberately waited for her own. They were kindred spirits, both needing to reconnect with someone.

Gradually, the woman became aware that a future version of the girl had appeared. Same lustrous chestnut-colored hair, same large dark eyes, same slim build. She, too, miraculously found a clean spot on which to sit, one that allowed her to put her arm around what could only be her daughter. Even if she hadn't wanted to, the elderly woman couldn't help but overhear.

"He would have loved knowing that you chose this way of keeping his memory alive," the mother said, rubbing the girl's shoulder. The girl just nodded and abruptly stood. Her mother followed, and the two were quickly swallowed by the summer evening crowd, leaving the woman to wonder.

She looked at the dates on the plate: 1995–2014. Nineteen years old. She then looked at the plate on her bench: 1940–2011. Seventy-nine years old. So much more life lived; such deeper memories made.

* * * * * *

Several days later, when the woman reached the boardwalk she found her own bench occupied. The young, dark-eyed girl was settled on the adjacent bench, again sitting sideways, dividing her attention between the phone and the ocean. The girl noticed the aged woman looking at her, and after a clear hesitation, gestured to offer a seat. The woman smiled and said, "No, thank you. I'll wait for this one." The girl nodded her understanding, then turned back to the phone.

Unlike the girl, the woman faced the buildings on the boardwalk while she waited. Many of the passersby waved to her. One young couple stopped to chat. The conversation included lots of smiling and a few chuckles, but children tugging at their father's hands cut the encounter short. Her eyes, whose acuity hadn't faded with their color, caught movement along the rundown upper floor of one of the few Rehoboth motels with an ocean view. The athletic couple in their forties had spent the weekend in a room positioned behind the antique clock tower—the only room without an ocean view. It had been a cold and rainy weekend, too, and the couple hadn't even bothered to stay for the final night of their reservation. They had realized that they hadn't really needed to get away from their everyday lives after all, so they had returned home to their own bed.

Distracted by the people at the motel, the woman didn't notice at first that her bench had become unoccupied. When she did, she sat carefully (*Oh! Those years of wear and tear on the knees and back*), just to the right of the brass plate. The woman and the girl, old and young, sat side by side as the minutes ticked on the tower clock and noiselessly changed on the digital display of the cell phone. The woman silently cheered to see that a fiftyish couple (more blue eyes and brown hair, although some thinning could be seen without looking too closely) had arrived at a remarkably fortunate moment to land a prized window-side table at Grotto Pizza. The elderly woman was pleased to see that tonight appeared to be a happy slice of their lives.

After a while, the young girl's voice startled her, but as she turned her attention toward the adjacent bench, she realized the intended audience was on the receiving end of the phone call.

"I thought that I would keep my connection with him on this bench. How many nights did I sit right here, watching him wait out the rollers for the right wave? But I look out there and all I see is water. Already I can't see him." The girl listened for a few more ticks of the clock, then abruptly snapped, "I gotta go," and brought her thumb down on the phone screen. She brought her elbows down on her knees and dropped her head into her hands.

The woman acted before thinking about the wisdom of intruding into this life seemingly so different from her own. Putting her hand on the girl's shoulder, she offered, "I'm sorry for your loss."

Without raising her head, the girl turned her face toward the woman. "How could he do this to me?"

"I'm sorry," the woman said again. "What was his name?"

"Chase."

"And he surfed?"

"Surfed, raced cars, snowboarded. All that dangerous guy stuff that always stressed me out, and none of that was what I really had to worry about. Who knew?" The girl's face turned back to the boards at her feet. "He didn't even leave a note."

The woman chewed the side of her mouth, deciding, then spoke again. "I apologize; I didn't mean to eavesdrop, but I heard you say you can't see him out there in the waves where you'd watched him. Did you ever really 'see' him? Maybe that's why you can't see him now."

The girl jumped up. "Are you kidding me, you old bitch? How dare you!" She ran off, leaving the woman to chide herself. How often in her life had she wished she had left well enough alone. Her distress was visibly apparent, and a young acquaintance stopped and sat. "Faith, what is it? Come on; I'll walk you home."

* * * * * *

Faith struggled with the decision to return to the boardwalk the next night. She did not want to be the reason the girl stopped coming to her bench. However, this daily hour of reflection and connection had been her own for three years, and she could not imagine her life without it. In the end, she could not resist what seemed to be an automatic motion of her feet toward the boardwalk.

The girl was already at her place. Faith's heart beat faster as she took her own customary spot. She considered whether to apologize or let the girl have her personal space, and decided to take the latter course of action. However, the girl eventually turned to her. With difficulty, she muttered, "I'm sorry I spoke to you that way."

Faith breathed a sigh of relief. "I'm the one who should apologize to you. I was totally out of line. In some twisted way, I thought I was being helpful."

The girl let out a sigh of her own. "Actually, you were right. I didn't wanna hear it, but last night, I just kept thinking, Chase. Wow—his name said it all. But I didn't want to know it. You just hope you're enough, you know?"

"Sometimes it's beyond you," was all the woman could offer. "Tell me who you are."

"Stacey."

"Stacey: Greek origin. Meaning 'resurrection.'"

"What are you, an English teacher or something?"

Faith smiled. "I was. I'm retired now. But once an English teacher, always an English teacher."

Stacey grimaced. "Man, no offense, but I hate English. All those boring stories and stupid poems that no one ever gets."

Faith chuckled. "You could have been one of my students. So what do you like, Stacey?"

The question seemed to require some thought. Finally, "Well, I like to hang out with my friends, do Facebook and Instagram and stuff. Listen to music; dance."

Faith brightened. "When I saw you, I thought you were a dancer! You have the right build, and you move so gracefully."

"Oh, I'm not a dancer, like someone who takes lessons and does shows and stuff. I just dance with my friends."

"Have you ever thought of taking dance lessons? Or maybe you're planning some other direction for your future?"

"Yeah, okay, now I know you've been a teacher. Teachers are always pushing you to think about your future. I don't know. There's nothing that really interests me."

Stacey began to draw back a bit, and realizing she'd pushed too far again, Faith just nodded. At that moment, another young adult stopped to chat with Faith. When he left, she noted, "I love seeing my former students." She decided not to add, "to see what they've made of their lives. Instead, she simply rose and said, "Well, I'd best get on home for tonight. The dog needs his walk."

* * * * * *

The next night found them in their now-familiar positions once again. Stacey pointed to the brass plate on Faith's bench. "Was he your husband?"

"For thirty-nine years. I was fortunate to have found him later in life, when I was more ready to understand love and life. I wish I had met him before we were forty, but I'm not sure we would have made it if we had been younger. We went through some rough times, but much more often, we went through some great ones."

"I used to think about how Chase and I would have great times.

He'd talked about surfing in Hawaii. I could see myself lying on a beach on Maui during the day, clubbing at night."

Faith laughed. "Oh, our great times probably would seem pretty lame to you. My best memories happened right here. We used to take power walks down the boardwalk, trying to avoid what we called 'Big People Wandering Aimlessly.' He'd zig right, I'd zag left, and then we'd each try to be the first to get out of the congestion before we could come back together. I guess that sounds pretty stupid, but it was something that was our thing."

Stacey's look clearly said that she did indeed think it was stupid. She simply said, "Oh." Then, as people do in awkward moments, she searched for another topic. She asked, "So how do you get through each day without him?" It was not the most sensitive of recovery tactics.

But Faith did not become despondent, and she replied readily. "It isn't the same, of course. But there are so many things to enjoy and appreciate in this life. I stay pretty busy. I love to garden and play the piano. I kayak, swim, bike and hike with friends, or sometimes by myself. And I write."

Stacey tried to envision Faith, who had seemed ancient to her, in a kayak or on a bicycle. After struggling to find those images, she focused on the writing. "What do you write?"

"Poetry."

"That's right; English teachers like that stuff, don't they. Do you ever let anyone else read it?"

"Sure; all the time." Faith started to say, "Would you like to read some of my poetry?" but she quickly reversed. "That's right. You don't 'get' poetry. Don't worry; I won't put you in a tough spot by making you read it."

"No, that's okay. I mean, I'd like to read it." Stacey may have been sincere, but Faith wasn't sure. She felt even less sure when Stacey added, "By the way, I won't be here tomorrow night. I signed up for a dance class."

"Why, Stacey, that's wonderful! I hope you enjoy it. You'll have to tell me all about it the next time you're here." As Faith reflected on her joy that her young friend had begun to search for some purpose in her life, a light rain began to fall. She hadn't noticed the gathering clouds, but as she looked skyward, she recognized that a downpour was imminent. "We'd better get going, young lady. Good luck with dance!"

* * * * * *

The storm had seemed to be the onset of an entire late-summer season of rain. There were few days when anyone would consider sitting at the boardwalk during the damp, cool evenings. Through September the days grew shorter, and the encroaching shades of evening made the dank air feel even more miserable. Stacey had weathered the seasonal turn well. It was warm—actually hot—in the dance studio where she spent increasingly more time. The surprise with which she had discovered that she had a talent for it soon grew into a passion. The passion necessitated responsibility: dance costumes and contests were expensive, so a job became part of her after-school life.

But on the first day of fall, Stacey made her way back to the boardwalk. For the first time in weeks, the clouds had dissipated and the sun's rays had gradually gained strength, creating a pleasantly warm autumn evening. The flyer in her hand advertised her first show. When the fliers had been handed out, her first thought had been that she wanted Faith to be there. She had hardly thought of the aged woman over the previous month, but that evening, the thought had hit her with certainty. She exited Baltimore Avenue onto the boards expectantly. Her phone display showed 6:59 p.m.

It had never occurred to her that Faith wouldn't be there. Shocked, she stared first at Faith's bench, then turned to look north, then south on the boardwalk. Her gaze trailed skyward, and for the first time, she noticed the tower clock. It read five o'clock. Relieved, she started back toward the street, to wait until the correct time to return, but then clarity hit her. If one of the clocks was wrong, it would not be hers. Feeling dazed by the unexpected circumstances she was experiencing, she turned once again to the bench, sure that she would see Faith this time. She became aware that a small crowd of people were in front of the bench. "I just didn't see her," Stacey thought, and relief washed over her once again.

When she approached the bench, a woman looking to be in her forties turned at the sound of her footsteps. Stacey looked into the pale blue eyes of a past version of Faith. At the woman's side was a miniature: an even more past version of Faith. A middle-aged man was affixing a brass plate next to the plate that bore the name of Faith's husband. Stacey stared blankly, uncomprehending.

The fortyish woman took a step toward her. "Are you Stacey, by any chance?" she asked. Stacey could only nod.

"My mother spoke of you in the days before she died. She had a present for you, and she made us promise that we would do anything we could to find you. My job was to ask for you at every dance studio nearby. My brother's assignment was to sit on this bench every night at seven o'clock." The woman laughed. "So like Mom. Thank heavens you appeared early on! And she would be so pleased to know that we found you on the boardwalk, where you and she had met."

Faith's daughter held out a slim book with a picture of an ancient sundial on the cover. The book's title, *Purpose,* shone out in brass letters. Under the title was the author's name: Faith Moore. Stacey stuttered, "Did she like the poet because they had the same first name?" Then she turned over the book and the insight came. On the back cover, a middle-aged woman with mousy brown hair streaked with white had her arm around a man with golden brown hair, slightly thinning. They were both athletic-looking and both had blue eyes. "She … said she wrote poetry. I thought …"

"You didn't know she was a well-known poet? You had never seen announcements of her readings or book signings? She began writing when my father died. As devastated as she was, she was determined to find a purpose for her life without him. One that honored him and their lives together, and that she hoped would help others find purpose and peace in their own lives. It turned out that she was pretty talented. And now, Stacey, you have the only signed copy of the first printing of Faith Moore's final book."

Stacey's fingers grazed the brass letters, as she whispered, "Who knew?" Behind them, the residents of Rehoboth were capitalizing on a burst of sunshine and warmth that had spread from the west toward the rolling waves of the Atlantic. Surfers ran into the waves. Others grabbed the chance to take one more walk on the boards— an athletic couple in their forties, zigging and zagging around Big People Wandering Aimlessly; young girls sharing earbuds and hip-hopping along; parents trying to keep a slippery grip on the ice-cream-smeared hands of their tumbling children; a middle-aged couple who hoped to land their favorite table at Grotto Pizza; and a solitary white-haired woman who smiled at them all.

Nancy Michelson is a former high school English teacher who is now a professor of education at Salisbury University in Maryland, where she directs a local chapter of the National Writing Project. "Purpose" is her first published fiction, after years of professional education writing. The story was inspired by the reactions of dear family members and friends to the inevitable losses of loved ones, and for its creation, she followed Wordsworth's advice to "fill your paper with the breathings of your heart."

The Great Rehoboth Race

by Chris Jacobsen

Do you have an older brother? I do. Growing up, I oftentimes wished I didn't.

The day I arrived home from the hospital, Mom gingerly pulled aside the fuzzy blue blanket to show Connor my tiny form. He toddled up on fleshy legs and declared, "No!" while bonking me on the head.

That pretty much set the tone for our relationship.

Just eighteen months apart, we did everything together. We had the same friends and attended the same birthday parties. Mom signed us up for the same sports, but Connor, having extra inches and pounds, bested me every time. At bat, he clobbered the baseball beyond second base while I only achieved dribblers out to the pitcher's mound. He booted the soccer ball downfield farther than anyone, and in football he got playing time, while I sat on the bench. No matter the sport, at the end of each game, Connor got the high-fives while my parents tussled my orange curls and offered, "Next time, Sean." As I trudged to the car with my shame and frustration, Connor would catch up, his green eyes smiling, and offer a word of big brother encouragement.

"Loser."

Our antagonistic rivalry entered a kind of détente during our summer vacations in Rehoboth.

My parents rented the same house every year from the time I was three. Owned by an elderly woman, it was five blocks from the beach. Three cement steps led up to the red clapboard house, accented with black shutters. The front lawn was partially shaded by the neighbors' large maple tree, from which dangled a birdhouse. Bushes and variegated hosta provided landscaping along the façade to where a wooden fence took over to encircle the backyard. The gate latch had succumbed to the salt air but, with some cajoling, allowed access to the patches of grass that supported a tired swing set and a sun-bleached shed. A screened-in porch with wicker furniture ran the length of the back of the house.

Connor and I shared an upstairs room. The twin beds, adorned with a seahorse motif, were separated by an oak dresser with a circular stain on its top, a lamp placed to cover it. I was assigned the bottom drawer, which had a long gouge in it, while Connor took the middle one. We each took a side of the top drawer for our underwear, bathing suits, and miscellaneous stuff. A round throw rug graced the wooden floor.

Having only each other, we had no choice but to get along. Whether we were on the beach digging a hole to China or in the backyard attacking the enemy camp that had holed up in the shed, we managed to play cooperatively, as long as Connor was in charge.

The summer I turned ten, our vacation started out like any other. Before we were allowed to even think of going to the beach, the car had to be unloaded. Suitcases to the bedrooms, beach towels on the shelf next to the side door, toys in the garage, and groceries in the kitchen. Connor and I knew the drill; we dispatched the process in record time and raced to put on our swim trunks.

We bounded down the stairs to find Dad waiting outside, his six-foot frame topped with a red Phillies cap encircled by black flips of hair poking out from underneath. Next to him was the wagon from the garage, laden with the afternoon necessities of chairs, umbrella, and cooler. Mom wore a large-brimmed hat, perched just above her auburn ponytail, her hazel eyes hidden by sunglasses. She clutched her beach bag, which was weighed down with lotion, T-shirts, and her book-club book. Being a school nurse, she had put together an impromptu first-aid kit of wipes, aloe vera, and Band-Aids.

Connor and I, with towels under our arms, grabbed the boogie boards and turned to run ahead of our parents.

"Not so fast, Sean. Fix your strap."

Mom had a phobia about stubbed toes, so the rule was we had to have our feet safely shod as we navigated the streets and sidewalks until, after crossing over the boardwalk, we hit the gritty entrance ramp to the beach.

"It keeps coming loose," I said. To accommodate her, I leaned over and pinched the Velcro tabs together on my right sandal.

My brother and I took off to the street corner, where we waited for our parents to catch up. Then we ran off again, repeating the game until the last block, when we were able to race down the sidewalk and up the incline to the boardwalk. Connor's competitive edge would show itself when he tried to stay ahead of me, but now that I was nearly his height I was able to keep up.

Once in the sand, I kicked off my sandals. The shifting grains welcomed me back with a warmth that permeated my whole body. I was home. I watched as my toes sank out of sight with each step.

Connor and I steered around sunbathers and chairs in search of a prime spot for our encampment. Mom grabbed the corners of the boldly striped beach blanket and floated it out over the sand until it settled into place. Then, attacking our backs, arms, and faces, she lathered us with suntan lotion.

"Go have fun, but stay where I can see you."

With my boogie board bouncing behind me, I made a beeline for the water. Connor splashed in next to me as I threw my belly onto the Styrofoam wedge and waited for a good wave.

"Hey, Sean, I'll bet I can ride farther than you."

"Who cares? Leave me alone."

I pushed my way through the water to widen the distance from my brother. Now I was in a bad mood, especially after seeing him ride a wave all the way onto the beach. I stayed in the water for what seemed a long time, riding some waves but missing others, and tried to submerge the gnawing realization that boogie boarding was not as exciting when doing it alone. I would like doing most things with Connor if he would just keep his mouth shut.

I trudged out of the surf, saltwater stinging my eyes, and collapsed onto my beach towel. The sun was hot but I welcomed it on my back. In minutes, I entered a semiconscious state. The shrieks of the gulls, the lull of the waves, and music from a nearby radio all joined together in a cacophonous lullaby. I was oblivious to everything outside this cocoon.

"Sean, honey, wake up."

I stirred. *Did I just hear my name?*

"Sean, you need more lotion if you're going to stay out in the sun," Mom said from her shaded chair as she rummaged in her beach tote. My fair skin had sprouted its summer crop of freckles.

"Yeah, Sean, put your baby lotion on," taunted Connor.

"Shut up, jerk," I said, as I swatted sand his way.

"You shut up," he retorted, as he threw back a piece of shell.

"I think maybe it's time for pizza," Dad said, as he winked a brown eye at Mom.

"Yea!" we both chimed, and scurried into our T-shirts.

I loved going on the boardwalk. It was like a big welcome-home party. There was an energy that zigzagged around and through me. The crowd buzzed with purpose; let's eat, let's shop, let's play games. Even those just strolling along for exercise contributed to the aura of activity. My mouth watered at the mingled aromas of juicy hot dogs, garlicky pizza sauce, and the smooth, sugary richness of chocolate. Bells, whistles, and clangs from the arcades teased me with their invitation of man versus machine. I wondered if the grains of sand embedded in the crevices of the gray weathered boards would ever find their way back to the beach. And the nail heads that polka-dotted the planks, how long had it taken someone to hammer them all?

"Don't forget your shoes, and wait for Dad and me when you get up there," said Mom.

"C'mon, Mom. Can't we go by ourselves?" asked Connor. He brushed the sand from his meaty hands.

"Yeah, we'll meet you there. Please?" I added, pulling at my wedgie.

Dad turned to Mom and raised his eyebrows. She nodded. "All right," he said. "But stay together. It's about five blocks. Don't go any farther than Grotto's, got it?"

Connor and I looked at each other with mouths opened. We had never been allowed to do this before.

"Cool!" each of us said after the other, and we took off running, our feet spraying out sand behind us.

We reached the boardwalk and dropped our sandals, sliding our feet into them. Hunched over to secure our straps, my brother bumped me with his butt. I stumbled sideways.

"Knock it off, Con." I reached down to secure my other tab.

Suddenly, Connor straightened up and yelled, "Race you to Grotto's! One, two, three, go!"

I jerked my head up to protest, only to see Connor's back as he sprinted away.

"Cheater!" I yelled in frustration. I took off like snot from a sneeze. I dug hard into the boards, pushing off with all my might. I dodged around an old lady who was digging in her purse. A family started to cross in front of me, so I cut to the left. My arms pumped with a frenzy as my lean legs stretched to their max. Up ahead, a teenage couple was having an argument. *Out of my way!* I managed to swerve around them and scanned the crowd for my brother.

There he was, about ten strides ahead of me. I saw him brush aside a little kid as he swept by, forcing the kid to tumble into his father. Shouts followed but I doubted Connor heard them. Anger fueled my momentum. I was gaining on him.

Just a half block away, a few individuals watched me coming toward them. *Move!* I thought I would have to squeeze through them, but they shifted over at the last moment. *Oh, no.* As they cleared out of the way, I saw a young couple with a child. The mother was crouched down, helping her little girl with a dripping ice-cream cone. People flanked both their left and right sides, leaving me nowhere to go. I could see I was closing the distance with Connor. Catching him was the only thought in my head. In one fluid movement I pushed off my left foot, extended my right leg in front of me, and flew up into the air. Suddenly, time stopped. I was caught in a frozen tableau, suspended in mid-hurdle. Below me, the woman had her child in a bear hug and the dad's mouth stood open in the middle of a curse word. Out in front of me, dangling at the peak of a high arc, was my sandal.

The tableau dissolved as quickly as it came and time resumed. My soaring sandal finished its flight by dropping into the crowd. My bare foot landed my hurdle and immediately fell victim to a searing pain, causing me to bobble my pace. *Great.* The errant sandal left me with a lopsided gait, but I couldn't stop now. Slap went the sandaled foot, thump went the bare one. Slap, thump, slap, thump. The pain was working itself deeper into my sole, but Connor was within reach. I pumped my arms and legs as hard as I could. Another two paces and I was shoulder to shoulder with him. He looked over at me and his eyes widened.

A radiating burn was making it difficult for me to put my full weight on my right side. Had I stepped on a jellyfish? Gotten cut by a piece of glass? Slap, hop. Slap, hop.

Still shoulder to shoulder, with Grotto's looming ahead by only a half block, our churning arms swiped against each other. The cords in Connor's neck were straining; my injury was screaming. Sweat seeped from our brows. *Ignore the pain.* A young girl, pushing her younger sibling in a stroller, was running right toward us. Connor broke left. I broke right. My muscles and tendons were stretched to the limit. I pulled ahead by inches. Just three more strides and the race was mine.

Slap, hop. Slap, buckle. I fell forward as Connor sprang past me and tagged the trash can at Grotto's Pizza.

"Hey, Sean, are you OK?" My brother rushed over to help me up.

I ignored his proffered hand and, without a word, hobbled into the shade and slid down the side of the building, wincing and breathless. My head fell between my knees. Once my heart slowed down, I checked out the bottom of my foot. Connor chewed on his fingernails.

"What happened here, guys?" asked Dad, as my parents approached. Their smiles were replaced by knitted brows.

From my seated position, I glanced up at my brother. He did not respond with the habitual smirk of satisfaction. Instead, he averted his eyes. "I was running and lost my sandal. I think I have a splinter," I answered.

My parents looked to Connor for confirmation but he kept his head down and tried to put his hands into pockets his swimsuit did not have. Mom and Dad were savvy enough to know a few key pieces were missing from my tale, but they didn't press. Mom inspected the wound and gently pushed on the tender area.

"Ouch! What are you doing?" I jerked my foot out of her hands.

"That's in there pretty deep. Looks like someone took a staple gun to you." Her attempt to lighten my mood didn't work.

Dad got some ice from the aproned kid behind the pizza counter. "Here you go, kiddo. Keep that on your foot until I come back with the car."

"I'll go with you," Connor quickly volunteered.

* * * * * *

I lay on the bed with my foot in Mom's lap. Armed with a sterilized needle and tweezers, she handed me a piece of gum. "Chew hard if it hurts."

I clenched my fists as she probed with the needle. I pounded my free leg on the mattress as she dug the point into my flesh. My jaws worked overtime on the gum except when I screamed into the pillow. "Mom, when will it be out?" My fists were hammering the bed.

"Almost there. I don't want it to break off."

Suddenly, the pain diminished. Mom whistled as she held up a nearly inch-long piece of wood clasped between the tweezers.

"Wow, kiddo. You have your very own plank of that boardwalk."

"Let me see," I said, as I reached for it.

Mom dabbed the wound with alcohol and applied a Band-Aid. She lay my leg back on the bed and patted my thigh, then kissed my forehead. "I'll call you when dinner is ready." She left the door ajar.

I lay there staring at the ceiling. Choppy scenes flickered through my mind: swerving through the crowd, the little girl with ice cream on her face, hobbling from the pain, the unfair start. I should have won the race. Heck, I could have, would have, if it hadn't been for that stupid sandal.

I gazed at the hunk of wood in my hand, a sword pulled from my stone. I had been a worthy warrior. That mattered, didn't it? I could have wimped out, but I didn't. That said something, right? I may not have been the winner, but I knew I was not the loser.

I swung my legs over the side of the bed and, with a yank, opened the dresser drawer to tuck away my souvenir, but then changed my mind. I didn't want Connor to see my keepsake, this trophy I had earned in battle. A witness to the day's events, my wooden saber needed a secret hiding place. I spit out my chewing gum, placed the splinter on top, and smooshed the whole thing to the underside of the drawer.

Connor and I never spoke about the race; he never apologized, I never accused. But that competition brought an end to another contest, one that I lived every day. I stopped caring about how Connor measured me. Losing that race lifted a wearisome weight off me. Instead of trying to excel in areas where Connor dominated, I realized I could pursue the direction of my own interests.

When it came time to pack up the car, I left the splinter still stuck to the bottom of that drawer. It was a piece of Rehoboth and belonged there, in my Rehoboth bedroom. Had I known it would be our last summer there, I might have taken it with me, but as luck would have it, Dad lost his job a month later. We never went back.

I thought a lot about that splinter and the role it played that fateful day. I didn't see it at the time, but my forte was right in front of my eyes, or should I say, right under my feet. I went on to become a standout on the track team.

And Connor and me? Well, let's just say we were each other's best man in our weddings.

"Hey, Sean, what do you think of this bureau?" my wife, Dianne, asked, as we wandered through a furniture consignment shop just off Route 1. Our goal was twofold: to find suitable pieces for her side business of refinishing furniture and also to furnish, on a budget, the little Rehoboth bungalow for which we had just signed the settlement papers.

"Looks solid. Go for it." I veered off to scope out some end tables and lamps. "Hey, babe, what about this? It would fit well on the guest-room wall." I pointed to an oval mirror that was leaning against a highboy.

"Possibly. Let's ask if there are any matching pieces." Dianne motioned for me to follow her as she trailed the bald storeowner.

"It's not in great shape, but with a little TLC it will fix up real nice," he said. "It's just over here behind this big bureau." We turned the corner and saw a small oak dresser that was the perfect size for our space. The manager cleared a few knickknacks from the top so we could see the whole piece. "There's a scratch on the front and a watermark on the top, but those are just cosmetic things. I can offer you a good deal."

"What about it, hon? We could …" Dianne cut off her sentence and cocked her head, knitting her brows. "What's wrong? You look pale."

"I, uh, yeah." Across the middle drawer was a long mark. Images of the dresser from my old Rehoboth bedroom flashed in my mind. That dresser had a gouge on the bottom drawer. In moving the piece, could the positions of the drawers been switched? I moved in for a better look. On the top was a round stain.

It couldn't be!

I reached for the top drawer and gingerly looped my fingers

through the handles. I eased it open, half expecting to see my old underwear. The interior was empty and nondescript. My palms started to sweat. *This is silly. I'm a grown man.* I bent down on one knee.

"Sean, is there something wrong with the drawer?"

The manager piped up. "Oh, it's well made, I can tell you that," and hitched up his belt over his stout belly. "This will refinish into a beaut."

I craned my neck to inspect the underside of the drawer. It was there. My heart started pounding like a teenager in love. "It's there. It's still there!" I threw my head back, laughing in amazement.

"What's still there?" Dianne asked, throwing open her palms.

I turned to the manager and pulled out my wallet. "We'll take it, just as it is." My smile was as wide as the dresser. "We'll pick it up tomorrow, but right now, I'm taking this drawer with me." I slid it out and carefully lowered it to my side, my trophy turned toward my leg. The manager shrugged and happily pocketed my money.

I turned to Dianne and swung her around in a bear hug as she asked in confused delight, "What is going on with you?"

The words tumbled out of my mouth. "Let's go to the boardwalk and grab some Grotto's pizza. I have a story to tell you."

CHRIS JACOBSEN FIRST REALIZED HER POTENTIAL AS A WRITER IN HIGH SCHOOL WHEN SHE TOOK A CREATIVE WRITING COURSE. OVER THE YEARS, OTHER CLASSES SHE HAS TAKEN HAVE INCLUDED WRITING FOR CHILDREN AND WRITING MEMOIRS. NOT LONG AGO, SHE RECEIVED AN HONORABLE MENTION IN THE NATIONAL FEDERATION OF STATE POETRY SOCIETIES FOR HER ENTRY SUBMITTED TO THE STATE OF NEW MEXICO. THIS IS HER FIRST TIME BEING PUBLISHED, BUT SHE HOPES TO HAVE BRAGGING RIGHTS AGAIN WHEN SHE COMPLETES HER MANUSCRIPT FOR A MURDER MYSTERY.

CHRIS'S STORY WAS BASED ON HER YOUNGEST SON'S EXPERIENCE AT THE AGE OF FIVE WHEN, AT THEIR FLORIDA VACATION HOME, HE GOT A SPLINTER FROM THEIR DOCK. HE TAPED THE SPLINTER BEHIND HIS DRESSER IN THE ROOM HE SHARED WITH HIS BROTHER.

CHRIS FREQUENTLY VISITS HER OLDER BROTHER AND HIS FAMILY WHO LIVE IN REHOBOTH BEACH.

JUDGE'S COMMENT:

Sibling rivalry at the beach. This could have been me and my brother back in the day. I can even smell the Coppertone.

The Case of the Artist's Stain

by Joseph Crossen

My friend, Mr. Sherlock Holmes, sat slumped in his chair staring fixedly at the initials "V. R." that he himself, in a moment of combined boredom and patriotism, had fired into the wall of our sitting room with his revolver. It was late July, and London was inordinately hot and humid. More so than usual, I must say, though mild compared to my memories of the hot seasons I spent in the Crown's service in India. The windows that looked out on Baker Street were wide open, but no air chanced to move through them and across our perspiring brows, only the sounds and smells of the great city. As to Holmes, he had been sitting and staring for over an hour. He rose only to go to the cold fireplace where the Persian slipper filled with dark shag tobacco resided on the mantle. He removed the tobacco and stuffed a large bent-stem briar pipe, lighting it and filling the hot room with blue smoke.

At length, he spoke as if we had been in dialogue all along. "So, Watson, what would you say to a trip to the colonies to escape this blasted heat?"

I must admit that I was somewhat taken aback by the suggestion. Sherlock Holmes was not given to taking holiday. On a rare occasion, he might repair to the country to tend to his beehives. Normally, however, boredom was relieved by a knotty problem to solve or, in its absence, cocaine.

"The colonies, Holmes? Why, India and Burma would be dreadful. Stifling, I must say."

"Not those colonies, Watson. I misspoke. I suppose I should have said the former colonies. America, my dear fellow."

"I've never been, Holmes, and as far as I know, neither have you. Why America all of a sudden?"

"For one, Doctor, the ocean breezes in, say, Rehoboth, Delaware, would cool our heated brows. I would think some time ocean-side would be refreshing. Bring our souls alive, as it were."

"I must say, Holmes, I don't know what to say. I've never heard of the place."

Holmes reached into the pocket of his smoking jacket—how he could stand a jacket of any kind in this heat I do not know—from which he withdrew a telegram and handed it to me.

"Pray, read it, Watson. Aloud, if you will, so that I may consider it again."

This is what I read:

My Dear Mr. Holmes,

I write you asking your assistance in a most dreadful and frustrating matter. In a form of communication so potentially public as the telegraph, I cannot tell you specifics. Suffice to say, I am in greatest need of your services.

I will gladly pay your travel costs and, of course, your daily rate, if you will come to America immediately and provide the assistance I so badly need.

Signed,
Howard Pyle

"Well read, Watson. What say you? Do we cross the Atlantic for Mr. Pyle?"

"Holmes, this is … what I mean to say is … it would be impossible to …"

"Excellent, my good fellow! Then we're for it! I've booked passage for us on the good ship *Countess Colleen*. An Irish vessel, but I'm sure she'll do. She sails from the London docks at first light tomorrow. Best to be packing now."

And with that, we were bound for Her Majesty's former colonies.

Holmes took it upon himself to send one of his Irregulars—a group of street urchins whose ubiquitous presence acted as a disguise for their deeds—to procure copies of Mr. Howard Pyle's books. Likely, the little wretches stole them from booksellers and the London Library, but the books gave us the opportunity to get to know the man through his works as we crossed the Atlantic. Pyle was a writer and, primarily, an illustrator of myths and legends, one of which was our own English hero, Robin Hood, a fanciful tale, but beautifully and precisely illustrated, as were other books of his depicting Arthur's Round Table and quite a variety of pirates.

We landed in Philadelphia and found it a bustling waterfront city, certainly larger and wealthier than when its denizens plotted revolution against the Crown. From Philadelphia, we rode by train south through the Delaware capital of Dover. We continued south from Dover across flat farmland and over estuarial rivers to the seaside town of Rehoboth. The Junction and Breakwater Railroad deposited us there safe but weary, and I must say the small towns, neat farms, and abundance of a striking variety of waterfowl were pleasant scenery for the trip.

Lodging had been arranged for us at the Bright House, a local hotel. After a brief rest in our rooms, we journeyed forth to explore this Rehoboth and found it to be a quaint seaside resort, the main attraction of which appeared to be a rather large combination pavilion, theatre, and ice cream parlor. From the sound of it, Horn's Pavilion also included a skating rink.

We strolled the boardwalk, noting the entertainment there: jugglers, mimes, charcoal artists offering portraits, and food vendors. On the beach, we stopped to watch a gentleman taking a photo of a young woman. She was smiling softly as she watched her three children playing in the sand. The man with the camera was slowly circling them, camera at his eye, as he presumably searched for the best picture.

"Come, Watson, we've found our man." And with that, Holmes was down the steps from the boardwalk and walking toward the photographer and his subject. I followed, sand filling my brogans, as I trudged after Holmes, who cried out, "Mr. Howard Pyle, I presume?"

The man turned, looking annoyed at the interruption.

"I am Pyle, sir. And who might you gentlemen be?"

"I am Sherlock Holmes, for whom you sent. This is my colleague and sometime Boswell, Dr. John Watson."

Howard Pyle tucked the camera under his left arm and shook hands with each of us. "Gentlemen, thank you for coming. But, how did you know it was I? Have we met before and I've forgotten?"

"Quite obvious, actually. You saw it right away too, didn't you, Watson?"

"Certainly. Quite. But, you go ahead, Holmes. Tell Mr. Pyle how we knew his identity."

"Not only who you are, sir, but that you are in a great hurry to finish a particular illustration."

"Come now, Mr. Holmes," Pyle began. "You can't possibly ..."

"Ah, but I can, as could anyone with an eye to see. Your light summer suit is stained just a bit at the cuff with silver paint. That identified you as an artist. That you have paint on a suit cuff identifies you as an artist in a hurry, too big a hurry to concern yourself with wearing a smock. And, finally, if I were to hazard another deduction, it would be that the paint is from a jousting scene at which you are at work and need silver for a combatant's armor."

"Amazing. As I was leaving to come to the beach and meet my wife, Anne, and our children, I noticed a spot of armor that needed a bit more paint. You are remarkable, Mr. Holmes."

"Hardly," said Holmes. "Now, Mr. Pyle, if you will kindly introduce us to your family, we can find a comfortable place to sit together and hear just why you brought the good doctor and me across the Atlantic."

At this, and anxious to discuss whatever it was that brought us to these shores, Howard Pyle, Sherlock Holmes, and I took our leave of Pyle's charming wife and their children and walked together a short way up the main thoroughfare, then turned north to a large, airy house with a wide porch where the artist showed us his studio and the painting of a mermaid and sailor that he was, he said, hurriedly attempting to complete. Pyle then led us to the porch and directed us to comfortable rocking chairs. Once his manservant brought cold drinks, and Holmes and I filled and stoked our pipes, Pyle began.

"It's infuriating, frankly. I've been totally incensed over the matter," he said.

"Quite," said Holmes. "However, Mr. Pyle, pray do tell us what it is that so infuriates you that you would go to the expense to bring us here."

"Well, certainly, Mr. Holmes, Doctor," he said, nodding at Holmes and then me. Leaning forward and lowering his voice, though no one could have heard us on that expansive, sea-breeze-washed porch, he said, "Someone has been forging my work and selling it to collectors. By the time the forgery is discovered, the money and the forger are gone."

"When did you first learn of the crime?" asked Holmes.

"Two months ago, at the start of the summer season, a collector in Philadelphia discovered that one of my paintings he had purchased was a fraud. I am, by turns since, angered and humiliated."

"And what, would you say, is the quality of the forgery?"

"Actually, quite good, Mr. Holmes. These collectors are not artists, but they tend to have a good eye. But for one of them closely studying the work and noticing a defect, I would not have known myself."

Holmes turned toward me. "Interesting, eh, Watson?"

"Yes, of course, quite, Holmes." Embarrassingly, my attention had turned during the conversation to a trio of ladies walking by on their way to the boardwalk and the beach. Holmes never failed to disrupt me at such times.

"Can you help me, Mr. Holmes? People are paying for inferior copies thinking they have bought an original Pyle, to say nothing of the damage to my income and reputation."

"I am certain we can help, Mr. Pyle. Dr. Watson and I should have something for you before too very long. Come, Watson," said Holmes as he stood, "we have work to do."

"I shall be here working most days if you should need me, gentlemen. That is, with the exception of dawn and dusk, when you will find me with my children at the boardwalk raising and lowering the flag. A family custom of ours," said the artist.

Holmes and I left the disconsolate artist in his rocker looking toward the sea. I had seen nothing to convince me Sherlock Holmes was correct in thinking the culprit would be found quickly, but he surprised me regularly with what he saw and others overlooked.

"So, Watson," he said as we walked toward our lodgings. "We must be at the boardwalk just before dusk if we are to catch our man."

"Why dusk, Holmes?"

"It will be a test of whether you are learning to observe and collect data, my dear Doctor, so I shall wait until dusk to determine your progress. It will also appear perfectly natural to be there at that hour, for that is when Mr. Pyle and his children strike the colors, as it were. It is their ritual to raise the flag daily at dawn and lower it at dusk. We will appear to be simple observers of their family gathering."

Holmes could be maddening at times.

We spent a lazy afternoon of reading and smoking, followed by a passable dinner at our lodgings, and dusk found us seated on a bench on the boardwalk, looking out toward England, the sound of skates like a swarm of bees coming from the pavilion, and the Pyle pater and children dutifully lowering their flag. That is, I looked—longingly, I must admit—toward England. Holmes seemed distracted by the charcoal artist we had seen earlier in the day. The young man was packing away his materials, his white artist's smock flapping in the evening breeze. As he tucked his folded easel under his arm and proceeded down the boardwalk away from us, Holmes stood.

"Come, Watson," he said. "I think we have our man."

"What man? Holmes, really?"

"No time to debate, Watson. Quickly and quietly."

We left the family to its ceremony and walked south on the boardwalk, staying behind the unaware artist. After a short distance, he turned right down what might be called an alleyway, though it wouldn't have qualified as one in London, more a wide space between a few buildings, but the growing darkness was advanced by the walls of the frame buildings on either side. Our man never seemed to suspect our presence, and he led us, as the buildings quickly thinned, to a small clearing which he crossed to enter a small house of the kind the locals called tents, though I think "shanty" would have been more apt a word for it.

As we crossed the clearing, it was full dark, and the darkness of the little building was replaced by the glow from an oil lamp inside, filling the windows with a yellowed tint.

"Close, Watson," said Holmes, and he motioned me to a small window under which he was crouched. He raised it just high enough to see inside and motioned for me to do the same.

I looked inside, then at Holmes, who raised his eyebrows as if to say, "We have our man."

What we saw in the little room was the boardwalk artist standing in admiration of the unfinished painting of the mermaid and the sailor shown to us in very much the same state of completion as the painting Howard Pyle had shown us in his studio that morning.

We left the shanty and maintained a crouch until we were across the meadow and hidden by the alleyway again.

"Good heavens, Holmes! He's stolen Pyle's painting," I said.

Holmes chuckled. "Not at all, my dear fellow. Our boardwalk artist is apparently quite a good forger. He slips up to Pyle's studio, memorizes what he sees, and in the evening reproduces it. I have dealt with forgers before, Watson, but I must say this is the first time I have seen the forgery occur as the original progresses. He imitates the original as it is being created. Remarkable, don't you think?"

"Criminal is what I think."

"Yes, agreed. But, a criminal with a gift, I would say."

"Holmes, tell me. How did you know our lowly charcoal artist was the forger?"

"As I have told you before, Doctor, you often see but fail to observe. The first time we passed that young man at his work, I saw a magenta stain on his sleeve. Why, I asked myself, would he have a paint stain on his smock given that his chosen medium is charcoal? Then this morning, when Mr. Pyle was showing us the work, his 'mermaid,' that he said he was in a rush to complete, I saw the same shade of magenta on the sailor's cap. Too much of a coincidence. So we followed the young man to his home, and there it was."

"Would that we all had your gifts of observation and deduction, Holmes."

"Then how should I make a living if everyone had them, Watson? I should be unemployed and destitute. But, come. Let us inform Mr. Pyle of our findings and see what steps he would like to take from here."

In this small town, it was but a short walk to the Pyle home. There we found Howard Pyle, attired in his artist's smock, sitting on the porch where we had left him, rocking gently back and forth and lost in thought. Holmes cleared his throat as we stood at the stairs to the porch.

"Ah, gentlemen. Forgive me. I was thinking on the day's work and what I planned to accomplish tomorrow. Do come up," said Pyle. "Would you like some refreshments?"

"Not at all," said Holmes, though I thought some of the lemonade we had shared in this spot earlier in the day would be a cool comfort.

"We have news of your forger," Holmes continued.

"What? You've caught the rascal?" asked Pyle.

"Not *caught* exactly, but we have identified him. I thought that perhaps you might like to meet him, and then we can call in the local constabulary."

"I certainly would. Where are you holding him?"

"He is not being held, except by his work, work which I think you will find fascinating. I suggest we go to him now, introduce the two of you, and confront him with your knowledge of his crimes."

Pyle was up and on his way down the stairs when he realized he was wearing his smock. Embarrassed, he removed it, placing it on the rocker he had been sitting in.

The three of us walked back the route Holmes and I had taken to Pyle's home, and when we reached the edge of the clearing, Holmes put up a hand for us to stop. He cautioned Pyle that he did not know if the forger was dangerous, though he doubted it. With that, we crossed the clearing, and Holmes rapped loudly on the little building's door. We could hear some movement inside, then silence.

"It will do you no good to hide. We know who you are and what you have done. Now open this door before we force it," Holmes said.

The door opened a crack, a sliver of yellow light widening onto the doorstep. Holmes put his hand on the door and pushed it open to reveal a slender young man in an artist's smock backing hastily across the small room that appeared to serve as both living quarters and studio.

Pyle's eyes went immediately to the painting. "My God. What did you—? How did you—? When did you ever—?" he stammered, then turned to the frightened young man and said, "Who are you?"

"I ... I ... I ... My name is Maxwell Conroy, sir. I am very ... v-v-very sorry."

"As you should be. You could go to jail for a very long time, young man. A very long time," Pyle said.

"Tell us, young Conroy," Holmes said. "How did you go about your theft? You do realize that is what it is, don't you? Theft. Forgery. Both felonies, I am sure. Tell us now. How did you commit these crimes?"

"Sir, I ... You don't sound American, sir. Who are you?"

"I am a loyal subject of Her Majesty Queen Victoria. Though that is of no matter here. Now, don't dally any longer or it will go worse with you. How and why did you steal this painting?"

The boy's look of fear was now mixed with confusion. He gave a halting, stammering explanation. "Very early in the morning, just before dawn, I would sneak close to Mr. Pyle's studio. When he and his children left to raise the flag—I knew this because I was at the boardwalk one morning early to sketch the sunrise—I would look closely and study and memorize what he had done. Then I had to hold it in my mind until night when I could come back here and put it on canvas."

To Pyle, he said: "It was the most exciting thing to me, sir, to see what you would do with the painting next. I am so sorry, sir." The boy hung his head.

Pyle appeared to have heard none of it. He had taken a lamp from the rough little table and was holding it to give light to the painting as he studied it, his face inches away from the canvas. The little room was quiet, except for the sound of Maxwell Conroy's rapid breathing as he sat hunched over, his head down and his hands hanging between his legs. Holmes broke the silence when he asked, "Well, Mr. Pyle. Shall we take our thief to the authorities?"

"A few questions of my own first, Mr. Holmes, if I may," Pyle said. Then to the boy: "How many paintings, that is, forgeries, have you sold?"

"Seven, sir."

"And how did you do that?"

"I have contacts, sir."

"Contacts, hmm? Where did you learn to paint?"

"I taught myself and studied pictures in the museum when I could, sir."

"And where," Pyle asked, "is the money from your sales?"

"I have it here, sir. Hidden."

"Well, Maxwell, I am going to give you two choices."

The young artist looked up slightly, not sure whether to be hopeful.

Pyle continued, "Maxwell Conroy, you may choose to go to jail. I am positive you would be convicted and that you would spend many years there. Or, you can give me the money you stole by copying my work. You may move into a small room off my studio and paint your own work for the remainder of the summer, then enroll in my school in Wilmington. The money will be used for your room, board, and tuition. When you begin to sell your own paintings, the money will be used to reimburse the victims of your crimes who bought your forgeries. You are a very talented forger. This is your chance to decide whether to go to jail or see if you can become a respected and honest artist. This choice is yours to make."

Holmes and I left the two artists to work out the details of the apprenticeship of Maxwell Conroy.

Anne Poole Pyle and her children, photographed by Howard Pyle at Rehoboth Beach, 1890.
Photo courtesy of the Delaware Historical Society.

Howard Pyle (1853–1911) was one of America's most popular and prolific illustrators at a time when top illustrators were celebrities. He and his family spent many summers at his cottage in Rehoboth, where the famous artist raised and lowered the flag each day. Maxwell Conroy is a product of the author's imagination.

Arthur Ignatius Conan Doyle (1859–1930) was a Scottish physician and writer who wrote sixty fictional stories about the detective Sherlock Holmes and his assistant Dr. Watson. This story is in the spirit of the beloved Sherlock Holmes stories.

JOSEPH CROSSEN, ED.D., HAS HAD SEVERAL POEMS PUBLISHED. HIS SHORT STORY "GALOOTS" WAS INCLUDED IN LAST YEAR'S *THE BEACH HOUSE*. HE HAS WRITTEN TWO CHILDREN'S BOOKS, *JOSHUA'S DREAM* AND *ZACHARY'S SHRINKITIS*, AND HE IS CURRENTLY WORKING ON A NOVEL AND A ONE-MAN PLAY ABOUT A HISTORICAL FIGURE. HE HAS BEEN A THREE-TIME FELLOW OF THE DELAWARE DIVISION OF THE ARTS CAPE HENLOPEN POETRY AND PROSE WRITERS' RETREAT.

Stolen Heart

by Terri Clifton

It was the last night of vacation and soon the summer of '87 would be at an end. The next day, his family would head back home and school would start a few days later. It was now or never. On his second pass by the pavilion, he made up his mind to just go for it, and crossed the currents of people being carried along the boardwalk.

He'd first seen her the weekend before, standing on the beach by herself at sunset, just out of reach of the waves, then later the same night in the electric glare of the water-gun game, laughing. Both times something in his gut had moved, and ever since he'd felt more awake.

He made his way toward her, slipping through the vacationers as if he were swimming. She looked up the moment he headed in her direction, tracked his progress with large dark eyes. He saw amusement there, and something else. She could laugh. He didn't care. He wanted to know about the something else.

Her bottom rested on the back of a wooden bench, tanned legs stretched before her, her feet bare. From her fingers dangled a pair of flip-flops. It wasn't quite dark, but lights were already coming on in the shops and restaurants, nighttime overtaking the beach town, the time each day when the sand became deserted and the bustle transferred itself to the boards and streets.

He should have just said hello, but it was the truth that came out: "You have beautiful eyes." That's what caught him, mid-stride. Dark eyes touching him. You don't just keep walking when something feels like that.

She just smiled, laughter dancing on her face, but nothing cruel in it. The kind of smile that made him smile back before he even thought about it. A wail erupted from a baby carriage, the parents steering out of the flow. The cries increased.

He couldn't just stand there and stare at her. "Wanna walk?"

"Where to?"

He shrugged. She straightened and moved forward. She was almost as tall as he was and he liked the way she seemed to glide along, never seeming to notice the congestion surrounding her.

He followed her into the arcade, wishing he'd asked her her name before they'd stepped into the din of a dozen electronic games. She put a dollar in a machine that spit out tokens, then walked to the air hockey table and dropped them in. The whir of the fan made it even more impossible to talk to her.

He let her score and it was the wrong move. She stopped, her hand poised above the table, the air blowing her shoulder-length hair.

"Sorry," he mumbled, and they started to play. He beat her, but just barely, and she made him work for it. He slammed the last goal home and she looked at him with the most interest she'd shown yet. Then she beat him squarely at a game of pinball. It wasn't even close.

"Let's take our picture." She pulled the curtain back on the photo booth. He slid in next to her on the seat and looked into the glass square, aware of her closeness, smelling her perfume. He leaned into her as they froze between flashes.

Outside, a stray breeze off the ocean brought the smells of salt and creosote and something sweet. She waved the strip of photos in the air to dry as they walked. She headed to buy cotton candy—blue—and perched on the back of a white wooden bench. That was when he told her his name.

She didn't offer hers, so he asked. She tilted her head to the side and narrowed her eyes. "What name fits me?" She exuded some kind of mystery, as if she might know answers to things he'd never even questioned.

He searched his brain for something beautiful, something bright and quick. He could only think of names of girls he knew, but she wasn't anything like those girls, and she was grinning at him. His brain froze as he stared at her, but she looked out at the silvery water and popped cotton candy into her mouth, still grinning.

After a while he didn't need to know. Just walking next to her in the sand had a rhythm. Like a heartbeat. Like a life beat. He didn't have enough experience to know the feeling was rare.

He watched her as she played Skee-Ball at Funland, aiming the brown wooden ball, scoring more often than not, and knew she would never ask someone else to win her the stuffed cat she wanted. She got prizes three times straight and traded a shiny starfish for the black cat she then tucked under her arm. He wanted to take her on a ride, but the bumper cars were probably a bad idea, the haunted house seemed too obvious, and the carousel would make him look like a dork. "Wanna get pizza?"

She shook her head no. He thought his heart stopped, the moment seemed so long before she finally spoke. "Ever had a Nic-o-Boli?"

He fell in step with her as they walked north along the edge of the ocean, the sea so smooth and the light so soft it was impossible to tell the horizon from the sky. She turned up the Avenue, weaving between people on the sidewalk. He alternated between watching her walk and avoiding collisions. She never looked back to see if he was following, but when she turned the corner onto First Street, she waited for him.

Across the street, a guy outside the record store shouted and waved at her. She smiled and waved back, before pushing the door open and walking into the bustle of the restaurant. At a booth in the window, she sipped her birch beer and asked him questions.

He told her things meant to impress her. He went to a private high school. He wanted to be a lawyer. He played soccer and was captain of the golf team.

She looked at him and smiled. "I'm sorry."

He laughed, not knowing what else to do, and wishing he'd told her something else, like that he played guitar when no one was around. That he used to dream about sailing around the world. She seemed like the kind of person you told those things to.

He tried to guess her name. He tried the basics: Ann, Beth, Donna. She shook her head. He tried again, going for more modern names: Jennifer, Kristin, Ashley. She sipped her soda and shook her head some more. When he tried the names of Greek goddesses she laughed. He tried rock stars: Chrissie, Joan, Debbie, Stevie.

"Nope," she said. "But I like the way you think."

He managed to learn a few things. She had another year of school, like he did. She thought maybe she wanted to travel before college. She spent her summers babysitting tourist children. She hated winter. They must have talked for a long time. He looked up and they were the only customers left.

Back on the street, the crowds had thinned. He passed a father carrying a sleeping child and remembered being carried just like that, exhausted from sea air and playing all day. This place had changed for him tonight, childhood setting quietly with the sun and night bringing a subtle shift in the way the world looked.

They strolled along, slow progress to nowhere in particular. It was dark; stars etched against a moonless sky. She balanced on the back of a white bench where the Avenue met the boardwalk, stuffed cat wrapped in her arms. The air was rapidly cooling. They just listened to the waves. Fewer and fewer people went by. Mostly couples. Some touching, some not.

"It's almost midnight," she said. "I have a curfew."

"Cinderella, then," he teased.

She tore the bottom photo from the strip and handed it to him. She was smiling into the camera, her head tilted and almost on his shoulder.

"You aren't going to tell me your name."

She looked at him a long moment, thinking. "You'll have to come back next year and keep trying."

He knew he would and told her so, but she was already walking away.

As she left him, he wished a dozen things. That he wasn't leaving in the morning. That he could know if she felt any of the things he had, and if any of those things were real. He watched her disappear up the street, watched until he couldn't see her anymore before he walked south to his parents' cottage.

* * * * * *

Every summer after, he looked for her. He looked in the arcade, on the beach, at the pizza place, everywhere she'd taken him. In the Dewey bars during college summers, he couldn't help scanning the faces of girls. His family still came down every year, and even after he was married, they spent two weeks at the end of August.

As the years passed, his one regret, or perhaps the beginning of all his regrets, was letting her go. His life had never again felt the way it had for a few hours one night, a long time ago. Maybe it had kept him from committing to what he had, and why he'd lost it.

He'd never seen her again and wondered if he had, if it would have made her more real, more flawed, than she'd seemed that one perfect summer night; if he would have been able to somehow settle, give his life over to what he'd had, not what he'd missed. Then maybe he wouldn't have had the unshakable feeling that he'd let something important slip from his grasp. No one could be as perfect as he'd imagined her. And no one could just steal a heart like that. He'd tried to tell himself that he'd made it all up inside his mind, but his soul never changed its story.

He still had that photo, tucked into his wallet, a sort of talisman, a tangible piece of a dream he'd once had, a hope that he could find something of himself, left from before he'd stopped believing in such things. He'd looked at it just before he'd come here tonight.

The crowd moved along, just as the years had. He wasn't in a hurry. The air was warm and the sea was the same still, silver-pink, as it had been that night. He'd sit right here, under the glow of the Dolle's sign, and just maybe he'd catch those eyes, the ones that belonged to the stranger who had taken his heart.

TERRI CLIFTON IS THE AUTHOR OF *A RANDOM SOLDIER,* A MEMOIR, AND HAS RECENTLY COMPLETED HER FIRST NOVEL. IN ADDITION TO WRITING, SHE SPEAKS ON ISSUES OF LITERACY AND THE IMPORTANCE OF STORIES WITH STUDENTS OF ALL AGES. A DELAWARE NATIVE, SHE LIVES ON A HISTORIC FARM AT THE EDGE OF THE DELAWARE BAY WITH HER SON RYAN AND HUSBAND, RICHARD, AN INTERNATIONALLY KNOWN WILDLIFE ARTIST. SHE IS AN ACCOMPLISHED PHOTOGRAPHER AND LOVES TO TRAVEL. SHE IS ALSO THE DIRECTOR OF A FOUNDATION BENEFITING VETERANS.

The Old Colored Man Breaks the Law (Again)

by Matthew Hastings

Editor's Note: This story contains language that may be offensive to some readers. This is a historical story and the terms used are required for authenticity. Thank you for understanding that no offense is intended.

What he was about to do was against the law. Then again, most everything he'd ever done in his life that'd gotten him anywhere near getting what he wanted, or gotten him feeling good about himself, had been either illegal or frowned upon. He smiled, thinking of this, holding the small cardboard box, sitting on the boardwalk on one of those benches where the back flips so that you can either face the parade of sunburned tourists or gaze out over the beach and the ocean. He was not looking at the tourists.

It had been his idea to scatter Emma's ashes on Rehoboth Beach. They'd never discussed funerals or burials. They had an unspoken agreement not to, and an even more unspoken understanding that he'd go first. He'd failed her once again.

For a half century they'd come down from Bala Cynwyd every June to open up Miss Charlotte's rambling fourteen-room beach house in the Pines. They'd stay all summer, doing the work that allowed Miss Charlotte to entertain an endless parade of family, old and brand-new friends, and people who just wanted something, usually money—her money.

He was technically the butler, just like his papa had been for Miss Charlotte's father. Emma was technically the cook. And what a cook. Everyone who ever tasted her cooking couldn't get enough and insisted that her food somehow made you feel better about yourself. He did everything to keep the place going and the guests happy. He looked forward to stripping and revarnishing the wood on the '49 Packard woody and the Rhodes 19 sailboat, and keeping track of Fergus and India, Miss Charlotte's two meandering, opinionated Westies (dogs would come and go over the years, but there were always two, and they were always named Fergus and India). He didn't mind changing the diapers on Mr. Lucas when his caretaker wasn't available. Mr. Lucas was Miss Charlotte's brother who had become a quadriplegic after a bad car accident. Emma was not only the cook who oversaw the daily girls who cleaned, but also the gatekeeper to, and protector of, Miss Charlotte. They'd do one big final party on Labor Day, pack up, and then head back to Philly for the season and to get the kids back to school.

No matter how many years they were in Rehoboth, they got the stares. Some of these Sussex County folks just couldn't keep their eyes off them and couldn't keep their ignorant comments and outrage about what they saw to themselves. Over the years he'd heard plenty, but he never said or did anything until "it" happened. Just once, once in all those years, did he lose control. Some ignorant cracker called six-year-old Annie a "half-breed" and said she shouldn't be allowed to be in the "whites only" amusement arcade. He'd cracked that fool's jaw half off his face before he'd known he'd done. Forty years later he got all hot remembering standing there, in the line for the bumper cars, with the cracker bleeding on the hard cement floor. He was ashamed that he'd lost his temper, horrified and disgusted with himself. As soon as he'd looked over at a shocked Emma and terrified Annie, he was filled with dread thinking he'd go to jail for the audacity of knocking down a white man who'd insulted his little girl.

In fact, he had been arrested, as had the cracker, much to the outrage of the cracker's wife and children. He spent a total of one hour and nine minutes in jail. That was how long it took Miss Charlotte to call her cousin, the president of the company that pretty much ran Delaware, who called the governor, who called the mayor of Rehoboth Beach, who told the police chief to release him and apologize to him. The newspaper people were waiting for him when Emma came to walk him back to the house. He said nothing. There was nothing they would write that would make it all go away or teach that cracker fool and his kind a lesson.

His three kids had played on that beach for hours. One good thing about being high yellow was, as his mama had said every time she inspected each of her brand-new grandchildren, they just didn't never sunburn.

After hero-worshiping the Rehoboth Beach lifeguards for fifteen years and taking endless classes at the Y, his tall, handsome, athletic, and gentle son Will tried out for lifeguard team. Will had tested first in a group of over one hundred boys. When he wasn't chosen, Emma was some rip-pissed. She had marched into the mayor's office, by this time quite familiar with his family. The mere suggestion of another of Miss Charlotte's phone calls immediately ensured that Will would become the first black lifeguard Rehoboth had ever had. Then Emma had second thoughts and was scared to death that some silly white girl would flirt with Will and claim he'd forced her to do the strange and the locals would lynch him.

After all, it had only been a few years since they stopped publicly whipping people (that meant coloreds) in Dover. But Will was way too smart to fall into any of those traps.

He'd busted with pride when Will joined up with the Army right out of Howard, and then immediately filled up with fear that something bad would happen to his boy. They'd all known he'd be in the service, what with his ROTC obligations. But they'd all thought he'd postpone it until after he finished law school, by which time, with any luck, that nonsense in Vietnam would have cooled off. But Will wanted to get it over with. He came down to Rehoboth just before he left for duty. He'd brought a girl with him, not one of the pretty, adoring coeds he'd dated at Howard, but a different girl: a very serious, very thin, and very white girl.

Emma was real quiet at his graduation from officer's school. From the second he shipped out she was a nervous wreck. Her cooking went from magical to edible. She went stone-silent when Miss Charlotte and Mr. Lucas came to tell them that Will had been taken prisoner in Vietnam, and spoke little after they got the word. When the general tried to hand Emma the flag that had draped Will's coffin, she'd turned her face and walked away. The skinny white girl walked away with her. He took the flag from the general. He still had it with Will's sports and debating trophies and annuals and clippings and scrapbooks, all in his old Army chest in the basement.

Annie had been a handful. So willful and spirited, but she was always a daddy's girl. He'd taken his hand to her only once. Afterwards, he felt sick with shame for losing control. Luckily, for some reason, the mere thought of disappointing her daddy kept Annie in line—more or less. At least as far as he knew. She was number one in everything she set out to do: Gold Award Girl Scout, first violin in the youth orchestra, president of student council, and class valedictorian. She was head girl at Candy Kitchen at fifteen, and then a summer supervisor, at age seventeen, for all five of their local shops. She was an easy child to be proud of.

When Annie got married to her Spellman roommate's brother, a fine young man named Charles, who was in medical school at Johns Hopkins, they'd had the wedding and reception at Miss Charlotte's beach house. Miss Charlotte had insisted and had paid for everything. She turned the entire place over to them for two weeks and moved into a hotel with Mr. Lucas, the caretaker, and the wee beasties. She even got some of her friends to loan out their beach houses for the overflow—for even then, black folks weren't exactly welcomed with open arms at most of the guest houses and hotels at the beach.

There was dancing and singing and music that went on and on. And the food, good Lord, the tables were groaning with every sort of food you could imagine, prepared by his kitchen-competitive sisters, cousins, and aunts. That wedding was the first and last time he'd ever danced with Miss Charlotte. She'd mentioned halfway through the dance that until that point she'd only danced with three men who could actually dance: her father, her brother, and her late husband. He had said he was honored. She'd stopped dead on the dance floor, which brought a lot of attention to them, as if this little white lady with the skunk-striped hair, in red Chinese pajamas, dancing with a black man in a room of black folks wasn't enough to attract attention. She'd told him in no uncertain terms that the honor was all hers. It was more or less a lecture. He smiled thinking of it.

His own wedding to Emma, he remembered, was quite different. There was no laughter, no singing, and certainly no food. It had been in March 1944, in a half-bombed-out chapel in London's East End. He was technically AWOL from the 761st Tank Division and he hadn't gotten permission from his CO to get married. He hadn't even asked. His CO was a racist animal who hated all white people and held a special well of wrath for the Jews. Emma was Jewish. This would have been double trouble.

Emma's people were mostly dead, killed in the blitz. Emma herself had lost half her hearing. But the moment he saw her handing out food while standing in line at the canteen, he'd known he was a goner. And that was before he'd tasted one mouthful of her magical cooking. He'd been listening to her talk to the soldiers in front of him. Her voice sparkled. He'd never heard anything like it. And she sparkled. He'd kept his eyes looking down when it was his turn. There was silence, and he'd had to look up. She'd looked him right in the face and said, "Black or white?" He was crushed and hot with shame, disgusted with himself—why would this beautiful English girl give him a second glance—but he said quietly, "a little of both." She'd burst into a laugh that then, and later, lifted his spirits. "I meant the coffee," she said. "Do you want it with or without milk?"

It took an hour, three trips to the bathroom, and every ounce of courage in his body to ask her out for a walk. After the words stumbled out of his mouth she had her apron off and her arm in his so fast he lost his breath. Very quickly, they'd fallen in love.

He seemed to live for Emma's touch, and thanks be to God, she for his. Emma's landlady who was the bossy kind and took matters into her own hands, found a sweet old minister who was not too concerned about Army regulations to marry them. Emma was pregnant by the time of the invasion and it was the thought of getting back to her and his baby that kept him going as his tank rolled from Normandy to Berlin. He was all Emma had in the world and he never let himself forget it.

He looked down at the little plain cardboard box with Emma's ashes. He hadn't cried yet. He supposed he would soon enough. He hadn't really cried since the last time he saw Cessy, his baby girl.

It had been in court. She'd been arrested for the last time and the judge had no option. She would be away for ten years, minimum.

What Cessy had been doing with drugs and the people who used and sold them scared him to death. The sweet little girl with the blue eyes, "from some long-ago Russian Cossack's pogrom exploits," Emma had said when she'd handed this squirming little bundle to him at the hospital, was never far from his thoughts. How had she gone from ballet recitals, spelling bees, and prom queen to drug addiction? She had done unthinkable things, stealing from her parents and putting herself out on the street, to feed her habit. And now she had been taken away from him.

The last time Cessy had come to the beach she'd disappeared right after supper. He'd spent hours looking for her and found her at two in the morning, facedown in the sand, a hypodermic needle next to her. He crushed it with his foot and kicked it into the ocean. He'd cried as he carried her black-and-blue bruised skeleton-like body to Emma, just like he used to carry her back to the house so many times, dead asleep to the world, after a day of playing on the beach. When her mama went to her room the next morning with her favorite breakfast, Cessy was gone.

The summers in Rehoboth came and went. Each one a little different but, now that he thought of it, not really all that much. Annie and Charles would come for a week, first alone and then with the babies. The first time he took his twin granddaughters to Playland he was shaking, remembering what had happened so long ago, thanking God that it wouldn't happen to these precious treasures.

But soon enough it had been just Miss Charlotte, Mr. Lucas, Emma, and him. Most of Miss Charlotte's friends had died off or had lost their buttons. Miss Charlotte made him promise that he'd never lose his buttons, and that he'd always remember. He was the last person who remembered what she remembered after Mr. Lucas had been taken.

When they stopped giving sunset barbecues, Miss Charlotte and Mr. Lucas started going to the beach to watch twilight on the ocean. Of course like everything associated with Miss Charlotte it was a production, but he'd been happy to be useful. They had a proper canopy, proper bamboo beach chairs, a proper table, and proper postprandials. He'd carry Mr. Lucas to the car and place him gently on the backseat, and Miss Charlotte would climb up front; she'd shrunk so much she barely saw over the dashboard. The Packard would crawl the two blocks to the beach, as if in a parade, which considering the stares they got it might as well have been. He completed the elaborate setup, got them both into the beach chairs, and the two of them would sit there holding hands and laughing as the sun went down. He'd leave them be and sit on the bench, this bench actually, on the boardwalk and watch them; going down to bring them back to the house when the first chill came in the air.

The last time they made what Mr. Lucas called "the pilgrimage," he'd seen Miss Charlotte get up from her chair, but not for a fresh cracker with caviar to feed Mr. Lucas. Instead, she put her arms around his head and rocked back and forth. He'd rushed down and stopped a few feet away. "Now there," Miss Charlotte said softly. "Now there, everything is all right." Then she looked up at him. Tears were making her trademark panda-eye mascara run down her cheeks like blue-black rain. He took her in his arms and carried her back to the Packard. He went back for Mr. Lucas and carried him to the backseat. They drove to the Beebe Hospital together. Miss Charlotte sat in the front seat while he took care of the paperwork. He never went back to the beach for the setup.

For a while afterward, Miss Charlotte seemed to spark up. She was having parties and going out again, ordering new wallpaper, and one day at breakfast announcing they were trading in the forty-year-old Packard for a powder-blue (her favorite color as it matched her eyes) Rambler American wagon she'd seen in Milford the day before. When he went to collect the Rambler, he'd taken Mr. Vinal Bennett at the dealership aside and told him to hold the Packard for them; they'd be back for it. The Rambler lasted one week and the woody was quietly reclaimed. Miss Charlotte claimed she couldn't think from all the noise the Rambler made; in fact, it was the quietest car he'd ever known. What she didn't like, but couldn't come out and say, was that no one in Rehoboth knew she was coming when they saw the Rambler. The highly polished and stately Packard and its owner and driver were well known— legendary in fact. Miss Charlotte had posed for umpteen lobster-red sunburned tourists' cameras in front of that car. The Rambler wasn't so photogenic. They were soon back in the Packard with the one-digit license plate. The Rambler had clocked a total of forty-five miles and lived under an oilcloth in the garage on blocks. They saw it daily, but it was ignored.

But after a while, Miss Charlotte didn't seem to have it in her anymore. There were no more parties. A good day was when she would ride her three-wheeled bicycle to Lingo's Market in the morning to get the Philadelphia papers and have a gossip with Mrs. Lingo, with whom she'd played on the beach as a girl. In the afternoon, she'd take yet another watercolor class at the Art League and then come home and listen to her opera records until it was time to share a postprandial and, more often than not, a dividend (her term for refill). She'd usually fall asleep looking at photo albums. He'd carry her up to her bed and Emma would take it from there. Miss Charlotte was a few years older than Emma and him. They hoped she would go before they did. They worried who would take care of her. There were only some scheming cousins, she'd say, "just aching to get their hands on Mummy's Flora Danica."

When Emma had her first stroke, it was Miss Charlotte who took over the nursing. She'd trained in the war as a WAVE and knew exactly what to do, or more accurately, what the twenty-four-hour nurse's aides should do.

It had been a week ago today that he'd kissed Emma good-bye as she set off on her daily "walk," pushed in a wheelchair by Jennifer, the aide. They would stroll down the boardwalk with the current Fergus and India on leashes. That day, they'd stopped for cotton candy. It had slipped out of her hands and fallen on Fergus. She had gone to her maker looking at the beach.

He thanked the Lord he'd not seen her go. He'd not seen her dead and wouldn't. Charles came down to identify his Jewish mother-in-law married to his colored father-in-law. They'd had a service at the little synagogue on Holland Glade Road, where Emma had taken to going after Will was killed. Annie's girls had recited a poem about their Nana, and he'd been real surprised to see Will's skinny white girlfriend paying her respects. Emma and she had apparently kept in touch all these years. But not totally in touch, because, with the white girl (still skinny but now a Philadelphia corporate lawyer) was a handsome, tall young man who was, as she introduced him, her son. No need to tell him more. The boy was the spitting image of Will. He sounded like Will. He laughed like Will. His name was Will. One loved one leaves his life, another enters.

He'd brought the box to the house where it sat for a couple of days. Finally, that morning, Miss Charlotte had said, "It's time." And here he was, once again, down to the beach with Emma. For the last time.

Miss Charlotte was right. It was time. She was waiting patiently at the house; told him to take his time. But he knew she'd be thirsty for her postprandial, something they now had together.

He took off his socks, folded them in thirds, and put them in his pocket. He tied his always mirror-polished shoes with the shoelaces and put them around his neck. He rolled up his trousers. He took a deep breath and walked out into the water. There weren't many people about. He'd chosen this time, dinnertime, for that reason.

He leaned over and put the box entirely under water. He opened it and watched the ashes float out. Gray, not black or white, like clouds that neither promise rain nor deny sun. Some came up on the surface. He timed it for when the wave came in, and when it went out it swept Emma away with it. Forever.

He walked back to the boardwalk and rinsed off his feet, putting his socks and shoes back on. He had to hurry home now. He had to get things organized for tomorrow. His daughter Annie had arranged a birthday party for Cessy at the prison. Tomorrow they were all going up to the Baylor Correctional Institute; everyone, including the new Will and his mother and, of course, Miss Charlotte. Odd as it was, when Miss Charlotte and the Westies went visiting Cessy, the warden herself greeted them and loaned them her conference room for their meetings and parties. When Miss Charlotte learned that Cessy was essentially running the prison kitchen these days, and that the guards and inmates were getting pleasantly fat as a result, she began counting the days until Cessy could take up Emma's apron and return things to the way they were supposed to be.

MATTHEW HASTINGS HAS BEEN WRITING STORIES AND LETTERS SINCE HE WAS SIX, INCLUDING TWO OVER-COMPLICATED MURDER MYSTERIES. UNTIL THIS BOOK, HIS PUBLICATIONS WERE LIMITED TO PROFESSIONAL AND TECHNICAL JOURNALS AND THE OCCASIONAL EULOGY. MAT WAS BORN IN DETROIT (WHICH EXPLAINS HIS IRRATIONAL PENCHANT FOR MOTOWN AND VERNORS), WENT TO A TWO-ROOM SCHOOLHOUSE IN THE BERKSHIRES, AND LANDED IN A COLLEGE IN A PLACE COLDER THAN SIBERIA. HE HAS HAD DRIVER'S LICENSES IN NINE STATES BUT NOW SPLITS HIS TIME BETWEEN DC, REHOBOTH, AND AN ISLAND SEVEN MILES OFF THE COAST OF MAINE WITH NO WI-FI. WHILE HIS WORK TAKES HIM OVERSEAS FIVE OR SIX TIMES A YEAR, HE INSISTS THAT HE IS NOT A SPY (BUT THEN HE WOULD). MOST OF MAT'S FRIENDS TEND TO BE CAUTIOUS ABOUT WHAT THEY SAY IN FRONT OF HIM AS IT COULD WELL END UP IN A STORY.

JUDGE'S COMMENT:

A poignant story worthy of publication and prize—the writer had me fooled into believing this was his memoir about working as a butler for a prominent Rehoboth family. He has come to the boardwalk to bury his sweet wife and to let go of life's resentments. A little work of art.

Granny in Funland

by Renay Regardie

It's May again. I'm glad that winter's over, glad that summer's around the corner, and glad that I can think about getting out of Washington, DC, and kicking back at the beach.

Of course, there's all that preparation to do, and, frankly, I don't do prep very well. Not at this stage of life. I like prep prepped for me.

But there's one task that only I can do, so that those damn kids (whoops, I mean my darling grandkids) remain clueless: prepping their dormitory. No, they won't know that Granny's hands touched—and removed—half of those ridiculous stuffed animals that clutter the bunk beds and trundles. They're the spoils of several hundred dollars spent at the Funland Wars for maybe $50 worth of keepable stuffed treasures, including teddy bears, puppies, snakes, horses, frogs, birds, kittens, and sea creatures.

A granny's got to be ruthless to cut this herd down to a manageable menagerie, and I've become an expert at it. In thirty minutes, I've readied the room to grow a new zoo as the fortunes of my grandchildren at the games of chance at Funland bring in another shitload (oops, I mean assortment) of stuffed toys.

There are, of course, some keepers. The giant burro my granddaughter won three years ago inhabits the top bunk. Her parents won't let her take it to L.A., so it resides here, awaiting her return. I sort out the more prestigious winnings (that is, the bigger ones), including two smiling puppies, a brown teddy with hungry tongue hanging out, a laughing turquoise monkey, a leering pink pig, a couple of fish, and a few snakes. I toss out the little crap, but the room still looks trinket-full, belying the thirty to forty trophies I've trashed.

The family arrives. My mission was a success. The kids are in the bunkroom, screaming and laughing, not missing what is missing.

The season's first trip to the boardwalk is at the top of the agenda after everyone settles in on Memorial Day weekend. We grab caramel corn at Dolle's, chocolate-marshmallow fudge at Candy Kitchen, and vanilla/orange frozen custard from Kohr's. We need sustenance as we move on to the premier family attraction of this boardwalk: Funland. Even more than the rides, it's the games of chance that these young risk-takers crave.

I'm always up for this first fling at Funland, but not the follow-ups. The kids go five or six times a season, but now I've finally learned the art of avoidance. It's not my pleas of old age or aching feet that excuse me, but the fact that I press a few greenbacks into the grandkids' eager little paws, so I'm there in spirit—or at least funding.

We hit the rides first. I've still got a very young one, so I must endure the boat floating along in brackish water and the fire engine with the clanging bell. I smile and wave as these fast flyers charge around a circle at two miles an hour. I dutifully and dizzily ride the carousel, smiling as my horse bounces up and down. The bigger kids head for the scary rides. They don't even ask me to accompany them, certainly not after I endured the Freefall two years ago, crying and screaming as my space commando seat went up and down at blistering speed. "Never again," I wailed. The kids, embarrassed by my cowardly performance, no longer cajole me to accompany them.

The real enticement, though, for the kids, Gramps, and me are the games. We've chanced most of them over the years. We have a hit list of our favorite four. We like them because we actually win some of the time.

First, we head to the Super Goblet Toss. This is a game of pure luck. You toss a softball- sized plastic sphere, hoping to land it in the lone center silver goblet to win a plus-sized stuffed pup. The yellow goblets bring a cute puppy, the red goblets, a tiny keepsake. I figure your odds of hitting the gold (silver in this case) are a thousand to one. At a quarter a shot, though, this is a bargain. Oodles of parents shell out a few bucks as little kids throw blindly and badly. We got hooked three years ago when our granddaughter, then only four, tossed her first ball smack into the silver cup and the giant burro had a new home. Since that time, we plow at least twenty bucks an evening into futilely aiming for that silver cup. Sometimes we hit reds and yellows, but it's not the same as winning The Big One.

Next, we're off to the Water Race. Aim your loaded water gun perfectly at the bull's-eye below your dancing puppy, then squeeze hard and fast. If your pup rises to the top first, the bell goes off and you're a winner. This is also a game that little kids can handle. It's not as popular as a lot of the other games, which is one reason I like it. With fewer people playing, I have a better chance of winning. The hook, of course, is that the size of the prize depends on how many people play. If you have only three competitors, you walk away with a dinky dancing puppy, but that's still better than losing. Often, there are children playing alongside me, but I pay them no mind. I win and grab my prize, ignoring their parents' disdainful stares. I've seen adults pass their toys to some crying kid, but not me.

The key to keeping you playing these games is the trade-up. In most of these games, even if you win, your plush kitten looks food-deprived. However, if you keep winning, you can trade up several so-so prizes for a bigger so-so prize, and so it goes. It's a Ponzi scheme for kids. The more you win, the more you play, hoping to make that jumbo bear, or jumbo panda, or jumbo whatever, perched tantalizingly aloft, yours.

On this year's inaugural Funland venture, we've scored a tiny lavender seahorse on the Super Goblet Toss and two malnourished puppies at the Water Race. I trade them up for a larger pink puppy, tongue hanging out in throw-up mode. My granddaughter whisks it out of my hands. I don't mind. It's not cute. It will be marked for extinction at the end of the season.

Next stop is Whac-a-Mole. This is a game for muscles. First Son, though not muscle-bound, can whack the hell out of the little turds—uh, varied colored moles—that pop up out of the little holes. We cheer him on. He usually scores a medium prize, but since no one else in the family has mastered this skill, we quickly move on.

Our last and favorite stop is Derby, also known as the horse race. It's my game of choice next to the Water Race. It's the game that my eldest grandson could letter in, if they gave letters for this skill. In Derby, you roll a little ball up a ramp, much like Skee-Ball, except you're sitting down. Up to twelve racing aficionados play. Everyone hopes to bring their horse in first across the finish line. You do this by rolling your ball into red (best), blue, or yellow holes, which somehow propels your horse along the track. You often miss altogether, but the ball just rolls back to you. Sports have never been my thing, but I have mastered the slow roll, angling my ball, and I have seen my horse charge (uh, trudge) first across the finish line a surprising number of times.

Here's the rub: where I've been lucky, Eldest Grandson is remarkably skilled. He takes on anyone—muscle-bound guys with tattooed arms, lithe ladies with sculpted biceps, white-haired grandpas, flamboyant teenage boys, squealing girls—and wins. His favored position is seat one. I like five. Why does he like position one? He doesn't give a reason, but I know it's because this kid believes he is number one in everything he does. A fancy numero uno will probably be his first tattoo.

Here's the deal: Last summer, I got lucky and beat him and the rest of the crowd twice, trading up to an extra-large panda, one size below the jumbo prize. That darn grandson conned me, pleaded with me to pool my panda with his. I did. Grandson won, traded up his winner and mine, and took the jumbo panda back to Washington, DC. That pissed me off. I envisioned jumbo panda living at the beach house, forever standing guard at the kids' dormitory, a symbol of family unity, fun, and skill. Wrong!

This year, I'm out for blood. I want to bring a jumbo bear home to my beach home, not see it carted off to some DC bedroom. My pitching arm is itching with anxiety. I am ready to kill.

It's Granny against Grandson and this Granny's out for Bear—the big cuddly jumbo one, that is. Whether you're eight or eighty, there's something about winning, and I feel it to the tip of my orthotic-enhanced Nikes. Grandson, in his flip-flops and shirt to his knees, runs his tongue over his lips, his eyes bright with anticipation.

Kentucky Derby music swells around us. Seat one opens up and Grandson slides in. It takes me two games, but then seat five, my lucky chair, is mine. It's a busy night: every seat taken, the watchers two deep. I'm rusty. My horse barely gets out of the gate the first two games, while Grandson scores a win. Third game, I am in the zone with a win, Grandson just behind me. I taste sweet victory. Some long-haired kid takes the next game, and a zonked-out-looking black-haired gal (must have stoned luck) nabs the next.

I plunk down dollars. We've set a limit—twenty bucks each. I'm down to my last five, and I win. Next game I come up short. I don't even know how Grandson is doing, but I hear a cheer, and I see, behind him, his dad—First Son, the traitor—holding an extra-large bear.

I'm down to my last dollar. Music blasts, the bell clangs, and they're off. Sweat on my hands, roll the ball, I miss. Focus, focus, roll, and I'm in the red. My horse jumps ahead. Roll again, another leap. My horse leads the pack. I roll, hitting a blue, and my horse jumps forward. I hit the yellow, just a smidgen of a move, but I am almost there. One more roll in any color hole will put me across the finish line. I roll and the bell goes off. Someone else has won!

It's Grandson. I relinquish seat five and move to him. He has a shit-eating grin on his face as he exchanges his winnings for that humongous jumbo bear, the super cuddly brown one with the red tongue. Defeated, but somehow exuberant (it is family, after all), I clutch my lesser bear to my breast, my heart pounding from a game well fought.

"Granny," he says, "you did really well. Wow, you almost beat me. Let's keep this jumbo bear at the beach house for all the family. And if you'll give me a few dollars and the bear you've won, I can come back tomorrow and win another jumbo bear to take back to DC."

I am touched. I hand him a few bucks and pass my bear to his dad. I put my arms around his shoulders. What a great, caring, sensitive grandson he is.

"Deal," I say, "let's get some Thrasher's." We walk off down the boards, Jumbo Family Beach House Bear cradled in my left arm, my right hand entwined in my grandson's, basking in the starry boardwalk night.

After building (and then selling) a business that provided market research, feasibility studies, and marketing strategy to residential home developers, Renay Regardie turned back to her first love, writing. Renay began by taking courses at the Rehoboth Beach Writers' Guild. Her story "Refuge," which focused on the relationship between a mother who has Alzheimer's and her daughter, won third place in the 2013 Rehoboth Beach Reads Short Story Contest and was published in *The Beach House*. She is trying to lighten things up a bit with this story. She has five grandchildren who are passionate about Funland, the beach, and all things that tire out grandparents. An upstairs "dormitory" in Renay's Rehoboth beach house features the loot these kids win each year.

Judge's Comment:

"Granny in Funland" portrays in delightful detail the appeal of a unique boardwalk experience to children of all ages. The reader will remember this spunky granny for her playful humor and her exuberant love for her family.

Elaynea and the Walk of Boards

by Robin Hill-Page Glanden

My name is Elaynea and I am from the planet Zerban. This is my report on the trip I made to Earth on my fiftieth birthday.

My people have been visiting Earth for many years and hope that some of us can live there one day in the future. We are peaceful and loving people and have been developing programs and procedures to help people on Earth save the air, water, and land from pollution. We also have medical innovations that will assist with disease and illness. Our elders are working on ways to introduce ourselves and our gifts to Earth without being seen as invaders and causing panic. Many Earthlings seem to be quite wary of outsiders.

Zerbanites look much like the humans that inhabit Earth, so we blend in easily. Our body structure and facial features are very similar to that of Earthlings, but we have pale skin because we do not have a lot of sunshine on Zerban, and we all have light blond or white hair and blue eyes. We have a special chip implanted under our skin at birth that enables us to speak whatever language is spoken to us. All adult Zerbanites are slender and stand between five and six feet tall. We enjoy exercising every day and most of our diet consists of wafers and capsules that provide optimum nutrition and health benefits. Our healthy diet and lifestyle plus the low incidence of illness serve to slow the aging process, so a fifty-year-old Zerbanite is similar in appearance to a twenty-year-old Earthling. Time is measured the same way on Zerban as it is on Earth, but our life span is about twice as many years as it is for Earthlings, so at fifty years of age, a Zerban boy or girl is just crossing over into adulthood. Our rite of passage is a trip to Earth. Those of us who wish to go, may travel to any place on Earth for one day to celebrate our fiftieth birthday. Last week, it was my turn to choose where on Earth I wanted to go for my birthday celebration adventure.

I decided on the place my oldest brother, Baylon, visited on his fiftieth birthday three years ago. He was headed for New York City in the United States, which is where many of my people go, but his pod developed a mechanical malfunction so he had to make an emergency landing. He contacted our flight control help desk and they landed him in a field on a large farm in a tiny state called Delaware. He repaired the problem with his pod, but because he was behind schedule, flight control suggested that he stay there and visit a popular summer resort located nearby. They told him that he would greatly enjoy this place because it is located right on the Atlantic Ocean, and it has a beach and a walk made of boards that has many wonderful sights, sounds, and activities. The town is called Rehoboth Beach.

Baylon was disappointed at not getting to see New York City, but thought a summer resort by the ocean sounded interesting. He got on his power bike and rode into the town. He was awestruck by the enormous mass of salty water that is the Atlantic Ocean, but what he liked best was the walk made of boards. He said he met many very nice people, ate some delicious food, and visited a place with bright lights, bells, and buzzers, where he played games and rode in small cars that bumped into each other on purpose.

We attend classes and are coached on protocol and procedures to follow when we spend time on Earth, but I was always worried about meeting Earthlings and wondered what would happen if someone found out I was from another planet. Although I was curious about the people of Earth and eager to meet some of them, I have always been a little shy and didn't see how I could ever feel at ease. Baylon is more outgoing than I am and was not concerned at all about fitting in. For his trip he wore blue jeans, a T-shirt, a New York Yankees baseball cap, and sneakers. He said he mingled with people on the walk of boards and had a very good time. The stories he told of the sun, sand, and ocean made it sound so pleasant and appealing. But it was that walk of boards that particularly intrigued me. So I booked my pod flight to Rehoboth Beach, Delaware, and left very early on the morning of my birthday.

* * * * * *

I landed in the same field my brother landed in. It is in an isolated area, surrounded by trees. I got out my power bike and headed for Rehoboth. It was a warm, sunny day, so I dressed in light clothes with long sleeves, long pants, and a wide-brimmed hat to protect my delicate skin. There were so many cars on the road into town. They were all lined up and barely moving. I noticed there was a narrow lane on the side that no one was using, so I moved into that lane and was able to ride quickly past the cars. The drivers were very nice despite their slow pace of travel—one fellow even gave me some sort of special wave with his finger when I had to cut in front of him suddenly to make a left turn. I smiled and cheerfully returned his wave with my finger. Then he called out something to me—I couldn't hear what he said, but I'm quite sure it was a friendly greeting.

I rode past shops and restaurants on Rehoboth Avenue and parked my power bike in front of a bookstore. From there I went directly to the ocean and the walk of boards. I took my shoes off, stood on the warm planks, and stared out at the Atlantic Ocean. I had seen pictures of the ocean, but nothing compared to seeing it in person. I was overwhelmed by the sight and sound of the waves. The water seemed to go on forever. Shoes in hand, I walked slowly onto the sand. It felt hot and scratchy on my feet and grains of sand crept in between my toes. The sand shifted as I stepped, making walking difficult as I moved unsteadily toward the water.

Someone behind me asked if I was okay. I turned around to see a handsome young man, who looked to be about my age. His feet were bare and he was wearing a bright red T-shirt and baggy blue shorts. He had black curly hair and his skin was dark brown. I think he had what they call a suntan. He came quickly toward me, having no trouble at all walking on the sand. I told him that I was all right, just having a little trouble keeping my balance, and I wanted to go down to the water. This nice fellow offered to help me. He took my arm to steady me and we walked together. A wave came up and washed over my feet. I jumped and screamed because the water was so cold. He guided me back a little bit away from the waves onto wet sand. It was a little easier to walk there.

He said his name was Jeremy and he was on summer vacation from college. I told him my name and said it was my first time visiting a beach. He couldn't believe I had never been to a beach or seen the ocean and asked me where I was from. I couldn't tell him I was from another planet, so I said I was from Kansas. Jeremy offered to show me around, so we left the beach and went onto that walk of boards my brother had described.

It was everything he said it was—lights, music, booths selling many types of merchandise and food, and there were lots and lots of people. There were young people, old people, dark people, light people, tall people, short people, large people, small people. I had never seen such a diverse group of beings.

I asked about the place with rides and games. Jeremy took me there and we rode on wooden horses that went up and down and around in a circle. We played a game where we threw a ball and tried to get it inside a metal ring with a net.

He bought me a slice of something called pizza. It was so good! If I lived on Earth I think I would eat a lot of this pizza. Then Jeremy took me to a booth where he got a cup of something called ice cream. He handed me a spoon and told me to taste it. It was smooth, creamy, cold, and sweet. It was so delicious. He laughed and told me that I was eating bacon ice cream. I have no idea what bacon is or what it's supposed to taste like, but apparently it's a funny thing to put in ice cream. I don't know about that, but I found the flavor to be quite wonderful.

We spent the whole afternoon together and I have never had so much fun in my life. Jeremy and I laughed and talked and he asked if we could spend the next day together. I told him I was only in Rehoboth for one day and couldn't stay longer. We were both sad. I did not want to leave Rehoboth, and I did not want to leave Jeremy, but I knew I had to go according to schedule.

We started to walk back to where I had parked my power bike. On the way, he pulled me into one of the shops. He bought a little ring carved out of a pink-and-white seashell and put it on my finger. He said he wanted to give me something to help me remember him and our day together. We walked out of the shop and back onto the walk of boards, and then he kissed me. We do not kiss on my planet, so this took me by surprise, but I liked it. I looked into his brown eyes. I had never seen brown eyes before. He told me that I was beautiful and asked me again if I could stay at least one more day. I had to say that I couldn't, although I wanted to very much. I told him that I have two big, mean, older brothers who would be very upset if I didn't get home on time. That wasn't entirely a lie. I do have two older brothers. I just didn't tell Jeremy that they are not that big, they are not really mean, and they are on another planet.

Then, a drop of water ran out of Jeremy's eye and down his cheek. I caught it with my finger. When I asked him what happened to make water come out of his eye, he said that he was sad to see me go. Then I realized that the water was a tear. I had heard of tears but had never seen a Zerbanite cry. Suddenly I felt something in my own eyes. Water welled up and ran down my cheeks. I was crying! I did not think it was possible for anyone from my planet to cry. Jeremy wiped the tears off my cheeks, then put his arms around me and held me tight. It was the most wonderful feeling ever.

When we got back to where my power bike was parked, Jeremy said he wanted to exchange phone numbers. Someone had left a yellow envelope on my power bike, so I told Jeremy he could write on that. He said the envelope was a parking ticket and handed it back to me. While Jeremy went into the bookstore for a pen and paper, I opened the envelope and found it contained an official-looking document. It seemed to be a check or voucher of some kind as it had a dollar amount written in. I guess they give rewards for good parking in Rehoboth. Too bad I would not have time to cash it in and spend the money.

Jeremy returned and wrote down his name and telephone number. When he asked for mine, I told him that I would be traveling for a while so he wouldn't be able to reach me. One of the rules for coming to Earth is to give very little information about ourselves and no information about our planet. I took Jeremy's number and put it in my shirt pocket along with the parking reward ticket, which I decided to keep as a souvenir. I thanked him for the ring and told him I would wear it always. He kissed me again. It sent a shiver all through my body. I got on my power bike. I felt such emotion for this Earth boy. Then without thinking I said to him, "Thank you so much, Jeremy, for making my fiftieth birthday better than I ever imagined it could be."

He looked at me with a puzzled expression. "Today is your birthday? And did you say *fiftieth* birthday?"

I quickly tried to correct myself, "Oh! No, I just said it's my birthday today and you made it so special. Thank you!"

"But I heard you say *fiftieth* birthday," he said. "How could you be …?"

"Good-bye, Jeremy," I said. "I'll call you soon." And I sped away before he could ask another question.

On the ride back to the field, I thought about everything that had happened during my day in Rehoboth. I really did not want to leave. I got back to my pod, contacted flight control, and asked the flight coordinator if there was any way I could stay just one more day. He told me what I already knew—that the flight schedule could not be altered and the countdown to my departure was already under way. I brought my power bike into the pod and got ready for takeoff.

My departure was smooth and I gazed longingly at Earth as I headed toward home. What a wonderful place is this Earth with its beaches, oceans, and sunshine. And I know of no other place in the universe where you can eat ice cream and pizza, play games, have kissing, and get monetary rewards when you park your vehicle! I hope that someday soon my people will find a way to send some of us to Earth to live there permanently. When they ask for volunteers, I will be one of the first in line and I know where I will choose to go: Rehoboth Beach, Delaware, with that magical walk of boards. I will find Jeremy and I will never leave him. We will kiss again and again and then there will be no more tears.

ROBIN HILL-PAGE GLANDEN GREW UP IN HARRINGTON, DELAWARE, AND HAS ENJOYED MANY SUMMERS IN REHOBOTH BEACH. SHE GRADUATED FROM THE UNIVERSITY OF DELAWARE (UD) WITH A BS DEGREE IN THEATRE ARTS EDUCATION AND A MINOR IN ENGLISH/JOURNALISM. ROBIN SPENT TWENTY YEARS IN PHILADELPHIA, NEW YORK CITY, AND LOS ANGELES WORKING AS AN ACTRESS AND MUSICIAN, AND BEING EMPLOYED IN THE BUSINESS END OF THE ENTERTAINMENT INDUSTRY. IN LOS ANGELES, SHE STUDIED IN THE UCLA WRITERS' PROGRAM, WROTE ARTICLES FOR LOCAL L.A. PUBLICATIONS, COWROTE A SCREENPLAY ON THE LIFE OF SILENT FILM STAR FATTY ARBUCKLE, AND WORKED WITH VARIOUS AUTHORS AS A COPYEDITOR. ROBIN MOVED BACK TO DELAWARE, AND AFTER THIRTY-FIVE YEARS SHE WAS REUNITED WITH HER HIGH SCHOOL BOYFRIEND. THEY ARE NOW HAPPILY MARRIED AND LIVING IN NEWARK NEAR THE UD CAMPUS. ROBIN IS A FREELANCE WRITER AND COPYEDITOR. SHE ENJOYS WRITING MAGAZINE ARTICLES, FICTION, CREATIVE NONFICTION, POETRY, AND LOVE NOTES TO HER HUSBAND.

The Edge of the World

by Bruce Krug

The place where the world ended in an abrupt collision of earth and sky was not miles distant but a mere three city blocks away. The place was the stretch of weather-faded wooden planks that made up the Rehoboth Beach boardwalk.

It was not the first time I had been in this very spot and it certainly wouldn't be the last. Unlike Pavlov's dogs, my mind stubbornly refused to learn from experience. There was no convincing my brain that things would change once I stood upon the raised grain of those sun-dried boards.

My view was from the backseat of the family Chevy. Chin resting next to the headrest of the front seat, knees pressing into the back of the same seat, and vinyl sticking to the backs of my sweaty thighs, there was no disputing my senses were all present and accounted for.

Our baby blue Belair pulled to the curb on Laurel Avenue in front of a two-story house with a wide screened porch and curling roof shingles. We rented the same place every year. The moment the ratcheting of the parking brake reached my ears I was out the rear door and onto the sidewalk. As always, my parents shouted that I needed to help unload the car and, as always, I responded that I needed just one look first.

I gobbled up sidewalk in my black-and-white high-top Keds. The first year I took off like this, my dad raced after me while my mom recited my name in panicky shouts. Now, both my parents accepted that I would somehow make it across both Bayard and King Charles Avenues without incident.

The point of no turning back was unpredictable. In my earlier years I could make it all the way to the boards before reality shifted. Now I was tall enough that there were still four squares of sidewalk between me and the boardwalk when things changed. Perception changed just as it did when staring at a drawing of overlapping rectangles that first form an open, empty box and in the blink of an eye change to a solidly closed box. Here on the sidewalk, just as I was sure I would reach that tantalizing edge of the world, the horizon sped away.

In the new expanse of geography lay summer. Bleached sand, peppered with pastel umbrellas and faded towels, reflected dazzlingly bright light. The same light captured salty spray rising from the crest of breaking waves seconds before the waves fell beneath their own weight. The resultant smack of water on sand sent reverberations all the way to where I stood.

As always, there was the desire to immediately immerse myself in carefree summer. As always, the desire was tempered by my parents' masochistic insistence that vacation did not begin until the car was unpacked.

Resentfully, hurriedly, I carried too-big loads from the trunk of the car to the interior of the house. Sometimes the loads made it intact and sometimes I finished the trip with a beach towel or windbreaker dragging from my foot. The trips back and forth did not end with suitcases and beach bags. Convinced that food was not sold at the beach, my parents always brought brown paper bags filled with purchases made at the Acme back home.

Finally, after every item had been properly stored in cabinets and bureaus, bathing suits were donned and we headed for the beach. *This* was what I had been waiting for all year.

By the end of day two I remembered why I hated the beach. SPF 120 sunblock was still years away. For a red-haired freckle-faced kid, SPF 4 was as effective as a generous coating of Crisco. When I stepped under the outdoor shower, each droplet of water was a stinging bullet.

I spent the next two days in the living room of our rented house. Camped out in the floral-patterned rocking chair with bottles of Coke and a strategically placed fan, I passed the time with science-fiction books and afternoon game shows. The rocking chair was the one piece of furniture that did not scratch, poke, or stick to my sunburned skin.

Tuesday evening brought an end to the monotony. With rusty-colored sunbeams stretching parallel to the ground, we headed to the boardwalk. Our first destination was an eatery where we slid into—ouch—vinyl-covered booths for seafood, chicken, and fries. While we ate, Rehoboth underwent a metamorphosis.

Pushing back through the glass doors of the restaurant, I discovered the tired afternoon had been resuscitated by the glare of impossibly bright sodium lights and a cacophony of bells, whistles, shouts, and screams. Endless conga lines snaked along the boardwalk in opposing directions.

Merging into one of those lines took the skill of an accomplished bumper-car driver. I watched for an opening, shot in, adjusted my speed, and then shot back out when I reached my next destination: the amusement park.

I have no doubt that "Funland" was one of my first words. Here was a world that offered the promise of endless excitement—provided you had the appropriate number of tickets. My parents and I never agreed on what an appropriate number was. Consequently, I was forced to deal with the stress of constantly weighing options. Once the tickets were gone, consolation was found only in something sticky or sweet.

My sister always went for cotton candy, while I went for snow cones. To me, the brain freeze that came from taking too big a bite of flavored ice was far preferable to having my treat evaporate in my mouth. The syrupy remains of the snow cones were a bonus. Diluted by melting ice, the syrup became a flavor-packed juice that seemed downright healthy.

While I succumbed to sensory pleasures, night settled heavily. The one or two sodium lights pointed at the ocean barely illuminated a curling line of white foam. The pounding surf so omnipresent by day was reduced to a muffled drumbeat. Uncertain whether the shiver that ran up my spine was caused by images of an approaching army or chilled air on my bacon-crisp skin, I was all too ready to return to the shelter of my home-for-a-week. I took a last look at the now dimly visible horizon and decided that Columbus had been wrong about there not being an edge to the world.

BRUCE KRUG IS A DELAWARE NATIVE AND HAS BEEN WRITING FOR FUN, AND SOMETIMES PROFIT, EVER SINCE HIS ELEVENTH GRADE ENGLISH TEACHER INSISTED HE READ HIS SHORT STORY ASSIGNMENT IN FRONT OF THE ENTIRE CLASS. MORE RECENTLY, BRUCE'S SHORT STORIES HAVE TAKEN PRIZES IN WRITING COMPETITIONS. IN OCTOBER OF 2012 BRUCE RELEASED A COLLECTION OF SHORT STORIES AS AN E-BOOK TITLED *EXPOSING MY SHORTS*, AVAILABLE ON AMAZON. CURRENTLY, BRUCE IS WORKING ON A SERIES OF NOVELS ABOUT THE PARANORMAL.

BRUCE'S CREATIVITY HAS PAID OFF IN HIS NINE-TO-FIVE JOB; HIS TRAINING PROGRAMS HAVE BEEN NATIONALLY RECOGNIZED FOR EXCELLENCE.

HUSBAND, FATHER, AND GRANDFATHER, BRUCE WEAVES THE IMPORTANCE OF FAMILY INTO HIS WRITING. SOME OF HIS STORIES TELL OF THE JOYS TO BE FOUND IN LIFE'S SUBTLE MAGIC, WHILE OTHER TALES LEAD READERS INTO PLACES THEY WOULD NORMALLY SEEK TO KEEP AT BAY WITH THE HELP OF A HUNDRED-WATT BULB.

Forever Fifteen

by Sandy Donnelly

It's a sizzling evening in July. You are standing in your kitchen at the beach, sweating over your grandson's favorite oven-roasted potatoes, dressed in shorts, gauze top, and flip-flops. You're swaying to the music on your i-something and sipping a glass of wine. Adele is singing "Rolling in the Deep." Just then, your fourteen-year-old grandson comes in from the porch. "Nana, I know what I'm going to get you for your birthday."

This blond, easygoing athlete is loaded with a perpetual smile. The minute he comes into view, you can't help but give him a hug. "Oh, Colin, you don't need to give me anything."

"No, Nana, this is perfect for you. I just saw it on TV. It's a medical alert bracelet."

Your mouth drops open. "Aw, Colin, do you really think I'm that old?" Can he tell by the crack in your voice that you suddenly see yourself trading in your flip-flops for orthopedic walkers?

The reality of his statement hits hard. It reminds you that you're past prime, well beyond the "sell-by" date. Yet the still-wannabe-forty lurks in the back of your mind. You wonder why time has played this terrible trick. When did your body concede to gravity? Wasn't it yesterday that you were an innocent teenager strutting down the boardwalk with your band of girlfriends in search of boys? And how did it happen that you, the least likely, became the prizewinner?

It started outside homeroom, in the hall by the lockers at Montgomery Blair High School. Orientation for freshmen had just ended and students clustered in groups designated by previous junior high attendance. Dejection started to simmer as you noticed that several of your girlfriends, all dressed in pleated skirts with new twin sweater sets and saddle shoes, greeted each other with conspiratorial high-fives like players on the field. No one, except you, could stop talking about all the adventures and misadventures they'd shared that summer in Rehoboth.

The closing bell left you mute, in a full boil of resentment. It flowed over as you came up the driveway from the bus stop, slammed the back door, threw your books on the kitchen table, plopped into a chair, and burst into tears when your mother simply asked, "How was your day?"

In that moment, it became your mother's fault for taking you to boring old Cape Cod each summer while your friends were having a super, fun, fantastic time doing whatever they wanted in Rehoboth Beach. They got to go to the beach without their mothers. They could sit with the boy who rented umbrellas and wait for Elvis's latest hit to come on his transistor radio, and turn for hours in the sun, lathered in baby oil and iodine, watching every move the lifeguards made. They got to have canvas rafts and float out beyond the breakers, singing the words to "Wake up Little Susie" almost as well as The Everly Brothers, until a wave caught the rafts and threw them onto the shore. They could swim out beyond the crowds, imagining one of the guards coming to their rescue. And, when they got hungry, they simply walked up to the boardwalk and got salty Taylor pork roll or juicy cheeseburgers with dozens of pickles sliding around in ketchup and mustard, and chocolate milkshakes or Cokes, and Thrasher's fries, in cups, sprinkled with salt and vinegar. And then at night, they got to walk the boardwalk, barefoot, wearing white Villager blouses, Bermuda shorts, and XL blue sweatshirts with "Rehoboth" printed in big white letters on the front. Boys would follow until they ditched them at Dolle's and ran down the boardwalk in the opposite direction. And when it rained, they laughed as the blue dye of the sweatshirts bled down their legs. They were supposed to be in by 10 p.m. but instead took turns sleeping at each other's places and staying up until 2 a.m. discussing which boy was the cutest that night, the recent breakups on Dick Clark's "American Bandstand," and the latest gossip about Ricky Nelson in *Teen* magazine.

"And, Mom, what did I get to do this summer? Nothing!" you said, stomping off to your room before she had a chance to respond.

Flopping on your bed, you had to admit it was fun to see your cousins each July. It was a family tradition that had started long before you were born. They rented the same white rose-covered cottage every year. You did have fun walking down the gravel road leading to the beach, throwing pebbles along the way. Swimming out to the old wooden raft, diving off, climbing back up, diving again or floating aimlessly in Cape Cod Bay. On the days your mother and aunts started drinking martinis at noon, you could sneak off into the woods with peanut butter and jelly sandwiches, Cokes, and chips, and read dirty romance weeklies for hours. And you did love those chunks of steamed lobsters, dipped in butter, served several nights a week. Going down to the wharf and getting baskets of lush briny fried clams with their bellies still intact. Picking blueberries in the patch behind the cottage and stuffing so many in your mouth the juice dripped down your chin, staining your shirt, forever, blueberry blue.

But it all paled in comparison to the freedom your friends had in Rehoboth. Plus, in Cape Cod there was no such thing as a boardwalk.

The following summer, the summer of 1959, the Gods of Vacation aligned their dates and your friends' mothers rented cottages in August instead of July. You were available and invited. You knew the date by heart. Saturday, August 8th, had been circled on the calendar for weeks.

It was a typical hot soggy morning outside Washington, DC. You woke in a tangled sweat of sheets, polka-dot pj's, and pink rollers that had escaped from your hair. With a couple of good stretches, you escaped the sheet's harness and pointed hot pink toenails toward the end of the bed in search of the suitcase. It was still there, waiting patiently (unlike yourself) for this day to arrive.

You knew the contents by heart. They'd been packed and repacked daily. The most important items were a pink Janzen bathing suit in the latest one-piece style with an apron front, a white bathing cap with a cluster of pink rubber flowers that would flap in the ocean breeze, and a terrycloth cover-up. And a surprise for the girls, Midnight in Paris perfume, which was a bestseller according to the sales clerk at Woolworth's.

Two white Peter Pan–collared blouses, washed and ironed, hung on your closet door next to your life-size Elvis poster. From the vantage point of your bed, it looked like his big brown eyes were lusting for your breasts inside that blouse. These blouses would go into the suitcase at the last minute, along with khaki-and-white Bermuda shorts and an extra-large navy Rehoboth sweatshirt that Katrina, who had two of everything, lent you. The must-have essential for the girls that march the boards.

Then you remembered. This *was* the last minute. You scrambled out of the sheets and took the blouses off the hanger, leaving Elvis staring at a blank yellow wall. Packed one outfit and put the other one on. Double-tied your white Keds, snapped the suitcase locks shut, and clanked it down the stairs.

"Mom," you said, dragging the suitcase into the kitchen where she was lecturing your younger brother and sister on water safety before they left for the neighbor's pool. "Can you believe it's really here? This is finally the day."

"I can believe it and couldn't be happier," she said.

"Why? You're not coming, are you?"

"No. Not a chance. I'm just glad I won't have to hear about this for another year. Now sit down and eat your cereal. Nina's mom will be here soon."

After crossing the Chesapeake Bay on the longest bridge you'd ever seen and passing endless rows of sagging cornstalks on the Eastern Shore, you finally pulled up to a gray clapboard bungalow with green shutters. The old porch door slammed shut at least a dozen times as you and Nina, her mother, and her aunt unloaded the car. As prearranged, you were to change into your suits and cover-ups; fill beach bags with towels, caps, lotion, magazines, Good and Plenty's, gumdrops, and Wrigley's Doublemint gum; and meet Barb, Kathy, Nancy, and Katrina on the beach in front of the bandstand. You couldn't wait to finally walk over the boardwalk onto the beach, spread your towel, lather that lotion into place, put on the cap with flowers, and jump those waves you'd heard so much about.

All was going better than anticipated; you'd met the beach umbrella boy, survived two bouts in the ocean without going down, and had the giant cheeseburger with shake and fries. Waiting the twenty mandatory minutes mothers always demanded after eating, you felt confident going into the water for another swim.

Suddenly, everything went wrong. Two waves came at the same time, tossed the bathing cap off your head, churned you up with sand, shells, and water like an agitator in a washing machine, and spun you out on the sand. Lesson #1: This was not placid Cape Cod Bay. Lesson #2: No guard was coming to your rescue.

And another issue became self-evident. Your friends—all a size 5 or 7—looked perpetually perky. You—a solid 13—not so much. Your mother spent many years and more than a few dollars grooming you in the "chubette" department of Peck and Peck. Which wasn't a bad thing. They managed to create an illusion with classic A-line dresses. But exposed to the elements, in a soaking-wet Janzen, with curls dissolved to a stringy sandy mantel accentuated by a scraped and bleeding nose, you were no longer an illusion of beauty. And that night was the night of your first stroll on the boards.

Then another discovery. Your friends were all working on "going steady." And those steady potentials would be meeting you on the boardwalk that night. Before this moment, the only intimate exposure you'd had with a boy was a five-minute make-out session on a hayride with the church group, which left you weak in the knees, with a pounding heart, to be humiliated as your arouser jumped from the wagon and skipped away through the pumpkin patch to the parking lot, leaving you with a strong distrust of the opposite sex.

So while the beauties were prepping for their boys, sharing makeup, and putting their hair up in pin-curls or ponytails, you were feeling less and less secure about going out and began to consider staying home. But then Mrs. Carmack entered the room.

She was not only Nina's mother but also your extremely discerning cotillion leader, and if anyone knew how to put on a show, it was she. She'd greet you each week at the side door of the church where the cotillion was held, dressed in a long velvet gown, hair rolled up in waves, with a long cigarette holder attached to her hand like a sixth appendage. At that checkpoint, she made sure every teen had on proper attire before she ushered you into the hall. This professional trainer of etiquette took one look at your beat-up face and led you to the shower, put your hair in rollers, sat you under her professional great-domed hairdryer, and got your nose to stop bleeding.

By the time you were to meet the boys, she had you looking like one of the group, with an identical board-walking outfit. And you were beginning to believe you just might make it through the night, despite wondering how something that sounded so good months ago could now be so terrifying.

The boardwalk at night was more magical than you imagined. You were mesmerized by the number of people, their voices echoing off the roar of the ocean. The blinking neon lights, whirling cotton candy machine, and popping corn. You felt like Alice in her Wonderland.

As planned, everyone gathered at Dolle's. Barb, the pixie redhead who was all about Tony, the Italian beach bum who slept under the boardwalk, was giddy when he showed up in his hoodie. When he flung his arm around Barb, her night was made. Katrina, the tall lanky blonde, had her eye on Rick, the town's local hunk. She'd met him last year at teen club and dreamed of him through the winter. When he showed up with some of his fellow football players, still in their bathing suits, she was beyond the moon. Nancy, the seducer, with her sexy voice, dark wave of hair over one eye, and fashion runway walk, had an ongoing thing with Eddie, the class vice president from home. And Kathy, who kept everyone in hysterics with a constant commentary on life as a Greek, was working on Greg, the high school football star. Eddie and Greg came up from DC earlier and had walked with you to the boardwalk, looking like male counterpoints in their khaki shorts and white button-down shirts.

By the time you arrived, handholding had started and Nancy and Kathy had that dreamy look you had after a hot fudge sundae with nuts. And finally, Nina, the tiny blond beauty who had run out of space on her high school notebook for any additional boyfriends' names, had plans to buy a new binder if she won over her latest conquest, Steve, an unrequited crush from junior high. He was coming up from Ocean City that night with a friend to show off his new used Corvette.

The moment seemed seamless and still does today. It started with a loud treble sound vibrating up Rehoboth Avenue as a car came into view. Steve, Mr. Beautiful himself, waved from the driver's seat, motioning Nina in his direction. The whole group followed like a TV news crew covering an epic event. His dark hair and wide white grin reflected in the boardwalk lights. The signature mole on his left cheek folded into his dimples as he smiled, got out of the car, and gave Nina her kiss.

But you weren't concerned with their embrace. Your attention was on his funny passenger, whose blond crew-cut hair was a sharp contrast to Steve's full head of brown. He sat at least three heads taller than Steve in that convertible. They looked like before and after hormone injections. His Roman nose was regal and masculine compared to Steve's cute pug. And those eyes. Those deep blue eyes. Those deep blue eyes looked like they could stop a heartbeat with their intensity. And those deep blue eyes were gazing at you.

As he got out of the car, dressed in crazy madras Bermudas and Chucks, Mr. Blue Eyes twirled a walking stick he'd won in a ball-toss game on the boardwalk. You were standing off from the group when he pointed that stick in your direction. Turning around to make sure no one was behind you, you pointed toward yourself and said, "Me?"

"Yeah, hi," he said. "My name is Carl. What's yours?"

"Uh, Sandy," you said. "That's right, my name is Sandy," you repeat, stretching your sunburned cheeks into a grin. "Like the stuff that killed my nose today."

"Well, Sandy with the killer nose, do you think you could get your posse here to walk down the boardwalk and find a milkshake?"

You don't remember exactly where you found those milkshakes. What you do remember is feeling like you finally belonged: to your friends, to a boy, and to the boardwalk where the moon's light reflected on the ocean like a thousand tiny crystals, the stars twinkling back in response. You floated next to that funny boy twirling the walking stick, and you trusted each other with bits and pieces of your lives. And as your friends' faces and laughter faded in and out of the lights, you fell deeper and deeper in love with those deep blue eyes.

* * * * * *

Fifty years later, you are in your own cottage by the sea. Three children with spouses bring grandchildren to visit for weeks at a time. Regardless of the number of days spent fishing, crabbing, boating, or swimming, one night is always dedicated to walking the boards. Other nights you may be sipping wine, roasting potatoes, singing with Adele while wearing your shorts and gauze shirt, or pretending you're forever fifteen.

And you can't help but smile.

You, the least likely, were the prizewinner. Those deep blue eyes are still gazing at you.

Sandy Donnelly is a freelance writer who has published several essays in regional magazines, most recently, *Delaware Beach Life*. She first realized her gift for writing through feedback from her letters home to family and friends during fifteen years of moving around the country.

Once settled back on the East Coast, she was an advertising and lecture bureau agent before becoming an RN. When she retired from nursing, she pursued her passion for writing through classes in New York City and the Rehoboth Beach Writers' Guild. She attributes any success to those inspirational instructors, especially Maribeth Fischer.

Sandy and her husband share their time between Fenwick Island, Delaware, and Washington, DC, with three adult children, their spouses, and six amazing grandchildren.

Judge's Comment:

I chose "Forever Fifteen" because it is a timeless story that could happen to anyone on the boardwalk. Sandy met her husband years ago as she walked with her girlfriends on the boardwalk. The same could happen to her grandson fifty years later during his visit to the beach. Anyone who has visited the boardwalk has seen the groups of teenagers noticing each other, walking down the boardwalk holding hands, and making memories that will last a lifetime, whether or not the romance does.

The Key to Winning

by Mary Ann Glaser

Things were slow at the Salty Dunes. A petulant weather front had wandered into Rehoboth Beach and decided to rain hard on everyone's cabana for three solid days. Thanks to lightning giving the ISP's main server center a rap on the head, the Internet was down for the count, which meant a better tip count today. When the weather was good and hot, Matt could count on selling beer the minute he opened the bar at eleven, but when it rained this long, trade didn't pick up until all the other indoor activities were exhausted and people were thoroughly annoyed with each other and in serious need of an attitude adjustment; but the blonde was different.

She'd come in every day since the storm hit, taking the two-top jammed into the worst spot in the joint, the table people only took on nights when the place was packed and they were desperate to take a load off. Only these past couple of days the storm was keeping the bar an echo chamber, open tables everywhere. None but those frantic to escape their beach hotels and the handful of regulars who would never let a little thing like a tropical storm come between them and a cold one at the Salty Dunes were coming in at this early hour, and she beat even those guys. She could have taken number ten, the four-top with the view of the boardwalk (more room to spread out those big yellow legal pads she pulled out of the battered tote bag), and given herself elbow room, a view, and a bit of light, such as it was with all the rain; but no, she sat hunched over the pad diligently working away, making just enough room on the table for the mug of coffee that would become a glass a wine after the

Mediterranean salad, dressing on the side, in the afternoon.

When she first walked in, with rain streaming off her rain jacket and water squishing in her wellies, Matt could have sworn he'd seen her before, but after careful consideration decided it was a case of didn't know, but wanted to. He found himself watching her a mite more than perhaps a barkeep should. Matt could tell when she got stuck; she had a way of tucking a strand of her long hair behind her right ear that was, well, fetching. He noticed that while she didn't look up when people came and went, nor when, at the four beers point, Donovan started the rest of the regulars guffawing over his inexhaustible supply of "a priest, a rabbi, and a minister" jokes, she was always pleasant and attentive when Myrtle waited on her. He figured her for a lawyer on a pretend-cation, pretending to be at the beach while she slaved away over a brief. He was not in her league.

The second day in, the storm was still rattling the windows and, in the Battle of the Tracked-in Water, Myrtle gave up on appearance for appearance's sake and left the mop and bucket by the door. Matt had decided he should give up on his silly attraction to the out-of-his-league blonde, when in she walked, just as wet as yesterday and just as intriguing. He decided maybe he should let *her* decide his league standing. He told Myrtle to take a long lunch and served the mysterious blonde himself. A guy can't count on a storm lasting forever. Chatted her up as much as he dared, talking about taking over the bar when his dad died, the history of the beach, the fate of the server center. All she'd given up was her first name: Alex.

Myrtle laughed right in his face when she described his efforts while they were closing. "For the love of Mike, you own a bar! You spend your days listening to other people's lives, you moron, and the only personal question you ask is 'what's your name'? If she's here tomorrow, take her lunch order and stop embarrassing yourself. You know I told your dad I'd look after you, but sometimes

… Her *name*. Unbelievable."

Day three and in she walks. Matt can't believe his good fortune, but plays it cool, just a smile and "Hey, Alex! Coffee?" He gave her a moment to settle in at her usual spot before heading over with the pot and a mug. "Okay, so here's the deal: tell me what you're working on and lunch is on the house."

"Is that a bribe?"

"Hey, I tried charming, informative, politely curious …"

"Politely curious?"

"Yes, politely curious indeed. At this point, extortion is a logical progression. Look, so, that didn't come out as smoothly as I'd planned, but you know, you gotta eat, so what do you say, Alex? How about one Mediterranean salad with conversation on the side?"

Alex looked up at him for a moment and then smiled. "I think I'd like that. And the answer is I'm working on a story."

"Not a lawyer, that's great!"

"A lawyer? What made you think that?"

"You're using yellow legal pads, so I just assumed. Lesson learned; never judge a person by their yellow legal pad."

"Oh!" Alex laughed. "I like to write out the first draft by hand so I'm not distracted by my poor typing skills and, well, I find there is something comforting about yellow paper. Weird, right?"

"Nah, writing's not for sissies. It takes what it takes to get the words down. So, what's your working title?"

"The title is 'The Key to Winning.'" Alex looked up at Matt and paused. "Working title is not a common phrase in bar chatter; you write?"

Matt pointed to the chalkboard displaying the beer and food specials for the day. "Every single day, more when we run out of the specials and we have to change up the menu." Alex laughed and Matt was surprised at how much that pleased him. "Actually, I was in my second year of the MFA program at Iowa when Dad died. I thought I'd go back and finish up in a year or so once I sold the bar, but no takers, and then my kid brother needed a leg up to get through his degree program, and then the economy tanked and absolutely nobody wanted to buy a bar, and staff here need their jobs, and well, you know, you think one thing, life thinks another."

"I'm sorry about your dad. That must have been rough. I lost my dad too, but not until after I'd graduated. He was sick, but he was there at the graduation, which was so great. Your brother still in school?"

"No, he finished up at Caltech and is working in Silicon Valley, happily plotting to take over the world, one line of code at a time."

Alex looked up at him. "So, an MFA at Iowa; I did the MFA at Berkeley. What are the odds?" Just then the door blew open as the storm decided to give the bar a good shake. He rushed over to muscle the door closed and then grabbed the mop, both to give Myrtle a break and to give himself a moment to think. He'd told her about Iowa! He didn't tell anyone about Iowa; it led inevitably to questions like what had he published (nothing), what was he writing (nothing), when was he going back (probably never), and did he miss it (without end). He was tired of explaining how hard it was to run a bar—the long hours, the need to keep on top of trends to keep the cash flow up, how hard it was to be so freakin' responsible. He'd become particularly tired of those who loved to lecture on how they'd read you only need to write one thousand words a day. Surely he had time to write a measly thousand words a day. At that point Myrtle would step in before Matt could dive over the bar. He'd been a bitter bastard for about a year and then just settled in; his brother needed him, end of story.

He propped the mop back in the bucket and looked back at Alex. It had felt right telling her about Iowa. He didn't know what that meant, but decided to let it play out and walked back to her table. "About the MFA thing, I hear you, a guy and a gal meet in a bar, yeah, and it's like, oh my goodness, we're both MFAs! What a coincidence! I can see the editor's red ink in the margins now, if you wrote it, I mean."

"True, that." Alex gave a brief laugh and then paused. "Did you study with Professor Hayford? He taught at Berkeley before he went to Iowa."

"I don't think so; the Hayford I knew taught at Yale before going west."

Alex visibly relaxed and her smile brightened.

"So," Matt said. "I passed, yeah?"

"What do you mean?" Alex blushed and quickly looked down at her writing pad.

"You knew Hayford was a Yalie. You thought I'd just pulled the MFA line out of the bullshit box, right?"

"Sorry, I *was* checking to see if you were playing me." Alex looked up at him. "Was it that obvious?"

"Hey, don't worry about it. It's a scary bad world, lots of ruthless MFAs out there just looking to break hearts for a giggle. So it's a sports theme, is it?"

"Sort of. Why don't you sit down and I'll tell you."

Matt turned to ask Myrtle to cover the bar and bring him a cup and almost hit Myrtle with the coffee pot he had forgotten he'd been holding all this time. Myrtle smiled.

"Already on it." She took the coffee pot in one hand, using it to hide a sly thumbs-up with the other hand, and walked back to the bar.

Matt turned back to the table and sat, pleased to see Alex had piled up her stuff to make room for him. Nice bit of welcome, that. "You were going to tell me the plot."

Myrtle's arm slid in front of him, cup of coffee in hand. "Aha, the plot thickens!" she said, giving a Snidely Whiplash twist to an imaginary mustache.

"Thanks, Myrtle," Matt said quickly. "Now walk on, nothing to see here." Myrtle raised her eyebrows before heading back to the bar. Matt turned to Alex. "Okay, again—plot, please."

"Well, I was researching the game of Monopoly, do you know it?"

"Is there an American alive who doesn't? It's not 'Call of Duty,' but it's still big here for sure, cause when a hurricane kicks over the power grid, the lanterns come on and Rich Uncle Pennybags comes off the game shelf."

"Wait," said Alex. "Who's Rich Uncle Pennybags?"

"The round-headed tuxedoed guy on the box and the cards, you know, *the Monopoly guy.* When the game was launched, that was the character's name: Rich Uncle Pennybags. It was right on the first game box in 1936."

"Seriously, how do you know that?" Alex pulled out one of the pads from the stack and made a quick note.

"I come from a long line of Monopoly players. My granddad had one of the early editions; I remember seeing it up on the shelf in his closet. Unfortunately, we didn't have a dad waving us off the soon-to-be-a-valuable-collector's-item, so it was played to rags. But you can see Rich Uncle Pennybags on Wikipedia. You have heard of Wikipedia, have you not, my dear, or are you still wandering the stacks?"

"Yes, I've heard of Wikipedia, wise guy." Alex wrinkled her nose at him and Matt responded with a smile. "But I missed that the Monopoly guy had a name; that's great, thanks! And yes, I still wander the stacks. I'm a sucker for the smell of books and, well, books are just a bit more friendly than a laptop. The battery never dies in the middle of a great chapter when you're a mile away from the nearest plug. Besides, books are big in my family. My dad was a book dealer. At one point, he told me he figured he had ten thousand volumes tucked away between the house and the shop. It was a pain to live with; boxes everywhere, and the first editions, the ones I wanted to get my hands on the most, I couldn't read any of them because their condition had to be maintained to retain their value. So annoying! I guess that's why I love the stacks—thousands of books and I can touch any one I want. But that was how he put my brother and me through college, so I'm grateful."

"Your family keep the business after your dad died?"

"No. We closed up shop when he got sick and sold off the remaining inventory before he died. He wanted to leave us with as much as he could. In a way, it was probably for the best he got cancer when he did. Now that everything's e-books, it's not as much of a collector's market anymore. That would have killed him." Alex pulled her coffee cup toward her and stared at it for a moment before taking a sip. Matt waited, not wanting to be the clod who stepped on the hem of that memory.

"I am sorry. He sounds like a great dad."

"Thanks." Alex drew in a breath. "Okay, 'The Key to Winning' tells the story of a couple in their early thirties. He's a computer programmer and she's a freelance writer. They have been dating a while and decide to go to Delaware for a beach vacation together. After a great first day, a storm blows in and they are stuck in their room. She finds a Monopoly game and as the game progresses they …"

"It *was* you!" Matt interjected. "I thought I recognized you when you came in. You were here at the start of the season. There was a storm; it didn't take down the Internet, but it rained solid for a day and a half. It was busy in the bar that day, but I remember there was a guy who came in yelling for a stein of our handcrafted Bitches Brew—always a giveaway that one—followed a bit later by a very choice blonde: you. An argument ensued, he stormed out, and after a shot of Jameson's, so did you. Nice touch by the way, the Jameson's. Most go right for the tequila." He waited a beat, but she was all eyes down. "So really, this isn't fiction; you're writing about a real guy, a real game, aren't you? So he kicked the board and dumped you, is that it?"

"No, he did not. I dumped him. That is, it is too fiction! I mean I …" Alex stammered, a blush sliding up her neck. "Well, crap. Busted, I guess. The professors always said write what you know, right?"

"See, this was always the point where I got bounced outta class, 'cause if there's one thing I know it's, I don't know shit about me, and I certainly do not know for certain why I do anything, much less the rest of the world. Not that I'm not self-aware. I'm very aware that I am a whirling storm of what-do-I-want-to-be-when-I-grow-up uncertainty. So how can I write what I know? Let me ask you this—you're writing about this because you lived it, so you know it, right?"

"Yeah, that's right," she said.

"So why did that moment happen?"

"Why?"

"Yeah, why fight over Monopoly?"

She sighed. "Well, because the fight wasn't really about Monopoly. We fought because I didn't take the game seriously. I approached it with the same childish outlook as I had when I played as a kid: picked my favorite playing piece and made my cards look like rainbows."

"Rainbows?"

"You know, instead of putting the property groups together as a set, red with red, orange with orange, and so on like most people do? Well, I make strips of rainbows: red, orange, yellow, green, blue, purple."

Matt smiled. "Got it, rainbows. So you were having fun with the game. You monster! And that proved what?"

"He had a very strategic adult perspective, and a competitive edge, and I was making rainbows and not taking winning seriously."

"And, pray tell, what is the strategic adult perspective of Monopoly?"

"Well, for example, he said the key to winning Monopoly is buying at least one complete color group on sides one and two of the board and knowing the probabilities of the dice. Seven is the most common roll and two and twelve the least probable. Did you know it takes five to six rolls to go around the board once and you have a 17 percent chance of rolling doubles?"

"You don't say?"

"Not only did he know the dice roll probabilities," she continued, "but he knew the odds on all the cards in the game."

"The Chance and Community Chest cards?"

"Yes. Chance cards have a high probability of moving you to another square and Community Chest cards have a high probability of giving you money. There are other probabilities for those cards, but I can't remember them right now." Myrtle appeared with Alex's salad and freshened up Matt's coffee.

"What are you guys talking about?" Myrtle asked as she finished pouring Matt's coffee.

"The key to winning Monopoly," said Matt.

"You're kidding," replied Myrtle. "Nobody wins at Monopoly! Somebody gets pissed, kicks the board, and game over. What's to talk about?" Myrtle shook her head and headed back to the bar. Matt and Alex both smiled.

"Let's see," said Alex. "Where was I? Oh, yes! The most important key to winning is to play by the traditional Parker Brothers rules, as those rules apparently give the strategic player the best possibility for winning. That started things off on the wrong foot right from the get-go, as I didn't even know there were traditional rules. I thought the way my family played the game was, well, the way everybody played the game, and I made the mistake of arguing for family tradition over Parker Brothers tradition and that was not, shall we say, well received. And then I made rainbows and bought a utility."

Matt laughed. "Let me guess, an adult never buys a utility."

"No. There is only a one in thirty-eight chance of profiting from utilities; they are a bad long-term investment."

"I gotta ask, what does Mr. Strategic Adult do for a living?"

"He's a biostatistician; he designs research studies with doctors, life scientists, people like that, and then analyzes the data from the clinical trials. He was fascinating to talk to; I'd never met a biostatistician before." She looked at Matt, who was staring at her. "Ah, so you see, clearly the game uncovered our inherent incompatibility and I was not the right fit for him."

"Or," Matt leaned in. "*Or,* maybe the guy's a dick about winning Monopoly, and probably everything else, and you dodged a major bullet."

"Well, I don't know about that." She laughed and looked down at her writing.

"My point exactly. You don't know, so how can you write what you know? I say just go way out there and write what you don't know and see where that takes you."

"What, are we talking steampunk freaky alien genre?"

"Not necessarily, but Ray Bradbury and Phillip K. Dick are icons now, Alex. Some exciting stuff is being written by those following in their footsteps. Look what William Gibson started with *Necromancer,* and then there's the whole magic realism thing that *Like Water for Chocolate* gave rise to." Alex was smiling, saying something in response to his points, but all he could comprehend was how good it felt talking with her about the craft, how good life suddenly seemed to him. Matt looked around; the storm was finally winding down and business was beginning to pick up. He gave Myrtle a sign and stood up. "I've really enjoyed this, but I've got to get back to the job." He leaned over toward Alex. "How long are you staying?"

"Well, I ..."

"I was just wondering if you were staying the day, and if you were, I wondered if you'd care to join me for dinner." Matt felt that slight electric jolt of fear. The storm was breaking up, she wasn't staying forever, and time was not on his side.

"It seems I have a major rewrite to do, so I may stay longer than I had planned." Alex stood and took his hand. "I would like to talk more over dinner and afterwards maybe take a walk on the boardwalk?"

"I'd say there's a high probability of that happening." He leaned forward, kissed her cheek, and whispered. "And by the way, I'm kinda partial to rainbows myself."

MARY ANN HILLIER, WRITING AS MARY ANN GLASER, WAS BORN IN CHICAGO, ILLINOIS. SHE GRADUATED FROM NORTHWESTERN UNIVERSITY WITH A BA IN ENGLISH LITERATURE, WITH HONORS, AND LATER FROM UNIVERSITY OF MARYLAND WITH AN MSM. SHE HAS THREE CHILDREN AND FOUR GRANDCHILDREN. CURRENTLY SHE RESIDES IN TRAPPE, MARYLAND. SHE WORKS FOR THE US GENERAL SERVICES ADMINISTRATION AND IS ALSO FOUNDER AND DIRECTOR OF PAPER AND PENCILS, INC. (WWW.PAPERPENCILSINC.ORG), A NONPROFIT ORGANIZATION THAT PROVIDES BACKPACKS AND SCHOOL SUPPLIES TO NEEDY SCHOOLKIDS THROUGHOUT THE MISSISSIPPI DELTA. SHE HAS BEEN WRITING FICTION AND POETRY FOR YEARS, HAS SERVED ON THE BOARD OF THE EASTERN SHORE WRITERS ASSOCIATION, AND, IN 2013, SERVED AS A READER FOR THE WRITER'S CENTER'S MCLAUGHLIN-ESSTMAN-STEARNS FIRST NOVEL PRIZE.

The Window

by Trish Bensinger Kocher

The woman pulled the baby in close, tucking him inside the large coat they shared. No one had seen the storm coming and she was not fully prepared for its fury. She could remember turbulence like this in the past, but she was once again surprised at how conditions could change in the blink of an eye; how adversity could arrive unexpectedly in the midst of life's most beautiful moments. And, in the same way that this storm had rolled in off the ocean at the end of a beautiful day, the woman was struggling to reconcile the joy of the baby's birth with her mother's sudden illness, which left them unable to share this precious time together.

Now, the ocean was roaring and waves crashed onto the beach. The water ebbed and flowed, like emotions, and foam swirled in eddies of grief. The skies were filled with rain, leaving the mother and baby in the dark on the lonely stretch of boardwalk. The occasional flashes of lightning provided brief illumination, like comforting words, as they moved through the storm. Despite the turmoil, she didn't fear for her life or that of the child. She knew they would be fine, but a sense of resignation descended upon her. She could not change the situation or what would happen next, so she put her head down and moved forward, holding the baby close. Oddly, she knew she was not alone; others must be finding their way through this storm, too.

She peered through the rain and saw a light in the distance. It was only a glimmer, but it gave her hope that what was ahead was not as bleak as her current situation. As she walked on, the light began to take shape, forming what appeared to be a window in the side of a small cottage. With each step, the light became brighter and warmer, like the eyes of a loved one opening after a long illness. She had not imagined that she would find respite in this storm, but she knew immediately that this window presented a unique opportunity. Her step quickened and she rushed to look inside. Her heart leapt with joy to see an older woman resting in a chair by a crackling fire. She was nodding sleepily, but she opened her eyes to gaze back through the tear-streaked window, staring directly at them. She smiled.

The door swung open as if the older woman had been waiting for them. They moved into the room and were enveloped by the warmth. The mother shed the wet coat, putting aside this vestige of the storm, if just for the moment. The older woman took the baby in her arms and settled into the chair. She rocked him gently, smiling at his delicate features. She told him he was a beautiful boy and spoke of how he would grow into a wonderful man. He curled his tiny fingers around hers. The two women sipped hot tea and remembered warmer, sunnier days on the beach. They talked about the sights, sounds, and smells of the ocean, and the painful beauty of the passing seasons: spring's delicate dance of the horseshoe crabs and the red knots; summer's glorious sunrises and the laughter of gulls; fall's cool breezes and melancholy sunsets; and winter's sleepy silence blanketed in snow.

The time flew by and the older woman's eyelids began to flutter. It was clear that she was tired. While neither woman wanted the visit to end, they sadly said their good-byes, knowing it was unlikely that they would see each other again. The mother took the baby, lovingly wrapped a blanket around the older woman's shoulders, and watched as she drifted off to sleep. Anticipating the storm outside, the mother again pulled on the sodden coat and approached the door with anxiety. She stood for a moment, then timidly peered out. To her surprise, the storm had subsided.

In contrast to the low light of the fireplace's smoldering embers, she was startled to step out into dazzling sunlight. The air was fresh and the ocean, placid. Gulls flew overhead, lazily riding the gentle winds. She looked to her left, down the boardwalk where she and the baby had traveled the night before. While the boardwalk remained intact, the storm had buckled a few boards and slightly altered the alignment of their path. In time, it would be repaired and the storm would become a waning memory, except for those who had been caught in its fury.

She turned to look in the other direction. While the wild winds had caused the sand to drift, this newly constructed end of the boardwalk had not been damaged. She shielded her eyes but found she could not see very far ahead. Tall sea grass grew along the dunes, dancing and waving across the boardwalk and partially obscuring her view, like stage curtains opening and closing. She caught a glimpse of people in the distance, laughing and beckoning her to move forward.

Remembering her conversation with the older woman, she took a moment to take in the beauty of the beach in front of her: the storm had pushed driftwood into piles, creating abstract works of art; children were picking up seashells and beach glass, polished by the churning sand; and sandpipers ran up and down at the water's edge, furtively digging for newly deposited food. From her vantage point, she could see that, despite the storm's destruction, a multitude of treasures had been left in its wake.

The mother released her grasp on the coat, letting it fall open so the sun could shine on the baby's head. She hoped he would not remember the storm or their travels the night before. Instead, she would tell him about the precious window of time they had spent with the older woman. This would be their shared treasure, delivered unexpectedly in the midst of the storm. The coat slipped to the ground and the mother took a deep breath of salty air. Turning to the right, she and the baby continued their journey down the boardwalk, moving in the direction of the happy voices.

Trish Bensinger Kocher grew up in Dover, Delaware, later moving to Wilmington, where she and her husband, Glenn, raised their family. She worked in historic preservation and land-use planning, and now works in admissions at Wilmington Friends School. She spends weekends and vacations at their fixer-upper in the Forgotten Mile, daydreaming about retirement. Trish was inspired to try her hand at writing a short story after reading last year's anthology, *The Beach House*, and by friends in her book club, who annually attempt to write a novel in one month. While this is her first short story, she admits that she carried the story line in her head for nineteen years—she is hoping it will not take that long to develop another idea.

Awash

by Emily Littleton

She heard a rush and a crash and vaguely considered opening her eyes. The washing machine on the blink again, no doubt. She exhaled slowly through her nose, preparing herself for the bathtub of half-washed soggy jeans and socks she always faced in the wake of its wheezes and sighs.

Then she heard it again, and again. She opened one eye and squinted into the light. The sun blazed in the afternoon sky. Her skin was tight with dried seawater. The pool of crisp shade under her beach umbrella had scrambled away. She heaved herself up on her elbows and took a squinty look around, a little suspicious that the washer was lurking nearby, waiting to cough up some dirty T-shirts.

Typical, she decided with relief, after a moment. A typical beach scene. A studious-looking woman reading a trashy magazine, the straps of yesterday's swimsuit in bright white relief on her angry red shoulders. Seagulls jackknifing across the sky, their French fry radars on full alert. Kids pouring water on sleeping fathers.

A man stretched out over a remarkably uncomplaining beach chair just a few feet away adjusted his bulk and turned an accusatory eye toward her stare. She looked away. She pulled herself up into a sitting position and brushed the sand from the backs of her calves. She felt a dull twinge. Bathroom. I need a bathroom. *Nuts.*

Hastily scanning her camp, she judged her tired towel with the imprint of an insurance company on it too ugly to steal and her limp beach bag with the sunscreen in it, too uninteresting to gain a shifty beachcomber's notice. She stood up.

The bathroom suddenly seemed much, much farther away in this position. And sweet mercy, that sand is hot. Seriously hot. She could feel the soles of her feet starting to scream silently. Hop. She hopped onto one foot, lifting the other. And hopped again. And hopped and raised her eyes toward the boardwalk—far, far, far away.

Why hadn't she bought the flip-flops at the beach 5&10? Why was $2.99 "too expensive" this morning? What price flesh? She hopped forward, targeting the tiny shadow of a partially demolished sandcastle as a waypoint on the trek.

Hop. Hop. Dear Lord, I hope that sandcastle comes with a moat. Each hop, a jelly roll and a jiggle. "There's some motion in that ocean," she heard a girl mutter to her friend as she passed, both girls splayed in the sun, gathering heat like stove coils. *See you in a dermatology textbook, ladies!* she thought but was too chicken to say out loud. Then she yelped as she hopped onto the prong of a broken seashell.

She thought of that Jesus poster, the one about the footsteps on the beach. Does a bathroom mission qualify for that kind of help?

The sandcastle was ten steps, five steps … *ahhhh.* She paused, both feet crammed into the tiny patch of shade next to the crumbling tower. She took a moment to look around and pick her next stop. A lazy breeze licked the sweat from her face; a lifeguard's whistle shrieked.

A sudden twinge from below drove her onward, lurching across the expanse without another thought, her feet sinking deep into the burning sands at every step, the boardwalk stretching farther and farther away by the moment.

This is not good. This is bad, she thought, urgency nearing a fever-pitch. She considered the awful scenarios that could arise from her situation. With my luck, I'd be written up in the weekly e-newsletter covering the beach town. The eyes and ears of that reporter were everywhere. Each edition included the town's till-now-intentionally-ignored scenes of mayhem—arrests in bars, flooded streets after rainstorms, disturbances involving wildlife and wild lives, and coastal ironies. Maybe next issue: Large Lady Spotted Desperately Seeking Bathroom.

She floundered over to the shade of the beach umbrella shack where a teenager was folding a canvas chair. He looked up at her sudden arrival. She'd seen him earlier, gathering abandoned umbrellas under his arms and balancing three beach chairs seemingly magnetically on his person. She was old enough to realize the value of a man who could carry things and put them away in a timely fashion. Who needs someone in red swim trunks with a whistle who can pull you out of a rip current when you could have a man who knows how to clean up?

She smelled his clean sweat and, in a flash, countered it by imagining how loud the group house was that he no doubt lived in, its musty sweet smell of males and mildewed carpet, and how little food was likely in the fridge.

"Can I help you, ma'am?"

And there it was: the *"ma'am."*

Her years washed over her like a cold dry wave, each one surfacing in her mind as distinct as the rings of a tree. Some wide with growth, others—much easier to remember—tight and hard. A familiar pain awoke.

She shook her head in answer, to herself as much as him, then turned and set out again. The sand didn't feel so hot anymore.

EMILY LITTLETON THANKS THE REHOBOTH BEACH PUBLIC LIBRARY FOR HELPING HER BLOW THE DOORS OFF HER ELEMENTARY SCHOOL'S SUMMER READING LIST A FEW DECADES AGO. TODAY SHE IS MORE FAMILIAR WITH WRITING COMPANY MEMOS AND DRAFTING POWERPOINT PRESENTATIONS THAN WRITING FICTION. THIS IS HER FIRST PUBLISHED SHORT STORY.

The Watch

by Keith Phillips

After many years of teaching history to college students, he has retired to this place, this Eden on the ocean. Daily, when the weather is good, and sometimes when it isn't, he drives into town, parks in front of Dave and Skippy's bagel shop on Wilmington Avenue, and walks from the Greene Turtle south to the big yellow house on the corner of Prospect and watches the sun rise. He walks on the beach, not the boardwalk, and so only sees Playland and Funland and other shops and hotels and houses from a distance. The walk is a half-mile south and a half-mile north and is his cardiovascular exercise. It is more peaceful, more satisfying, than a treadmill. Each sunrise is an affirmation of life renewed.

This is a good morning to walk; the crispness of early fall invigorates him, helps him feel younger than his seventy-odd years. As he walks across the boardwalk, he sees the clouds along the horizon are no more than indigo daubs and splotches with rosy streaks through them. He crosses the dune and walks to the water line. Offshore, maybe five miles away, is the dark silhouette of a ship backlit by the dawn's increasing light. He watches, wondering what cargo it's carrying and where it's bound. The light of the not-yet-visible sun continues to intensify. Suddenly, in a moment, the sky's colors shift and change. The rising sun, still not breaking the horizon, transforms the glassy sea, changing its indigos and blacks into an intense rosiness. The sea seems to burn as the ship sails toward the sun. He thinks of the phrase "a sea of blood," but that is not this sea; it's too light-toned, too beautiful. No, not the color of blood, but the essence of rosiness. He is so moved by the beauty his eyes mist.

Atmospheric conditions continue to play with the scene and his mind. Beyond the silhouetted ship, out along the horizon, are seven or eight dark blobs—puffy clouds, he thinks, but his imagination sees them as ships. He has read memoirs from the early forties, when it was a blood-red sea and convoys were attacked just offshore by U-boats, and ships burned at night. As the sun breaks the horizon, the rosiness becomes more intense, almost blinding, beautiful beyond compare. He is so drawn by the spectacle he wants to join the ship and sail into the rosy sea and what lies beyond it.

He wants to share this moment with someone, but whom? Who would see the convoy? Who would know about U-boats? Who would understand? He smiles, thinks sometimes he is too imaginative. Those dangerous days are long gone, and most people know nothing of them.

The sun fully breaking the horizon ends the illusion. A cold brightness erases the "convoy" lying offshore, and leaves a single ship sailing on its mundane path to an unknown port. He has stared at the sun so long the brightness has almost blinded him. Everything has an aura.

He resumes his walk, and his peripheral vision catches something. It is so unexpected he almost misses it, and at first doesn't realize what it is and wonders if his eyes are playing tricks on him. He stops, stares at the numbers lying on top of a small cliff carved by last night's high tide. A man's watch lies completely exposed. Its white face is marred by two small spots of rust, and water has entered the crystal. He picks up the watch, tries it on, and immediately sees why the watch has been lost. The locking mechanism on the band is broken. He looks at the face and sees the name of the watch's maker: Tissot. Is it an expensive watch? Who lost it? How had it been lost? When? Where? How had the watch's owner felt when he discovered it missing? There's a story here, he thinks.

******

Sometimes there is justice in this world, she thinks. Sometimes, not often, but sometimes, working hard is rewarded. She had caught a mistake on a contract prepared by a senior partner. It was a small mistake, really, but it was a critical mistake. The partner who had prepared it had already left, so she took it to the managing partner. "Can you fix it?" he had asked and she nodded. She had finished at midnight and handed it to him when he came in at six. "Okay," he had said. That had been on Tuesday. Thursday noon he had called her into his office, handed her a check for $500, and told her to have a nice weekend. "See you Wednesday," he had said.

In two hours she packs, leaves her apartment in Arlington, traverses the Beltway, and crosses the Bay Bridge. Soon, Kent Narrows and Stevensville and Denton are behind her. It is early May and traffic is light. Her swift trip stops in Georgetown—a coal train heading for the power plant in Millsboro ka-thunks as it slowly bumps its way along the tracks. It blocks all the crossings. She has no patience for lines, so she pulls into a parking spot just vacated by a state trooper and runs across to the pawn shop on the corner. She is a browser and loves to look and touch and imagine. With the pawn shop's bounty she could equip a large rock band with guitars, a brass section, and several sets of drums. She could play their CDs on stereo after stereo and dress the musicians in a weird assortment of coats and jackets, adding bling until they sparkled. She stops at a display case close to the cash register. In the left rear, alone, overwhelmed by the gold glitz of the Rolexes and the magnificence of a Patek Philippe, is a no-nonsense watch, a competent-looking watch. She likes it. It has functional beauty; it's a watch for the twenty-first-century man, stainless steel from band to bezel.

"It's a Tissot," the store manager tells her. "Company's been in business since the 1850s. It retails new for $1,100. Guy going through a divorce, needed the cash. Nice guy. Known him for years. For you, $750."

Her mother had taught her to never buy at the first price. They settle on $550.

"Mind the clasp," he says. "It's not working quite right."

Yes, she thinks. Steve will love it. He's never owned a really nice watch. The train clears the crossing and the backed-up traffic inches its way through town. Thirty-two minutes later she is at the house on Robinson Drive. It had belonged to her grandparents and now belongs to her parents and someday it will belong to her and her sister and two brothers, and they'll mock fight about what weeks each will get and she won't care. It's off-season now and her siblings' children are in schools and academies. Steve is staying at the house, working on his dissertation, and he will be surprised to see her and will love the additional days they'll have together. He is expecting her to arrive Friday evening, maybe Saturday morning. She usually calls to let him know which but decides today is special; it is a day for surprises not to be spoiled by a phone call.

The door is locked and when she enters, she senses he is not there. The house feels unused, un-lived in. There are no dirty dishes in the sink, and that's unusual; it is not Steve. His only fault, she thinks, is that he's messy. The milk in the refrigerator is sour, and she remembers telling him the previous weekend he needed to replace it. She is more curious than worried. When she checks the bedroom, she sees throw pillows on the bed. Steve hates them, never puts them on the bed or makes the bed. It is just as she had made it Monday morning. Now she is worried. She takes her phone out of her jeans pocket and calls his cell.

"Hey, babe," he says. "How you doing? You coming down tomorrow night or Saturday morning?"

For a moment, she stands, mute, uncertain, scared. She doesn't let the tremulousness of her body sneak into her voice as she tells him Friday night. After a moment's hesitation, a moment that seems to last a long time, a moment she's never expected, she asks him, "Where are you?"

"At the house," he replies. "Working those damn statistical analyses. Think I'll catch a pizza soon," he says. "Maybe I'll get it delivered so I don't have to stop work."

She says "see you" and for the first time in two years doesn't end with "love you."

She sits at the kitchen table and is numb and then angry and then sad, and she uses a paper towel to wipe her tears. Where is he? Who is he with? What are they doing? There are no answers Steve could provide that wouldn't be lies. Two years of happiness and love end at 5:15 on a Thursday afternoon. She leaves the house, crosses the bridge, follows the banks of the lake, and finds Prospect Street, the end and the beginning of the boardwalk. She pays no attention to the big yellow house on the south corner or the age-darkened cedar house on the north.

She turns left onto the boardwalk. There are few people on the boardwalk and she easily threads her way through the strollers. She sinks into herself and becomes cold and remote and she ignores other people. She passes hotels and shops and beachfront homes and white-painted benches and they are all the same to her. She refuses to cry; she refuses to mourn what is lost. Should she call again and tell him she's at the house and listen to more lies that cannot change the truth? No, she won't do that.

She walks on and on and she ignores the shouts and laughter in Playland and the little boy carrying a stuffed tiger as big as he is and she ignores the smells of hamburgers and hot pizza and the mewing of the gulls as a little girl throws them beach fries and ignores the shouts of a group of teenagers playing tag football on the beach in front of Dolle's and ignores the young couple who lean against a light standard, kissing, smiling. She is at the end of the boardwalk. She stands and stares toward the sea, shivers in the Henlopen's shade, and thoughts and emotions roll through her mind like waves. She turns and begins the walk south. Suddenly, in front of the Railroad House, she stops and turns toward the sea. She opens her purse and removes the watch. She stares at it and then, expressionless, crosses the dune and walks toward the water. It is low tide and it seems a long walk, and when she reaches the water, she raises her right arm and with all her strength, all her sadness, she throws the watch. As it passes its arc, it catches the sun, reflects it, and then falls into the sea.

* * * * * *

The walker, now at home, puts the watch in a plastic bag and makes it a part of his beach-finds collection, setting it next to a pair of barnacled sunglasses. He boots his computer, opens Word, and begins to type.

"Sometimes there is justice in this world …"

KEITH J. PHILLIPS, A LIFELONG RESIDENT OF SUSSEX COUNTY, GRADUATED FROM DICKINSON COLLEGE IN 1963. COMMISSIONED A SECOND LIEUTENANT IN THE US ARMY, HE SERVED FOR SEVEN YEARS, INCLUDING THREE YEARS IN GERMANY AND A YEAR IN VIETNAM IN AN INFANTRY BATTALION. IN 1971, HE BEGAN TEACHING SOCIAL STUDIES AT LAKE FOREST HIGH SCHOOL IN FELTON, DELAWARE. AFTER BEING IN THE CLASSROOM FOR TWENTY YEARS, HE WORKED AS A GUIDANCE COUNSELOR UNTIL RETIREMENT. IN 2011, HE BEGAN TAKING CLASSES WITH THE REHOBOTH BEACH WRITERS' GUILD. HE AND HIS WIFE, RUTH ANN, MOVED TO REHOBOTH BEACH IN SEPTEMBER 2013.

JUDGE'S COMMENT:

This is a beautifully written story that, on the surface, seems to solve the mystery of a discovered object. What is real? What is imagination? The author impressively uses an everyday object—a watch—to create as many possibilities as answers.

The Watch

Come Fly with Me

by Russell Reece

Do you know what some of your people call us? Wind Rats. Yeah. And it always hurts when we hear it. We don't understand the need for name calling. We try to treat everyone with respect, no matter who they are. We go out of our way to get along. Why can't you feeders do that?

Oh, I see you're confused. I'm a seagull and you're wondering how you're able to understand my words, how I know the things I know. Let's just say seagulls are pretty darn smart and we know a lot more than you think. So, stop with the questions and let your imagination do what it's supposed to do. Come on, take a little fly with me. I'll show you around the boardwalk and fill you in on a few things you and all the other feeders should know. Get off that beach blanket, brush the sand off your belly, and spread those spindly wings. There you go. That wasn't so hard, was it? This off-shore breeze makes it easy. Let's head over to the north side.

The main thing everyone needs to be clear on is that all food belongs to us. It always has and it always will. And we count on feeders to deliver our food. That's what you're here for. Now, don't get defensive. We realize we're all in this together. We have to share. That's never been a problem. You can eat as much of our food as you want, but *you* have to do what *you're* supposed to do.

Who am I? Well, Jonathan Livingston I'm not. What a wuss that bird was. I can't believe they actually wrote a book about him. He made such a big deal out of flying, why not breathing? It's the same thing. JL wouldn't have stood a chance in my flock with his new-wave, idealistic views. My name's Solomon and I run things in this place you feeders call Rehoboth Beach. My mate Delicious and I have been together for twenty years now. That's her right there on your left. Hey, honey. Say hi. Talk about flying, have you ever seen it done better? Oh, I get excited every time I look at her.

Isn't this a great view? That's the Delaware Breakwater up to the north, and down the beach, off in the hazy distance, is the Indian River Inlet Bridge. I love it up here with Delicious and all my other brothers and sisters, hovering in this perfectly clear sky. We are so blessed. You poor feeders have to scrabble around on the ground and make the best of your two-dimensional lives. We can soar out over the ocean, float inches off the water, or zoom up into the sky and ride the currents for miles, just drifting along over the beach or anywhere else we choose to go in this beautiful world.

Look, there's your hotel. I watched you come out this morning with your flip-flops, your baggy orange swim trunks and blue-striped beach umbrella. And you had a cooler for us, which I was happy to see. You walked onto the beach, spread a blanket, and rubbed yourself with lotion. Then you sat with a goofy look on your face and checked out the other feeders, especially the long-hairs. I noticed they didn't pay much attention to you … just saying. Anyway, I was thinking you were one of the good guys until you laid down and got comfortable with that book, resting your head on that rolled-up beach towel. You never did open the cooler. See what I mean?

Oh, you're surprised I know so much about you? Don't be. We're always watching. We've been doing it for as long as your kind has been around. Did you know seagulls have an average life of thirty-five years? I knew one old bird who was forty-nine and his mate was forty-seven. That's another thing. When we pick a mate, it's for life and, thank goodness, I hit the jackpot. Right, honey? You bet I did.

Delicious and I haven't always been here at the beach. We've followed the fishing boats and the farmers on tractors. We've prowled the marshes and wetlands and lived up on the Nanticoke for a while. You can live anywhere you want when you're a seagull. I happen to like the ocean and the bay. I also have a thing for seafood, especially shellfish. There's nothing like scarfing down a tender mussel or a fat clam. But clams are a lot of work. You've got to find 'em, then fly up high and drop 'em on the road to get 'em open. After a while you get tired of that. I don't do it much anymore.

Of course clams still come in handy. There's a feeder over near Dewey who has a restaurant on the bay. He's miserable, never gives us our food like he's supposed to. He even keeps a dog to shoo us away. But too bad for him his restaurant has a tin roof. I dropped a clam on that roof twenty-seven times one day during his dinner service. I can still see him standing by the door, looking up at me red-faced, shaking his fist, the dog spinning around in circles and barking. Oh, it was a beautiful thing.

But, enough fond reminiscences; let's drift on down the boardwalk. It's starting to get crowded now. Just stay a little above the buildings and glide in the current. See that place at the end of the road with the big Dolle's sign? I always keep some of our brothers and sisters assembled there, even in the winter. There are lots of French fry and pizza shops clustered around, so the feeders don't have to go very far to give us our food. We try to make it easy on the feeders whenever we can.

Look, there's a little one bringing us some pizza slices. Watch Flip and his crew go pick them up. Oh, those beautiful white-and-black wings parachuting down, the joyous cheers and cries of thanks. I'm so proud of my people.

Oh, no. See, this is what happens. The little feeder doesn't know what he's supposed to do. He tried to snatch the food back. Look at him spin away from Flip's mate and run to that big feeder with the cream on his nose. The big one's so busy waving his hat and yelling at us he almost crashed into the old long-hair in the wheelchair. Now look at her; she's whacking him with her cane. Amazing! How are seagulls and feeders supposed to live together when feeders can't even get along? I'll never understand.

The little feeders can really be confusing sometimes. One day, they'll spread our food out all over the boards so it's easy for us to get. They seem so delighted when we fly in and land next to them. And the long-hairs sometimes join in and it all feels so good, so communal. We gather around them offering thanks as we eat the food. But then another day, a group of us will just be standing on the boards relaxing and a little feeder will charge right at us. We scatter apart so they won't hurt themselves. We realize they don't understand what they're doing, but it does bother us when the big feeders don't correct them. Instead they often laugh and encourage the bad behavior. That's disappointing, especially since we always try so hard to get along.

We keep our little ones in the nest and out on the dunes until they've matured and are well trained. We think it's the only responsible thing to do.

Hey, check out the bandstand at the end of the avenue. Sometimes feeders make music down there. If there's room on the boards we land in a group, stand around, close our eyes, and listen. It's really nice. But often it gets too crowded, so we lift off and hover overhead or go out onto the sand. There's something about music that slows everything down and warms the soul. And I have to admit, it gives us hope. If there are feeders sensitive enough to make wonderful music, then maybe someday they'll all realize how things really work and we can, like that old song says, live together in perfect harmony.

Now tilt your wings and let's drift a little farther down the boardwalk. See those stores? That's where feeders like to buy shirts, hats, and all kinds of junky trinkets. We don't understand the need for that kind of stuff. It's so much easier to live a minimalistic life, unencumbered by possessions. We don't have to carry things or remember where we left things. We don't have to take anything with us when we travel. The feeders would be much better off if they tried that. But then again, if hats and trinkets make them happy, who are we to question?

There're a couple more food places down here so there're always a lot of us around. We only have a few birds stationed at the ice cream store next to Funland. We don't like ice cream, even though feeders seem to go crazy over it. They can have it all as far as I'm concerned, as long as they remember to hand over the cone when they're done.

Now look, here's something that really gets my gall. See that long-hair down there next to the bench, arms out, popcorn piled in her outstretched palms? And the big feeder with the camera who's putting more popcorn on her head while she tries not to laugh? Isn't that ridiculous? You know what they want, don't you? They want us all to fly down and pick up our popcorn so the big feeder can snap a picture while the long-hair giggles. We don't make feeders perform tricks to get their food. That would be demeaning; we would never do it. But they do it to us all the time. And we probably shouldn't, but we go along with their silly games. I don't want anyone to ever say the Rehoboth seagulls don't have a sense of humor.

Uh-oh, I think they've spotted you. They're all pointing at us, covering their open mouths and, of course, everyone's got their cell phones and cameras up, snapping pictures. It's probably those ridiculous orange trunks you have on or, more likely, your big hairy belly hanging down. Whatever it is, we should head back before the boardwalk turns to chaos. If some of the feeders should bang into each other, fights will break out and they'll all start screaming and yelling. We hate it when that happens.

Come on, your stuff is just up the beach. See the umbrella? Swoop on down, aim for your blanket. Oh, I didn't tell you. Taking off is easy. Landing is another thing. You're gonna crash, probably be knocked unconscious for a few seconds. When you wake up you'll wonder if this has all been a dream.

When you do, just look up. You'll see me. I'll still be up here watching like I always do. And now that you understand things, now that you really know the score, I hope you'll make a point to educate the other feeders. Tell them what you've learned and remind them that there's always another side to the story. Hey, you might be the one who helps us solve this coexistence thing once and for all.

But do me a favor. Before you go off and start proselytizing, take a minute, bend down, and open up that cooler. Give us our food. It'll make you feel good.

RUSSELL REECE HAS HAD STORIES AND ESSAYS PUBLISHED IN *MEMOIR (AND)*, *CRIMESPREE*, *VINE LEAVES LITERARY JOURNAL*, *SLIVER OF STONE*, AND MANY OTHER PRINT AND ONLINE JOURNALS. HIS WORK HAS APPEARED IN SEVERAL ANTHOLOGIES, MOST RECENTLY *ALL THAT GLITTERS* AND *SOMEONE WICKED*, BOTH RELEASED IN 2013. HIS PROSE CHAPBOOK, *THE MUD LAKE TRILOGY*, WAS RELEASED IN 2014. HE HAS RECEIVED TWO BEST OF THE NET NOMINATIONS AND WAS A FINALIST IN THE 2012 WILLIAM FAULKNER-WILLIAM WISDOM CREATIVE WRITING CONTEST. RUSS CO-HOSTS 2ND SATURDAY POETS IN WILMINGTON, DELAWARE, AND IS A UNIVERSITY OF DELAWARE ALUMNUS. HE LIVES NEAR BETHEL, DELAWARE, IN RURAL SUSSEX COUNTY ALONG THE BEAUTIFUL BROAD CREEK.

Boardwalk Bound

by Kimberly Gray

My name is Lottie Gershwin. I'll admit to being over forty, but that's all you'll get out of me. Last week I went away with my mom for our annual jaunt to the beach. I go to have some time away from my husband and two daughters. Mom goes to meet ghost. You read that correctly: ghost.

By the time I was seventeen, Daddy had had enough of Mom's search for haunted hotels and bought me a brand-new red Toyota Celica to cart Mom around on her ghost-hunting adventures. Everyone was happy. Daddy got a peaceful vacation, Mom searched out ghost, and I had my own car. That was twenty-seven years ago. Don't try to do the math, just keep reading. Now every Mother's Day, Mom and I take off on our ghost-a-way.

We've stayed at some interesting places along the Atlantic coast over the years. This year, Mom chose a spot called The Lakeview Hotel in Rehoboth Beach. I love Rehoboth. I've spent a lot of time shopping with my daughters there during our vacations in Ocean City, but this would be the first time I'd actually stayed in Rehoboth. I don't like traveling too far from our home in Baltimore.

Mom was excited the morning I picked her up. She had her white-blond hair pulled in a chignon and wore her favorite pink pedal pushers. Daddy had packed us a lunch fit for a trucker. "We're only going to be in the car a few hours," I tried to tell him, but he pushed the basket on me, along with a rocket-shaped thermos of coffee.

"He's rented the entire Sopranos series and bought a gallon of Pudgy Hubby ice cream," Mom said, sliding into the passenger seat.

"He thought a bag of frozen peas would hide it."

I waved to Daddy, but the storm door had already closed behind him. Mom opened her trusty book of haunted hotels on her lap as we drove away. We'd been to most of them already and the scariest things we'd found were bedbugs.

"This one is it; I feel it in my bones, hon." She'd said that exact sentence every year. "Really, listen to this." Mom cleared her throat. "'Viola Woolcraft, daughter of a prominent Philadelphia doctor, died tragically on her wedding day at The Lakeview Hotel. The high-spirited Miss Woolcraft was engaged to an up-and-coming politician, but threw him over mere days before the wedding in favor of a hotel bellhop she met during her stay at The Lakeview. Her parents were horrified but chose to carry on with the wedding with the replacement groom.'"

Mom stopped reading and elbowed me. "She sounds a lot like you."

"Could we not talk about that again?" I said, taking my eyes off the road a second to glare at her.

"I think it was the best decision you ever made. I love Carl, hon. As for that Schramm boy ..."

"Mom!"

"Anywho, where was I? Right," she continued, reading from the book, "'The wedding guests had arrived on the sunny afternoon of May 9, 1939. The bride was dressed in the gown her mother had worn at her own wedding, and an orchestra was set up to play in the hotel lobby. As the hours ticked by, the embarrassed guests gradually took their leave. Viola had been abandoned by her bellhop. The next morning, her body was found on the boardwalk, still dressed in her wedding gown. It appeared the jilted bride had jumped to her death. To this day, the mystery of the broken-hearted bride remains, as does her spirit, which roams the halls of The Lakeview

Hotel in search of her wayward groom."'

A chill cut across my back and I rolled up my window. The story was sadder than most of the others in Mom's book.

"I know you're gonna get a hit on this one, hon."

"What does that mean?" I knew what she meant. Mom was absolutely convinced I had been born with a gift to communicate with the dearly departed. A gift, in her opinion, I ignored and stored away, much like the old Toyota I kept in my garage. You see, I was born with a caul, a membrane over my face. Mom has it tucked between the pages of her Bible. She guards it, convinced that, in the wrong hands, it could destroy me. My grandmother told her to burn it when I was born, but Mom seems to think it holds secret powers, as if it were Green Lantern's ring.

"Mom, I do not see spirits unless you put a gin and tonic in front of me."

"Lottie, you're sensitive and you know it. Remember when Uncle Joe died? You told me before the phone rang. How could you have known he'd be killed at work? And just last month you asked how Miss Edna was doing before she even had the heart attack. How else could you have known?"

I didn't want to nod, or agree, or encourage her in any way. The truth was I knew those things because I'd seen them in dreams. I had never encountered a ghost—much to Mom's disappointment. But because I've been able to predict a few deaths, she's convinced I can talk to the dead as well.

"I must have overheard Miss Edna complaining she didn't feel well," I said.

That wasn't true. For a week, every time I passed our neighbor's house, I felt a squeeze in my heart and my palms sweated. I even popped in one day and asked her if she'd seen Doctor Elliott recently. She laughed and claimed to be healthy as a horse. The next day it was all over. I guess I should have insisted.

Fortunately, before Mom could argue further we pulled into the lot behind the hotel. I could feel myself relax as I inhaled the salty scent of the ocean.

The hotel hardly resembled the old black-and-white photo in Mom's book. The aging Victorian was now surrounded by a concrete facade and had shops, an enclosed porch, and a pool. A wooden sign that read "Lakeview Spa" hung from an iron post out front. It seemed that more than the building had changed. We passed several shops with darkened windows and Help Wanted signs posted as we made our way up the walk to the front entrance.

The clang of a bell on the door announced our arrival, but the front-desk clerk didn't budge. She was a plump young girl with purple-streaked black hair that hung over her face as she studied the palm of her tattooed hand.

"Hello?" I was standing close enough that I could smell the coffee on her breath. Or was that my breath? "Hello?" Still no response. I put my hand over her iPhone screen and she jumped, dropping the phone on the counter.

"Geez, you scared me," the girl said, pulling her ear buds out and placing them in a drawer with her phone. "Sorry. Welcome to The Lakeview Hotel, I mean spa and resort."

"Which is it?" I asked. She rolled her kohl-lined green eyes at me.

"It's a hotel, but we're going for a new image, so I guess it's a spa." She took my credit card and license. I made sure she saw my photo. I had finally achieved the perfect shade of blond.

"Do you have things like manicures and massages?" Mom said.

"We're working on it. We've got a hot tub, though, and whirlpool tubs in the rooms." She smiled at us, revealing gold studs in her gums.

What about bedbugs? Or ghosts? I wanted to ask. She handed me back my things, along with a room key that had "Tranquility Number 4" stamped on a brass ring as heavy as my purse. Aja—at least, that's what her name tag read—pointed us in the direction of an antique elevator shaped like a birdcage. Mom slammed the door shut and we pressed the button for the Tranquility floor. The elevator gave a shake and made a sound similar to my washer on the spin cycle. As the elevator climbed, so did my pulse. I could hear blood swishing in my head. It was close to the feeling I'd had for Miss Edna, but more intense, more emotional.

"Lottie? You okay, hon?"

"Yes." The last thing I wanted to tell Mom was that I saw shadows in the halls as we passed each floor. She would pester me to no end. "I think I need some lunch."

"You can't fool me, I know what's happening. You think I can't feel the air changing and see the expression on your face? You know, you get your gift from my side of the family." The scalp under Mom's platinum hair was growing pink. "Is it Viola? Do you see her?"

"For heaven's sake, I do not see dead people." Just then, I saw a man watching us from the far end of the hall. He wore a gray morning coat and striped pants. The elevator creaked slowly by and he turned his head to watch us ascend to the next floor. I hoped he was an employee.

Our room was bright and comfortable and had a huge tub with a whirlpool, just as Aja said it would. Mom and I stepped onto the balcony, admiring the spectacular view of the beach. A man sat on the edge of the boardwalk, playing a light melody on a flute. The happy sound filled the air and a woman in a white gown swayed to the music. I glanced at the ocean for a second and then back down at the couple on the boardwalk, shielding my eyes from the sun with my hand. But the woman was gone.

"Did you see her?" I asked, pointing down.

"Lottie, that's a man. He just has long hair," Mom said as she laughed.

"Not the flutist, the woman who was dancing." Had I really seen someone? "Never mind, it must have been a reflection off the water. Let's get some lunch." I hurried Mom out before she could ask me any questions. We took the stairs. I told her it was to save time, but it was really because I didn't want to risk seeing the strange man in the hallway again. But there he was, standing at the bottom of the stairs.

"Excuse me, I wonder if you have the time?" he asked. Mom walked straight by him without a glance. I grabbed her elbow and hustled her out into the lobby. My hands and knees were shaking so badly I thought I might fall down.

"You look like you've seen a ghost," Aja declared as we came rushing from the stairwell. "Geez, you haven't, have you? Please don't tell the boss. I doubt he could take it."

I tried to get control of myself. Mom had her worried face on. She hadn't noticed the man in the stairwell. It couldn't be. I absolutely refused to see ghosts.

"Your boss doesn't like ghosts?" Mom asked.

"He's been trying hard to put that ghost stuff in the past," she said, motioning for us to come closer.

"You know that 'Haunted Hunters' show? They filmed here and made a real mess of things. Boss thought it'd be great for business, but instead it came back to bite him. Now, everybody thinks this place is haunted."

"By Viola, the jilted bride," said Mom.

"Yep. It has brought in a lot of business. We had all kinds of clubs and societies wanting to hold séances here. Guests have claimed to hear moaning and sobbing in the halls. I don't believe in that crap, but my boss, he grew up here. He told me his father was here at the hotel the day she jumped. My boss thinks he saw her ghost when he was a kid."

Mom and I listened attentively as Aja told us about how the hotel closed for business during the filming of the show. They held a party on the night the show aired. To their surprise and disappointment, The Lakeview was portrayed as a dive in a rundown area, owned by a scheming fraudster.

"That was the end of our bookings. Mr. Capri, my boss, he was furious, but not with the show, with Viola. He brought his priest in and had them say prayers and throw holy water in every room. Then, and I know this sounds crazy, he screamed at Viola to get out."

"He evicted a ghost?" I asked in disbelief. "It didn't work."

"But it must have, because we haven't had any exploding lightbulbs or electrical problems since that day."

* * * * * *

"Can he do that?" Mom asked later, as we walked down Rehoboth Avenue toward Browseabout Books.

"You probably know more about ghost etiquette than I do. I believe he did put Viola out. I'm sure I saw her on the boardwalk earlier." We were at the doorway of the store. The scent of books and coffee was intoxicating. I knew I'd have to confess to Mom about the man I saw as well, but coffee came first. Mom barely let me order once I revealed all I had seen. Soon we were back on the street, hightailing it to the boardwalk.

"Show me exactly where she was standing," Mom instructed. I pointed between the street lamp and the trash can. The beach and boardwalk were empty. It was a few weeks before the start of the summer season. A light tingling began in my arms and ran up my back and neck, filling me with a rush of pure happiness. I could barely contain the joy I felt. I grabbed Mom's hand for fear I'd float away.

"I know you can hear me, girlie." The squeaky voice rang in my ears. A woman stood next to me, wearing a white gown with a lace blouse and a pin-tucked skirt with embellishments trimming the hem. A Juliet cap was perched jauntily on her head, and a cascading veil was draped over her shoulders and down her back. Her black hair was cut in a bob and curls framed her face. She winked at me.

"Now don't get yourself in a lather," Viola said. Her image became clearer to me as she spoke. I could hear the cell phone in my purse begin to beep, alerting me that its battery was dying. "Those others, they were full of baloney. But not you, right, girlie? You're the real deal. Those movie people made a sap outta Capri. He gave me the bum's rush."

"Tell me what's happening." Mom's blue eyes were huge.

"Viola's explaining her situation," I said to Mom. "I'm Lottie and this is my mom," I said to Viola.

"Happy to meet you, hon," Mom said to the trash can.

"Charmed, I'm sure," replied Viola. "Lottie, right? I'm out here all balled up, not knowing what to do. I gotta get to my Harry."

"Harry is the groom?" I asked.

"He's the love of my life. I knew he'd come back to me," Viola said, becoming more upset as she told the story. "Capri's being a pill, and I had to take a powder. Now Harry's back and I can't get to him." Viola sobbed so hard Mom could hear her.

"Don't let your pride get in the way. March back in there and get your Harry," I said, with Mom nodding in agreement.

"I've tried," Viola said. She sniffled a few more times and wiped at her saucer-shaped eyes. We went single file toward the hotel, Viola in the lead and Mom bringing up the rear. The closer we got to The Lakeview, the more transparent Viola became. By the time we arrived at the entrance, she had faded completely.

"Where'd she go?" I asked Mom, who only threw up her hands and shrugged.

"I'm here." Viola was back on the boardwalk. "I can't seem to go any farther." She slunk back against the lamp post.

"I know!" Mom brightened. "Viola has to be invited back in by Mr. Capri."

"That'll never happen. He blames me for ruining him."

"I have an idea," said Mom. "I think Mr. Capri is going to be more than happy to have you back." Mom turned and clicked up the walk in her kitten heels, disappearing inside.

"Is she on the hooch?" Viola asked, staring after Mom.

"Well, she has had quite a bit of coffee today."

"You're gonna help me, ain'tcha?" Viola's shoulders slumped.

"How old are you, Viola?" I asked.

"I was eighteen my last birthday."

"You were so young. I understand how much you love Harry, I have a husband back home, but, well, nobody is worth ending your life over."

"You're off your nut," Viola said.

Maybe I was crazy. I was standing there talking to thin air.

"I was upset and went out on the balcony just to look at the ocean. Then this thing," she held a clump of her veil, "tangled in my feet. The next thing I know, I'm on the balcony watching my body being hauled off in a meat wagon."

Mom came to the door and waved me over. I wondered what kind of plan she had concocted. I went into the lobby and Aja grinned at me as I passed her desk. I figured she was in on whatever Mom was up to. Mom and I headed for the stairwell where Harry stood, looking around confusedly.

"Say, do you happen to have the time?" Harry asked.

"Yes, I think it's time for you to be with Viola," I said.

At that moment, Mom let out a scream. A small, wiry man with a shiny head came running over.

"Is there a problem, ladies?"

Mr. Capri, I presumed.

"We want our money back. I had no idea this hotel was haunted. And I can't even get a massage here. What kind of spa is this?" Mom was going a mile a minute. Mr. Capri held her hand, then dropped it, looking at me for an explanation.

"Mr. Capri, is it? I'm Lottie and my mom and I were on our way to our room when this man in a morning coat approached us for the time and then, poof, disappeared."

"Dear God." He made the sign of the cross. "Another one. I am sorry. I thought this problem was resolved. You see, it is true, we had a ghost, but she is gone. I will need to take care of this one too."

"The ghost you got rid of wasn't a bride, was she?" I smiled. "Because the man we saw was dressed for a wedding."

"It cannot be." Capri held his head. "After all these years, he has returned for his wedding. You see him now, really?"

With both Mom and Mr. Capri watching, I did what I swore I never would.

"Harry? Viola wants to know why you're late."

"Golly, I bet she's sore," said Harry as he stepped into view. He rubbed his cheek as if he'd been hit. "I never meant to be this late. A few of the guys from down the road said I should celebrate my last night of freedom. I've been begging them to bring me back for hours. Am I too late? Is she still here?"

"She's still waiting for you, don't worry," I said, then turned to Capri. "The only way to be rid of them is to reunite them."

"I don't know about this. You're not filming me, are you?"

"My Lottie knows what she's talking about," said Mom. "You get out there and ask Viola to come in. You ask her nicely, you hear?" Mom pushed Mr. Capri out the door and followed behind him. Harry smiled at me and I motioned for him to follow me to the lobby. Aja started snapping photos with her iPhone. I stifled a small laugh as Mr. Capri stood on the front porch, begging Viola to come back. She held out for a few minutes before rushing in and throwing herself into Harry's arms. The lightbulbs in the chandeliers flickered before exploding, sending a shimmering rain of glass over the happy couple and casting them in a momentary glow that revealed both of them to all of us. For a few seconds the air was filled with the scent of lilacs and roses. Aja's phone died, but not before she captured an astonishing photo of an outline of two people in a sparkling mist.

The next morning, Mr. Capri brought in a manicurist to do our nails and afterward treated Mom and me to lunch. He said he was relieved that his ghost problems were over and wanted to discuss a friend who believed his house was haunted. Mom agreed immediately and said we would investigate. I ate my salad quietly, not having the heart to tell him that, at that very moment, Viola and Harry were making themselves at home on the Tranquility floor.

KIMBERLY GRAY IS A BALTIMORE NATIVE AND FORMER SCHOOL TEACHER. SHE WAS THE 2009 WINNER OF THE WILLIAM F. DEECK-MALICE DOMESTIC GRANT FOR UNPUBLISHED WRITERS. SHE IS CURRENTLY WORKING ON A MYSTERY NOVEL AND IS STILL TRYING TO FIND THE TRANQUILITY FLOOR.

2014 REHOBOTH BEACH READS JUDGES

RICH BARNETT
RICH SHUTTLES BETWEEN HIS WORK FOR AN ENVIRONMENTAL THINK TANK IN WASHINGTON, DC, AND HIS WRITER'S LIFE IN REHOBOTH BEACH. HE WRITES THE POPULAR "CAMP STORIES" COLUMN IN THE MAGAZINE *LETTERS FROM CAMP REHOBOTH* AND IS THE AUTHOR OF *THE DISCREET CHARMS OF A BOURGEOIS BEACH TOWN: REHOBOTH BEACH STORIES* (2012). HIS WORK HAS ALSO APPEARED IN *CHELSEA STATION MAGAZINE, SAINTS AND SINNERS 2014: NEW FICTION FROM THE FESTIVAL; THE BEACH HOUSE; SHORE LIFE;* AND *NO PLACE LIKE HERE: AN ANTHOLOGY OF SOUTHERN DELAWARE POETRY AND PROSE.*

SARAH BARNETT
SARAH BARNETT RETIRED TO REHOBOTH BEACH FROM A CAREER IN PUBLIC AFFAIRS. SHE WRITES ESSAYS AND SHORT FICTION, SERVES AS VICE PRESIDENT OF THE REHOBOTH BEACH WRITERS' GUILD, TEACHES CLASSES IN SHORT STORY WRITING, AND LEADS "FREE WRITES" FOR OTHER WRITERS. HER WORK HAS APPEARED IN THE *DELMARVA REVIEW* AND OTHER PUBLICATIONS.

ALEX COLEVAS
ALEX COLEVAS IS A LONG-TIME EMPLOYEE—AND NOW ASSISTANT MANAGER—OF BROWSEABOUT BOOKS IN REHOBOTH BEACH, DELAWARE. SHE IS A VORACIOUS READER WHO OFTEN SCREENS SAMPLE BOOKS TO HELP DETERMINE WHICH TITLES THE STORE WILL STOCK. KNOWING WHAT READERS ENJOY, AND PARTICULARLY WHAT CUSTOMERS OF THE STORE LIKE TO READ, HELPED HER SELECT STORIES FOR *THE BOARDWALK.*

LISA GRAFF
LISA GRAFF HOLDS AN MA IN THEATER FROM NORTHWESTERN UNIVERSITY. OVER THE YEARS, SHE HAS PUBLISHED MORE THAN 100 ARTICLES, INCLUDING FOUR PERSONAL ESSAYS IN *THE WASHINGTON POST.* HER 1991 ESSAY, "NO TEACHER CAN COMPENSATE FOR NEGLECT MANY KIDS SUFFER AT HOME" WON THAT YEAR'S AAUW MASS COMMUNICATIONS' AWARD. HER WORK HAS APPEARED IN *WOMEN'S WORLD MAGAZINE, SHORE MAGAZINE,* AND *DELAWARE BEACH LIFE.* HER ESSAY, "GETTING MY FEET WET" WAS THE NONFICTION WINNER IN THE 2012 REHOBOTH BEACH WRITERS' GUILD/*DELAWARE BEACH LIFE* MAGAZINE CONTEST. MS. GRAFF CHRONICLES HER RETIREMENT JOURNEY IN HER COLUMN *RETIREMENT 101* FOR THE *CAPE GAZETTE* AND IS A FREQUENT

GUEST BLOGGER FOR RETIREMENTANDGOODLIVING.COM. SHE HAS TAUGHT WRITING CLASSES AT DELTECH, FOR THE REHOBOTH BEACH WRITERS' GUILD, VINE AND VESSELS CHRISTIAN WRITING CONFERENCE, AND THE RAL ARTIST/ WRITER RETREAT.

KRISTEN GRAMER

KRISTEN RECEIVED HER MASTER OF LIBRARY SCIENCE IN 2000 FROM THE UNIVERSITY OF MARYLAND. PAST LIBRARY EXPERIENCES INCLUDE POSITIONS IN SEVERAL SPECIAL LIBRARIES IN THE WASHINGTON, DC, AREA. UPON MOVING TO DELAWARE, SHE WAS THE DIRECTOR OF THE LAUREL PUBLIC LIBRARY FOR TWO YEARS AND HAS BEEN THE ASSISTANT DIRECTOR OF THE LEWES PUBLIC LIBRARY FOR OVER TEN YEARS, WITH A FOCUS ON ADULT LIBRARY SERVICES. KRISTEN MAINTAINS THE ADULT COLLECTIONS, ORGANIZES ADULT PROGRAMMING, AND IS ON THE DESIGN COMMITTEE FOR THE NEW LEWES PUBLIC LIBRARY. SHE LIVES IN LEWES WITH HER HUSBAND, MARK, AND, AS A LIFELONG READER, IS NOW INSTILLING A LOVE OF READING IN HER TWO YOUNG SONS.

RAMONA DEFELICE LONG

RAMONA DEFELICE LONG GREW UP ON THE GULF COAST AND HAS LIVED IN THE MID-ATLANTIC FOR THREE DECADES. HER FICTION AND CREATIVE NONFICTION HAVE APPEARED IN LITERARY AND REGIONAL JOURNALS, MOST RECENTLY IN THE *DELMARVA REVIEW, LITERARY MAMA,* AND *LUNCH TICKET.* SHE HAS RECEIVED GRANTS AND FELLOWSHIPS FROM THE DELAWARE DIVISION OF THE ARTS, THE MID-ATLANTIC ARTS FOUNDATION, THE VIRGINIA CENTER FOR THE CREATIVE ARTS, THE REHOBOTH BEACH WRITERS' GUILD, PHILADELPHIA STORIES, AND THE SOCIETY OF CHILDREN'S BOOK WRITERS AND ILLUSTRATORS. IN HER DAY JOB, SHE WORKS AS AN INDEPENDENT EDITOR AND INSTRUCTOR SPECIALIZING IN MYSTERY NOVELS.

Also from Cat & Mouse Press

www.catandmousepress.com

A Playful Publisher

Beach Reads with Local Settings

The Beach House

If you liked *The Boardwalk*, you'll love *The Beach House*. There is something for everyone here, from romance, history, and intrigue to jilted brides, NASCAR drivers, outlaws, and even a ghost or two. A collection of short stories set in and around Rehoboth. *The Beach House* is the first book in the Rehoboth Beach Reads series.

Sandy Shorts

Bad men + bad dogs + bad luck = great beach reads. You'll smile with recognition as characters in the stories ride the Lewes-Cape May Ferry, barhop in Dewey, go to "OC," stroll through Bethany Beach, run into the waves in Rehoboth, and visit the Wildwood amusement pier.

Great for Kids

A Rehoboth ABC

From swooping seagulls to frolicking dolphins, the sights and sounds of Rehoboth Beach are captured in this charming book, which children will beg to read again and again. The delightful rhyming text is complemented by amusing illustrations of children on the kiddie rides, sipping snow cones, examining jellyfish, and even reluctantly taking a nap.

Adult Humor

You Know You're in Rehoboth When

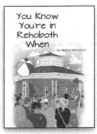

How do you know you're in Rehoboth Beach? The dogs are smaller than the martinis, you won't get ketchup with those fries, and happy hour starts at 9am. Whether you are a visitor or a local, you will recognize the unique charm of Rehoboth in this hilarious book.

For Writers

Resources for Writers

Cat & Mouse Press offers a variety of resources for writers. Check the website for current information.

Writing Contests

Cat & Mouse Press writing contests can be a great way for new and emerging writers to gain experience and perhaps even get published. Follow the Cat & Mouse Press Facebook page for updates.

When You Want a Book at the Beach

Come to Your Bookstore at the Beach